RISEN

RISEN

The Novelization of the Major Motion Picture

A Novel by
Angela Hunt

Based on the Story by
Paul Aiello
and Screenplay by
Kevin Reynolds
AND **Paul Aiello**

BETHANYHOUSE
a division of Baker Publishing Group
Minneapolis, Minnesota

© 2015 by Sony Pictures Worldwide Acquisitions, Inc.

Published by Bethany House Publishers
11400 Hampshire Avenue South
Bloomington, Minnesota 55438
www.bethanyhouse.com

Bethany House Publishers is a division of
Baker Publishing Group, Grand Rapids, Michigan
www.bakerpublishinggroup.com

Printed in the United States of America

ISBN 978-0-7642-1845-3 (Trade Paper)
ISBN 978-0-7642-1884-2 (International Trade Paper, United Kingdom and Australia)
ISBN 978-0-7642-1885-9 (International Trade Paper, Excluding United Kingdom and Australia)

Library of Congress Control Number: 2015915997

Scripture quotations are from the *Complete Jewish Bible*, copyright © 1998 by David H. Stern. Published by Jewish New Testament Publications, Inc. www.messianicjewish.net/jntp. Distributed by Messianic Jewish Resources. www.messianicjewish.net. All rights reserved. Used by permission.

This is a work of historical reconstruction; the appearances of certain historical figures are therefore inevitable. All other characters, however, are products of the author's imagination, and any resemblance to actual persons, living or dead, is coincidental.

Angela Hunt is represented by Browne & Miller Literary Associates.

15 16 17 18 19 20 21   7 6 5 4 3 2 1

Once you eliminate the impossible, whatever remains,
no matter how improbable, must be the truth.

—Arthur Conan Doyle

Clavius

Quick-moving shadows of clouds scuttled over the barren landscape as wilderness gave way to civilization. An inn, if one could call it that, lay upon the horizon, so I adjusted my angle of approach in order to reach it without wasting energy.

The building I trudged toward was built of sunbaked stone the same color as the sand beneath my feet. The place did not appear large enough to offer overnight accommodation, but if it could provide water and food, that would suffice.

I pushed on the wooden door that swung on leather hinges, revealing a table, a bearded man with a curved back, and a floor of stones set into packed sand. The owner bobbed before me and gestured for me to enter as if I were royalty and his establishment fit for a king.

I walked inside, stepped over the roughhewn bench, and sat. The man placed a cup of tepid water before me. I swallowed it in one long gulp.

A ghost of a smile flickered across the man's face as he refilled my cup. "Roman, eh?"

For an instant I considered giving a snide reply, but then realized I did not resemble my usual self. I had not been able to shave in days, and I had ditched the red *paludamentum* of a Roman officer weeks before. I now wore a tunic and a brown cloak, my only protection against the blowing sand. Perhaps my manner gave me away, or perhaps this man was more observant than he appeared. "Yes," I said.

His eyes widened as he lowered the pitcher. "And . . . is that a tribune's ring?"

I lowered my weary gaze to the silver circle on my left hand, a ring engraved with X FRETENSIS, the name and number of my legion. No wonder the innkeeper looked surprised. Not often did a Roman tribune wander about dirty, disheveled, and alone.

The man slid onto the empty bench across the table. "Have you come far, Tribune?"

How could I answer? I had spent the last forty days wandering in Judea, crossing and recrossing the same territory. But moving from the man I was to the man I had become was a journey of enormous length and breadth.

I lifted my cup and drained it again, then studied the innkeeper. With no other customers, he had to be bored. And like all bored men he thirsted for a story.

Perhaps I was finally ready to share mine.

1

Clavius

Under Tiberius Caesar, Rome's armies controlled a vast empire—from Britannia in the north to Aegyptus in the south, from Mauritania Tingitana in the west to Mesopotamia in the east. But no post was less desired than the wasteland of Judea. Pontius Pilate governed Judea for Caesar, and as prefect Pilate commanded me, as *tribune cohortis*, to wield the military might of Rome and keep the peace.

The winds of revolution were blowing strong, however, and at no time more so than the yearly ritual of the Passover, when the Jews celebrated their supposed exodus from enslavement in Egypt. The Jews prayed to their single god, Yahweh, for the arrival of a mystical messiah who would free them from the yoke of Roman rule. Yet there were zealots who were not content simply to pray but foolishly desired to die challenging the power of Rome. So we granted their wish. With our swords and spears we taught a lesson they had failed to learn: Rome was always right.

A few days before the festival of Passover, Pilate left his palace in Caesarea and traveled to Jerusalem to be nearby in the event the Jews' fervor instigated turmoil. Along with my men—the Augustan cohort of six hundred auxiliaries and one hundred mounted cavalry—I had prepared not only for the prefect's arrival but also for the battalion of Italian legionnaires that always accompanied Pilate from Caesarea. The Italians would stay at the praetorium and be under Pilate's direct command, and my commander and I would be responsible for making sure they were fed and housed.

The Jews' holy city, ruled by religious men who scorned nearly every aspect of Roman civilization, grew louder and more clamorous during religious festivals, the population increasing as thousands of Jews came to celebrate the Feasts of Passover and Firstfruits at their Holy Temple. Jews from birth and proselytes; Jews from Crete, Arabia, Parthia, and Mesopotamia; from Cappadocia, Pontus, Phrygia, Pamphylia, Egypt, Libya, and Rome; Medes and Elamites—the streets were overrun with them.

Within hours of Pilate's arrival, my commander summoned me. I found *Tribunus rufulus* Gaius Aelius in full battle dress, his molded cuirass gleaming with medals and the insignia of his rank. His slave stood behind him, adjusting the folds of the scarlet paludamentum, without which no commander would ever set out for war.

Who would we be sending to the underworld today?

I saluted my superior, then removed my helmet to receive my orders.

"*Salve*, Tribune," he said, acknowledging me with a cursory glance. "I trust the new arrivals have settled into the barracks at the praetorium?"

"They have. And their horses have been stabled."

He nodded. "Good, because Pilate may need them later today. A zealot, name of Yeshua Barabbas, has robbed the high priest and several members of the Sanhedrin. The council has called for blood."

I lifted a brow. "Have we located this thief?"

"Oh, yes." Aelius's mouth curved in a mirthless smile. "The brigand knew Caiaphas would not stand for such a violation, so this time he's gone beyond thievery and committed murder. He and his men have taken control of a tower outside the city."

I glanced at the map on the tribune's wall. "At the south gate?"

"The very one. I dispatched a century just after sunrise, but apparently the zealots are better fighters than we expected. You and I are going to finish them off."

Only by tremendous effort was I able to repress an expression of surprise. High-ranking officers usually sent cavalry and infantry to handle small skirmishes, and to my knowledge Aelius had never participated in any sort of battle. But perhaps he wanted to earn glory . . . or hoped I would praise him in a report to Pilate.

Aelius strapped on his helmet and dismissed me with a nod. "I'll meet you at the tower."

Upon reaching my quarters, I called for my slave to help me

into my armor. After I donned the padded vest worn under the breastplate, Titus helped me fasten the molded cuirass, which protected the torso. Finally he fixed the paludamentum to my right shoulder and clasped it with a fibula.

"Will we be sparring later today, master?"

"I think this morning's duty will negate the need for training, Titus. But if you want to practice, one of the auxiliaries might be willing to spar with you. Just don't hurt him."

I turned in time to see a half smile cross his face. My slave had been sparring with me for years and was as good a rider and swordsman as any man in my cohort.

"Anything else I can get you?"

"Fill a waterskin for my saddle. It's going to be as hot as Dis's oven out there."

As Titus stepped away, a bloodstained messenger brought a status report: "The brigand Yeshua Barabbas still holds the south tower. They murdered the tower guard and threw his body over the railing."

"Was the guard a Roman citizen?"

"No."

No need to worry about retrieving the body then. "Anything else?"

"The centurion was felled by a rock. He lives, but is no longer conscious."

"Then let us go."

I rode out with twenty mounted men. We found the dazed centurion at the bottom of a slope, where his legionnaires battled not only the zealots but also the blazing heat and taunts from an angry mob. I shouted a command to the new arrivals, "You six spread out and barricade the crowd from this area. Arrest anyone who crosses the line. The rest of you bring water to the men who have been fighting." I squinted and looked up at the tower, where a zealot with wild hair waved a blade and grinned down at us. He held the high ground, but only for the moment.

As I watched, one of the centurion's men broke formation and charged up the slope, roaring in frustration. For his efforts he was struck with a stone tossed by one of the zealots. The rock slammed into the soldier's face, knocking him off his feet and sending him tumbling down the hill like a straw doll.

"Dis take you," I muttered. "Only a fool charges alone."

With their shields up, the remaining men struggled for a foothold on the scree as stones and curses rained down on them. Battered bodies, both Roman and Judean, littered the slope beneath the swirling dust.

I squinted up at the tower again, then ducked as a javelin sailed past my ear. The zealots had done enough damage; it was time to gain the high ground.

I found the injured centurion, who staggered and looked at me as if confused. "Remain here," I commanded, noting that Tribune Gaius Aelius had just arrived. "I will rally your men and show this rabble how Rome handles insurrection."

The centurion nodded, and then a rock from a zealot's slingshot pinged his helmet and knocked the man senseless. He collapsed at my feet like an empty feed sack.

To celebrate this small victory, the zealot leapt over the short wall around the tower base and danced on the slope, taunting us. He bent to pick up a helmet from a fallen legionnaire and popped it on his head.

I bent to the centurion and checked the lump rising on his forehead. I picked up his pilum, which he had not yet thrown. Balancing it in my palm, I took aim at a man on the tower wall, then threw it and nodded when the spear pierced the zealot's thigh and sent a spray of blood arching into the air.

"Form up!" I commanded the troops, who hungered for direction. *"Testudo!"*

On my command, the remaining legionnaires grouped themselves around me in a tight oval configuration. With shields raised to protect the top and sides of the formation, we climbed the slope, the zealots' stones and spears skittering harmlessly off the legionnaires' heavy wooden shields. Once the testudo reached the top of the hill, we knelt down. Then the men at the back pulled away and ran over their comrades' shields, scaling the wall by way of our improvised ramp. Out came their gladii, double-edged swords designed to be thrust beneath an opponent's ribs, and in very little time most of the zealots lay dead around the base of the tower. Three legionnaires ran into the structure, where I knew they would make short work of any insurrectionists who remained.

"Tribune!"

I turned to see a pair of legionnaires holding up the Judean scarecrow who had worn the Roman helmet as he mocked us. "Meet the infamous Yeshua Barabbas!"

I waited as my men dragged the beaten zealot over and dropped him at my feet. The man lifted his head and gave me a bloody smile. "I know how this ends."

"Then tell Yahweh," I said, lifting my gladius, "that you are soon leaving for the underworld, courtesy of Mars."

The fool would not be cowed. "It must pain you," he said, rising to his knees, "to know the one true God chose us over you."

I felt my mouth twist. "Not today, he didn't." I lowered my sword and sliced the tendons at the back of his heels, effectively hobbling him. He would suffer, but he wouldn't die. Though this man was no citizen and did not deserve a trial, I wanted Pilate to see that we had done our part to maintain *Pax Romana*, the peace of Rome.

Not until I started walking down the hill did I spot Tribune Gaius Aelius among the fallen.

2

Rachel

Because it was a holy day, I should not have gone to the market-place. But the distance was within a Sabbath's walk, and I wanted to be sure I had secured my booth in case of windy weather.

I was standing behind the counter, tying down an awning, when a litter passed my booth. A jeweled hand lifted the curtain, and a woman's voice commanded the attendants to halt.

I straightened and smoothed my tunic. Few Gentiles ventured into this marketplace, but the few who did nearly always stopped to buy bread.

"No braided loaves this morning?" The upraised curtain revealed the woman's face, her hair worn in the Roman style of tightly wound curls. "I was hoping you'd have that lovely bread. My husband is entertaining guests tonight."

"My apologies." I dipped my head in a slight bow. "But today is Passover. At sunset we celebrate the first day of our Feast of Unleavened Bread. I cannot sell anything today, and tomorrow I will offer only unleavened *matzot*."

"That's a shame." The woman's lower lip edged forward in a pout. "Surely you might make an exception and bake a braided loaf for me. My husband is an important man—he supplies silks to the prefect's wife."

I shook my head. "I'm sorry."

The woman chuffed and let the curtain fall. As her litter-bearers continued onward I couldn't help overhearing her complaints: "These Jews and their joy-killing god! I'll never understand why they can't be more accommodating. One has only to placate a god and then one can do as one pleases. . . ."

I blew out a breath as the litter moved away and propped my elbows on the counter that usually held rows of freshly baked breads. I deserved the woman's criticism, but not for the reasons she mentioned.

I was such a hypocrite. Why did I bother to keep the traditions of my people? Why did I obey the law when my heart had so thoroughly led me astray?

Leah, another seller, stopped to say hello. "A blessed feast to you! How did you do yesterday? And where did you eat the Seder?"

I forced a smile and deliberately ignored her last question. "I stayed busy yesterday. Sold every bit of my matzot."

"I kept busy too. Between the selling and the baking and the Temple . . ." She shrugged, then waved a quick farewell and went on her way.

I felt my smile fade. Yesterday had been particularly painful. Though I did keep busy with customers, I couldn't help feeling left out of the joyous hubbub of the preparation for Passover. Mothers had filled the marketplace, calling greetings to friends and neighbors as they bargained for spices and ingredients for their Seder meals. Merchants charged premium prices for the apples, figs, and nuts that would be mixed for the *charoset* to represent the mortar our forefathers used to make bricks in Egypt. Eggs sold briskly as well, for they had a special place on the traditional Seder plate, along with *karpas*, celery, or parsley to represent the coming spring; *maror*, a bitter herb such as horseradish root to represent the bitterness of slavery in Egypt; and of course the roasted lamb.

After leaving the market, most families went directly to the Temple, fathers leading their wives and children while carrying the sacrificial lamb on their shoulders. The lambs had been selected and set apart for sacrifice four days earlier, tied to a post outside each home so that the animals might be carefully observed and tested. No family could offer a lamb that had either a blemish or spot.

On preparation day, thousands of priests and Levites from all over Judea went to help with the bloody work of sacrifice. The crowds were so large that the Temple gates had to be opened and closed three times so each family had an opportunity to offer its perfect lamb. The air trembled with the bleating of terrified animals as the priest offered them as both a sin offering and a peace offering. "The only annual sacrifice that serves a dual purpose," I could still hear my father saying. "That is why Passover is so special to us."

After selling all my matzot, I went to the Temple as well. Standing in the Court of the Women, alone among so many mothers with their children, I heard my heart break with a crisp snapping sound. I had hoped to find comfort by being with my people, but the presence of so many happy faces stung like salt on an open wound.

As the scent of roasting lamb drifted through the streets of Jerusalem, I walked home and quietly closed the door behind me. Sinking to the bench at my small table, I pressed my palms to the bare wood and relived the preparation rituals of my childhood.

While my father roasted the meat, my mother encouraged me to sweep the house, cleansing it from any *chametz*, crumbs of leavened bread, for leaven represented sin, which had no place in our lives. Mother scrubbed every dish and cooking utensil while I carried every storage basket outside and thoroughly thumped it so the house would be entirely without leaven.

Last night, every Hebrew family in Jerusalem had gathered around their crowded tables and shared the story of God's miraculous provision for our freedom from slavery in Egypt. Because every table had to have at least ten guests, people invited neighbors, friends, even strangers to fill up the empty spaces and share the Paschal meal.

No one invited me . . . because no one knew I was alone.

As the entire Judean community ate and prayed together, I sat alone in my chametz-free house and lit the Shabbat candles for myself. My late husband's family no longer approved of me, and I had been too ashamed to let anyone else know I had no place to go. I would have been welcomed if I'd confessed I had nowhere to eat Passover, yet I didn't want to force my company on anyone.

If the community discovered my secret shame, I would be completely cast out, perhaps even stoned.

So why did I refuse to bake with leaven during the weeklong Feast of Unleavened Bread? Why did I still bow my head and recall God's deliverance during Passover? And why would I refrain from eating or tasting any bread at all until after the sheaf of new grain had been waved at the Temple?

Old habits, I told myself. Ingrained tradition.

But habits and tradition did nothing to explain why I still yearned for the God of my father, the God with many names: *el Roi*, the God who sees; *Yahweh-Jireh*, the God who provides; and *Yahweh-Shammah*, the God who is always there.

I shook myself out of my reverie as another litter passed my booth, this one carried by foreign slaves with shaved faces and thick wigs. Because this special Sabbath had fallen during the middle of the week and caught them unprepared, the Roman inhabitants of Jerusalem were probably desperate for bread and other services.

But no matter—by sunset, Jerusalem would surely resume its ordinary rhythms.

My husband had been in the grave six months when his parents, Benjamin and Leah, arrived at my home with their younger son, Daniel. I welcomed them, served them lemon water and fig rolls, then sat to hear the reason for their unexpected visit.

They wasted no time. "Rachel," Benjamin said, pressing his hands together as he leaned toward me, "we want you to come live with us. A woman should not live alone. People will talk."

"It is not safe," Leah hastened to add, reaching for Daniel as if he might be exposed to danger simply by being in my house. "With the streets so filled with Romans, we will worry about you unless you are safely under our roof."

I looked from one earnest face to the other. "I like living here. The marketplace is not far, and as you can see, I've made renovations to the oven for my baking—"

"It's not safe," Leah repeated. "You really should have gone back to your family after Aaron's death. We would have sent for you when the time was right."

I blinked in confusion. "What time?"

"Really, we had no idea you would want to stay in Jerusalem," Benjamin continued. "A woman belongs with her people."

I drew a deep breath and tried to smile. I had no people, not really, and my in-laws knew it. My parents died when I was ten, and my aunt and uncle raised me along with six children of their own. Because they put their children first in all things, I was twenty before they arranged a marriage for me. They would not welcome me if I were to return to their home in Hebron.

"My aunt and uncle are older now," I said, trying to explain the situation without implying criticism of my relatives. "They are busy with their children and grandchildren."

"You could sell the house," Leah suggested. "The money would go a long way in paying for your keep until you are ready to marry again."

A muscle in my eyelid began to twitch. "I love my house. Since it was purchased with money from my dowry, it is fulfilling its purpose and sheltering me now that I have no husband."

"Then you shall not move to Hebron." Benjamin waved his hand, dismissing the topic. He laughed. "We are not trying to get rid of you. Like Ruth to Naomi, you are a daughter to us, and we are only concerned for your safety, your welfare—"

"And your reputation," Leah added. She squeezed Daniel's shoulder again. "And that is why we have agreed: if you do not want to go home to your people, you must come live with us."

"You are welcome to join us," Benjamin said. "You will live with us, and next year, or when you are ready, you will marry Daniel."

Leah released Daniel, then leaned forward to grab my hand and place it in her son's.

"No!" I pulled away, recoiling from Daniel's smiling face. "He's an unbearded boy!"

"He's seventeen," Benjamin said, his retort hardening his features. "He can father a child as well as any man in Jerusalem."

I snapped my mouth shut, stunned by his bluntness. "You want me to have a son for Aaron. A levirate marriage."

"Of course." Benjamin tugged on his beard. "It is written in the law. 'If brothers live together, and one of them dies childless, his widow is not to marry someone unrelated to him: her husband's brother is to go to her and perform the duty of a brother-in-law by marrying her. The first child she bears will succeed to the name of his dead brother, so his name will not be eliminated from Israel.'"

I could not speak for a moment. I absorbed the horrible revelation in silence, then shook my head. "I know the law, but a levirate marriage will not work in our situation. I am too old for Daniel. He will not want to marry me."

"I would," Daniel said, still smiling. "I would marry you today."

"But we would not be well suited." I injected a note of firmness into my voice. I had watched Daniel for the last five years and knew he was intensely attached to his mother. Even if he were my age, I would not marry a man who still clung to his mother's skirts.

"Our Aaron has died without an heir," Leah said, her voice breaking. "You can correct that mistake by marrying Daniel."

"I'm truly sorry." I looked from Leah to Benjamin. "I'm sure Daniel will make someone a fine husband, and they may be blessed with dozens of children. But I have no wish to marry, nor do I want to leave my home. I'm perfectly content to live here, and if HaShem wills that I live here alone, so be it."

"How could Adonai be pleased with a young woman living alone and unmarried?" Leah's sympathetic smile held a touch of sadness. "A woman's purpose is to bring new life into the world. How can you be happy just baking bread?"

Her question snapped like a whip and made me flinch. I had no answer to give her, but of one thing I was certain. I would never be happy married to a boy.

3

Clavius

I had no sooner returned to my desk when my slave announced a visitor, Marcellus Drusus, the injured centurion.

I gestured for him to enter, not surprised that he'd come to my quarters immediately. After a formal greeting, the weary and bloodstained centurion gave his report: "Three score wounded—twelve seriously. Sixteen dead, including Tribune Gaius Aelius."

I ran my hand over my face, still stunned by the commander's action. "Why did he engage the enemy? The situation was well in hand once the cavalry arrived."

"He charged up the hill as you called for the testudo formation. His slave thought he might have been caught up in battle fever. Apparently he was planning a return to Rome and hoped to embellish his name with glory."

I closed my eyes, understanding completely. Glory was one of Rome's most cherished ideals, granted to those who had selflessly defended their country with great dedication in the face of danger. Once received, glory could be passed on to one's descendants, forever gilding a family name. Gaius Aelius had been the son of a senator. Despite the senseless nature of his death, his family would hear that he had died in a brave assault. His action, however reckless, would raise the stature of the family name.

If he were still alive, my father would want me to follow Gaius Aelius's example.

I walked to the window and looked out on the centurion's returning troops, many of whom were hobbling through the courtyard and washing blood-spattered faces in the fountain. "Double the ration tonight," I said. "Especially the wine. And have those lumps on your head looked at—see my physician."

The centurion saluted and walked away, leaving me to wash my own hands in a basin. As I was drying them, Titus appeared in my doorway. "A letter, Tribune," he said, a barely controlled note of excitement in his voice. "I believe it's from your sister."

"Which one?"

"Adorabella, of course. We never hear from Chloe, do we? But she didn't share a womb with you, so perhaps it is only natural that you and Adorabella would be closer."

I smiled, silently indulging my slave's inappropriate fondness for my twin sister. My father had purchased Titus when I was twelve, and the slave had been my near-constant companion ever since. He went with me when I enlisted in the cavalry at eighteen, obeying Father's wish that I choose a military career while my elder brother, Crispus, carried on the family business of horse breeding. Adorabella obeyed Father and married a noble young man from the equestrian order. For my younger sister, Chloe, an unexpected late addition to the family, Father arranged a lifetime as a vestal virgin, one of the veiled women in white who tended the perpetual fire in the Temple of Vesta, goddess of the hearth. The last time I visited Chloe in Rome—to bury our father—she mentioned that while she might never know the pleasure of marriage, at least vestal virgins were emancipated from their fathers' control.

"Everyone," I had countered, "is under *some* authority. I am under the prefect's command. We all must obey the emperor. And the emperor must obey the gods."

"Ah, but the emperor," she said, an impish light twinkling in her eye, "can bend the gods to his will, can he not? An offering here, a sacrifice there, an auspicious augury—you cannot persuade me that the gods control the emperor."

I then warned her about the dangers of tempting the fates and promised to offer prayers for her safety. Service in Vesta's temple had flamed Chloe's independent streak, but Adorabella had never been a rebel.

I crossed my arms and settled in my chair, eager to hear my sister's news. "Proceed."

"I'm glad she found a way to send it through the military post," Titus babbled, breaking the seal on the scroll. "She has always been a clever girl. Both your sisters are clever, nearly as bright as you, and of course your brother—"

"Read," I interrupted. "My patience dwindles."

Titus cleared his throat. "'My dear brother Clavius, how I hope you are well! I have asked a friend to give this to her brother, who serves with a legion in Gaul. Can you believe the distance this parchment has traveled? Of course, I have no idea when this will reach you; perhaps you will have a niece or nephew by the time you read this.'"

I held up a hand. "Did she date the letter?"

Titus skimmed the page. "No."

"Read on."

"'Yes, that is my big news. At long last, Herminus and I will have a child, and I plan to name the baby Crispus Clavius after my two darling brothers. Herminus is delighted, of course, and Mother plans to offer sacrifices to Lucina so that the birth will proceed smoothly. She worries I am too old, but I remind her I am the same age she was when Chloe arrived. So rejoice, brother, for you are to become an uncle in the spring. I will write as soon as the baby is born, though you may not read the news until the child is weaned—ha! I'm jesting. Much love to you, dear twin. Yours always, Adorabella.'"

Titus lowered the parchment and smiled. "She certainly seems happy."

"Indeed." I was thrilled for her, but would let Titus's delight speak for both of us.

"Wonderful news. Her baby should be born anytime now." He rolled the parchment around the spindle. "Would you like to reply?"

I hesitated. I had not changed out of my sweat- and blood-stained tunic, plus this was a busy time, with so many dignitaries in Jerusalem and so many legionnaires moiling about in the barracks. But if I did not reply soon, I might not revisit the notion for weeks.

"I will reply later, in my own time."

Titus had just begun to unfasten my breastplate when a

white-robed messenger appeared and saluted smartly. "Tribune, Pilate summons you."

Of course he would. With Gaius Aelius dead, I was the highest-ranking officer at Antonia Fortress.

I glanced at my spattered apparel. "I am yet sticky with blood."

"No matter, it's urgent. There's more trouble afoot."

Sighing, I reached for my helmet and motioned for Titus to refasten my breastplate. I had been right to postpone my response to Adorabella. In Judea, a spark of trouble could blaze to a conflagration within minutes.

4

Rachel

Bored with watching passersby, I double-checked my knots and left my booth. Enjoying the rare luxury of free time, I wandered the streets, only partially aware that I was moving toward the Temple and the Antonia Fortress. I did not expect to see anyone I knew loitering outside the Roman garrison, but something drew me toward the fort nonetheless. . . .

Until I noticed that the streets were unusually crowded. I expected the Temple area to be congested, for the priests would soon offer the *hagigah* or second Passover lamb, a sacrificial offering for the entire community. Yet the crowds around the Temple were anything but reverent and dutiful. Highly agitated men milled about the outer court as if afraid to carry their conversations inside, and at one point a frowning group of Pharisees spilled from the court and began walking toward the praetorium, the stately structure that had once been King Herod's palace. Because everyone knew the prefect of Judea would be staying at the praetorium during Passover, my feet turned westward and I followed the Pharisees. What sort of trouble had Pilate instigated this time?

I was not the only curious observer. In no time I was swallowed up by a crowd that surged through the narrow streets, a mob of tense faces, furrowed brows, and flushed complexions. Romans on horseback waited and watched in narrow alleys, but none of them moved to disperse the people. If trouble erupted, however, they would not hesitate to drive us away with whips and sticks.

Finally I came upon the tall gates of the praetorium. The gates were opened wide, inviting access. Nearby, dozens of people stood in close proximity, peering toward the street as if watching a parade of dignitaries. I rose on tiptoe and tried to peek over their shoulders but couldn't see anything. I tapped a woman's arm next to me and asked her what spectacle lay ahead.

"The Nazarene," she said, her voice choked with emotion. "The one said to be our Messiah."

"Who is this Nazarene?" I cupped my hand to my ear, hoping she'd speak up. "Who are we watching?"

"Criminals!" The man beside her scowled at me. "Thieves and murderers. And one would-be king who could tempt the emperor to squash Jerusalem like a bug."

Knowing I would never be able to see clearly at the intersection, I doubled back and ran down a narrower alley that opened onto the same road. A knot of women stood alongside a mounted Roman cavalry officer, all of them facing the street. The women were weeping, some loudly, some quietly. One woman appeared older than the others, and her face had gone the color of parchment. She did not wail or sob, but stood silently, her hands fisted, her gaze intent on the road.

I wriggled into a tight space between the women and the mounted soldier and watched the procession. More legionnaires appeared, one carrying a royal ensign, the other slowly beating a drum. They were followed by condemned criminals. The first staggered under a heavy crossbeam, but his eyes sparked with rebellion as he roared at those who taunted him. The second condemned man seemed resigned to his fate, neither looking around nor speaking to anyone who jeered at him.

The third man . . . I grimaced when his face came into view. Like most Judeans, he wore a thick beard, but I could see bald patches where portions had been pulled or ripped away. A gruesome crown of acacia thorns had been wrapped around his scalp, and his arms, raw with reddened slashes, trembled beneath the weight of the crossbeam. He staggered beneath his burden. As I watched, he stumbled and fell, his knees hitting the street first, followed by his head. The impact drove the thorns deeper into his scalp.

That's when I saw his back. His was not the striped back of a man flogged thirty-nine times, the maximum allowed for a Roman citizen, but the back of a man who had been flogged until the barbed lash had torn away most of the flesh.

A Roman officer riding at the rear of the procession stopped and pointed to a fellow in the crowd. "You there! Carry his crossbeam!"

The bystander's eyes widened, yet he did not dare argue. He murmured something to a woman next to him, then stepped forward, glanced at the fallen criminal, and bent to settle the crossbeam on his broad shoulders. After giving the condemned man an apologetic look, the bystander straightened and followed the two who had gone before.

Something moved in my heart. I can't explain what propelled me forward, but I found myself kneeling only inches away from the brutalized man. Our eyes met, and in his expression I beheld pain as I have never seen it—raw, powerful, and shattering. He opened his mouth as if to speak, but the snap of a lash came between us. The man gasped as the end of the leather scraped across his lacerated back.

At another crack of the whip, the man managed to stand. He did not curse or insult the observers but turned to look at the weeping women who stood next to me. "Daughters of Jerusalem, don't cry for me," he said, his voice as ragged as his flesh. "Cry for yourselves and your children! For the time is coming when people will say 'The childless women are the lucky ones—those whose wombs have never born a child, whose breasts have never nursed a baby!' Then they will begin to say to the mountains 'Fall on us!' and to the hills 'Cover us!' For if they do these things when the wood is green, what is going to happen when it is dry?"

The whip snapped again, and the bleeding man obeyed, following the fellow who carried the instrument of his execution.

The road filled as soon as the procession had passed. One of the weeping women tugged on my sleeve. "Did he say anything when you were near him?" she whispered, her voice in tatters. "Did he speak to you?"

I shook my head. "Who was that? And what did he mean about childless women being lucky?"

"That was Yeshua," she answered. "And I don't know what He meant, but Yeshua is the hope of Israel and the hope of the world."

I cast her a sidelong glance of utter disbelief. *That* man? That man was beyond hope. If the world had staked its hope on him, the world was surely lost.

The woman and her friends began to follow the procession. Propelled by curiosity, I followed too.

5

Clavius

My journey to see Pilate took me to the western side of the city, to the luxurious palace built by Herod the Great. The sky began to darken as I made my way through the crowds around the Temple, and by the time I arrived the sky was as dark as slate, the air thick and still. A guard immediately ushered me into the prefect's presence.

Pilate took one look at my bloody garments and frowned. "Did you win?"

"I was told to hurry."

The prefect shook his head. "In truth, you're well dressed

for this job." He began to pace along the balcony, wordlessly demanding that I keep up with him.

"I have heard," he began, one hand resting on the folds of his toga, "about the demise of Tribune Gaius Aelius. It would appear that the heavens themselves mourn him."

"I am sorry about his loss. I know you appointed him as a friend—"

"I didn't summon you to discuss the past. We have a problem *now*."

"Has something happened?"

"Passover." Pilate stopped at the balcony railing and sighed as he looked out on the dark city. "Every hothead and holy fool in Judea is here in Jerusalem, stirring the pot. Some ascetic won a following by working so-called miracles, and the Sanhedrin decided to put him down. Sent a lathered mob here screaming for his blood because he claims to be their messiah."

"Is that a punishable offense?"

"It is when his followers call him *king*. I had to crucify the man. He hangs on Golgotha even now."

I swallowed hard. Crucifixion was a heinous death, usually reserved for the most horrible crimes, yet Pilate's order had been based on hearsay. But Rome was always right. If Pilate's decision was not good in the moment he made it, it would be proved good later.

The prefect's mouth thinned to a straight line. "Even my wife holds me responsible. She thinks I surrendered to the mob."

I bit my tongue. Though I did not know Pilate well, I knew he had valid reasons for surrendering to the religious leaders. Our prefect had antagonized them on several occasions, most notably by marching his troops into Jerusalem at night while they carried images of the emperor on their standards—images the Jews considered blasphemous. After the event, the religious leaders went to Caesarea and protested for six days. On the sixth day Pilate surrounded himself with legionnaires and met with the Jews. He boldly stated that unless they stopped protesting, he would immediately order their executions, at which point the religious leaders lay on the ground and exposed their necks, daring Pilate to strike them down for their beliefs. The prefect backed down, and the Jews left Caesarea in peace. They had not written Rome about the incident, saving Pilate's career, but neither had they forgotten the lesson they learned: Pilate feared the emperor above all else.

No doubt remembering his troubled history with the religious leaders, the prefect's brows rushed together. "Don't give me that disapproving look, Tribune. I've had enough already." He gestured to the courtyard below, where potted plants had been overturned and fountains toppled. "I had a situation—something you don't seem to understand. In six weeks the emperor arrives, and he expects to find order here. Roman peace and *order*!"

He stepped forward, inserting himself into my space. His sour breath wafted past my nose. I kept my expression steady and my eyes open beneath his glare. "What is it you want of me, Prefect?"

Pilate backed away, dipping his hands into the rippling water of a nearby fountain. "You're in charge of operations at the Antonia now, and that includes overseeing executions. I need you to take control out there and finish things before the Jews' high Sabbath. This execution has gone on long enough. Do this Nazarene a small mercy and break his legs."

He tilted his head as if recalling something, then gestured to a fresh-faced young man who stood at a respectful distance.

"Oh, and meet your new *beneficiarii*, Lucius Tyco Ennius, fresh from Caesarea. His father's a friend."

I bowed my head, wordlessly accepting his unspoken command even as I examined the lad. Lucius Tyco Ennius was a good-sized youth, broad through the shoulder and long-legged, though from where I stood his hands appeared soft and pink. He wore an infantryman's uniform, complete with sword and pilum, so he was well equipped for the work.

I would take responsibility for this new aide. Train him, teach him, and rebuke him if necessary, because he came from a noble Roman family and had high ambitions. I would do these things without complaining because today we had lost our commander and the post of tribune rufulus now stood empty.

As tribune cohortis, I stood first in line for promotion.

Following Pilate's orders, I hurried to the stables with Lucius in tow. The young man tried to make conversation as we walked, but I had no time for small talk. I wanted to handle the job and leave. Already I had seen more than enough death for one day.

The stable master had my horse ready and waiting when I returned, but Lucius had no mount. "Another," I informed the stable master, who smiled and turned to Lucius. "Any preference, sir?"

Lucius looked at him with a slightly perplexed expression, as if he had a question but lacked the courage to ask it.

I lifted my hand and caught the lad's attention. "Do you ride?"

The young man's brow creased. "I can drive a chariot, but I have not had many occasions to mount a horse."

I bit back an oath and turned back to the stable master. "A

steady mount then, with a bridle and a wide saddle. Perhaps you have an older mare?"

As the man hurried away, Lucius fastened his helmet and looked at me. "I do not intend to be a burden, Tribune. In my family, a working knowledge of livestock was not considered an asset."

"You were more suited to books, I suppose."

"Of course. I studied the arts, languages, poetry, and architecture."

Could the lad be any more useless? He had clearly been reared in a patrician home, and his father probably meant for him to become a senator one day . . . unless he was the second or third son, and there were not enough senate seats to go around.

"I'm not sure you'll find those lessons useful here," I said. "The work is far more . . . physical."

"Do not be concerned for me, Tribune. By nature I am a man of action and organization."

"Let us hope so."

I blew out a breath and looked to the busy street beyond the stable. The stable master had better bring out a calm mare or I'd be spending much of the day teaching young Lucius how to ride.

The steady clip-clop of hooves drew my attention. The stable master reappeared, leading a large *Bellator equus*, a draft horse with a wide back, a thick neck, and colossal legs. I rubbed my chin, smothering a smile, as Lucius warily approached the beast. "How do I . . . ?" He pointed up to the saddle.

The stable master dropped the reins and fell to his knees, offering himself as a human mounting block.

I pressed my lips together, suppressing my impatience as I watched Lucius step up onto the stable master, then gingerly lift one leg over the four-horned saddle. When he was finally astride the beast, the stable master handed him the reins and backed away.

"Shall we go?" I asked. I pressed my calves to my mount's side, signaling him to move out.

"Wait!" I glanced over my shoulder in time to see Lucius flapping the reins. The stable master offered a word of correction. Then, finally, Lucius's mount started walking away from the stables.

Since we could not travel at a fast pace on account of the crowds—a situation that definitely worked to Lucius's advantage—we let the horses pick their way through the shadowy streets. As we rode toward the southernmost city gate, the long wail of a shofar echoed over Jerusalem.

"What was that?" Lucius asked.

"The sound of the shofar. The priests have just sacrificed the Passover lamb."

"Does that happen often?"

"Every year."

The lad frowned. "Sounds mournful."

I glanced at the gray sky overhead. "The weather influences your opinion."

"What brings on a sky like this?" Lucius gestured to the boiling clouds. "A moment ago the sun was shining, but suddenly—"

A deep rumble cut him off, startling the horses while sharp bones of lightning split the sky. Like a roar of outrage, a crescendo of thunder trembled the ground beneath the horses' hooves.

"Tremor!" Lucius struggled to maintain his seat on the nervous mare. "Earthquake!"

Lightning continued to spider-web the sky as the city wall behind us groaned and cracked. Zigzag fissures appeared in the mortared stones, and my stallion skittered beneath the saddle. A caravan of travelers broke apart and scattered in all directions, one woman falling not more than a few paces from my horse. A pair of chickens escaped from a wagon and flew beneath my mount's hooves, adding to the beast's confusion.

"Poseidon's unhappy," Lucius yelled, struggling to hold his mount in check.

"Some god is."

The ground continued to shake, the sky swirling with dark clouds. As my horse wheeled, I saw movement from a nearby graveyard—steles and rock formations swayed as the earth shivered, many of them toppling over. I stayed in the saddle while my horse fretted, leaning down to pat the beast's flank as the ground finally stilled.

I gave my new companion a quick look—by some miracle he hadn't lost his seat during the quake. "Truth to tell, you're a quick learner," I admitted. "One might think your family was of the equestrian order."

"Patrician," he said, completely missing the intended humor in my comment. "My father is a senator."

Of course he was.

I sighed and turned my mount toward the path leading to Golgotha. When Lucius pulled up beside me, I gave him a nod. "Is this your first post?"

"It is. Father thought I should experience a coarse environment like Judea. He said it would enlarge my horizons."

"That it will. Have you ever witnessed a crucifixion?"

"No. But I've witnessed several public executions in Rome. Hangings mostly. One decapitation."

Searching for a familiar landmark, I peered through the gray murk that had descended with the earthquake. "Crucifixion is more than a death sentence. Death on an execution stake comes slowly, and only after hours of torture. It is not easy duty. In fact, we rotate the battalions so that no particular group of legionnaires becomes overburdened by the Golgotha detail."

"You worry about them becoming sloppy?" Lucius asked.

"I worry about them forgetting they are men."

I glanced at Lucius again, who was examining my face with considerable concentration. "But you, Tribune—do you not oversee executions on a regular basis?"

"Aye." I kicked my mount, urging him to pick up the pace.

The place of the skull lay outside the city near a ravine, a convenient spot for conducting executions. The treeless hill could be approached from the south, yet the steep incline on the north made it easy to dispose of unclaimed bodies. No burial necessary.

As we approached I spotted the familiar face of another centurion from the Antonia. He and his men had been responsible for escorting the prisoners and carrying out the day's executions. The centurion stood off by himself, and at the sound of our horses' hooves he spun and looked at me with a resolute face and eyes that appeared deeply sunk into caves of bone.

Three upright timbers rose up from the barren hilltop, a condemned man hanging on each. The men had been stripped of their clothing, and at a glance I realized what had become of it all. A cluster of soldiers in the foreground were gambling for the prisoners' garments.

I dismounted, handed my reins to a legionnaire, and looked around, hoping to spot what had caused the centurion's distress. The condemned men looked like dozens of others I'd seen before, their wrists nailed to horizontal crossbeams with iron spikes, heels nailed to the vertical execution stake. A sign hung above the center stake, and only after stepping closer could I read it.

YESHUA HA-NATZRATI, THE KING OF THE JEWS

For the first time I looked at the men on those instruments of torture. The first and third man were still pressing down on their wounded heels to catch a breath, then quickly sinking as agony overcame their exertions. The man in the center, however, did not move. His eyes were open but unfocused, even when I stood before him and searched for signs of life. The chest did not rise, the eyes did not blink, not even when thirsty flies landed on his face. Trickles of blood marred his wide forehead and the cheek above his patchy beard, but the blood had coagulated into a thick stream that no longer flowed.

"Kill me." The man on the first execution stake spoke when I turned to look at him. "Kill me . . . please. My arms . . . end this."

A soldier from the gambling group stood and barked at the condemned man. "Shut up!" Then he looked at me. "Wish I could put an end to his misery, believe me. Wish we could all just go back to the barracks."

The centurion stood alone between his gambling soldiers and a handful of observers, most of them women. They were wailing, arms around each other, their faces streaked with tears.

I had a feeling they weren't weeping for the two thieves.

Another guard stood with his hands over his ears. "I hate it when they scream—hate it." He stared at me and jerked his head toward the third man. "That one could last for days. But you should have heard him talking. Plans on going to paradise when it's all over."

I looked to the centurion for confirmation, but he gave no sign of having heard the guard's comment. He stood with his jaw clenched, scanning the dark sky above the hill. When I approached, he lowered his gaze and gave me a halfhearted salute.

"How goes this, Centurion?" I asked.

The man shook his head. "A strange day, Tribune. First the darkness, then the earthquake—"

"It was just a tremor."

"Was it? Yet we have this king"—he nodded toward the Nazarene—"and something's wrong here. The mob felt it. I felt it. The heavens still feel it."

"Apostate!" a woman from the crowd yelled. She threw a stone past the guards and struck the dead man on the center stake.

Lucius stepped forward, his palm wrapped around the hilt of his sword. "You can't allow that," he told the centurion. "Smite a few. Show them the rod."

I held up my hand, silencing my overeager beneficiarii, and looked at the unmoving body on the center stake. "The Nazarene—obviously dead."

"After only six hours?" Frowning, the centurion stepped closer to the body.

I turned to observe. "Has he spoken?"

"Just before the tremors," the centurion said, pausing and swallowing hard, "he said . . . 'It is finished.'"

"See that it is," I commanded. "And wrap this up quickly. The populace is agitated on account of the festival, and the prefect doesn't want any trouble."

One of the soldiers pulled an iron bar from an equipment bag and stepped to the base of the first execution stake, where he broadened his stance. He positioned the bar behind his shoulder and then swung without warning, breaking the thief's legs. The criminal screamed with his last solid breath, then hung in silence as the legionnaire spoke softly, assuring the sufferer that he would not suffer much longer. The thief attempted to support his weight on his legs, but the futile effort only rubbed the raw edges of broken bone against skin, eliciting waves of fresh agony.

Lucius turned away from the sight, and the women wailed anew. One fainted into the arms of her companion.

The centurion looked at me with reddened eyes. "The Nazarene's mother was here earlier," he said. "She did not scream, but you could see suffering on her face—looked like she'd been turned inside out. I didn't think she could last until the end, and neither did the Nazarene. He told one of his followers to take care of her, and the man led her away."

I lifted a brow. I had spent years working as an executioner on Rome's behalf, and I had heard many things from condemned criminals—curses, protestations of innocence, impotent threats, and insults. I could not recall hearing any tortured prisoner use his last breaths to demonstrate mercy for someone else.

The guard with the iron bar stepped up to the Nazarene's execution stake. Since the supposed king of the Jews was no longer breathing, I caught the guard's attention. "Use your pilum."

The guard dropped the bar and picked up his spear. He pressed the iron tip to the lower edge of the Nazarene's rib cage and thrust it up into the dead man's heart before stepping back. Blood and water flowed over the graying skin.

"He's gone," the centurion said, his gaze fastened on the dead man's face. "Surely this was a righteous man."

The guard withdrew his pilum and looked at his commander. "Wouldn't be the first time we killed a good man, eh?"

"Watch yourself," I warned. "Rome is always right."

The guard couldn't see the tears in the centurion's eyes, but I couldn't ignore them. I gripped the man's shoulder. "Steel yourself to the job. Rome expects more from you. Go along now and tell the prefect it's done."

I shoved the centurion toward the road, who walked through the gloom with a shambling step. I turned then to face the remaining witnesses. Some of them wept, some beat their breasts, and some watched me, probably wondering what atrocity Rome would commit next.

Behind me I heard a thwack and another anguished cry, followed by soft words as the legionnaire with the iron bar talked the thief through his final breaths. Amazing, how long it took some men to die. Sometimes death came without warning, striking perfectly healthy people in the prime of life. During executions, however, the living tended to struggle, resisting with their last breaths against impossible odds.

At least the Nazarene had surrendered quickly.

When the prisoner on the third execution stake finally hung motionless, the legionnaire turned to me. "We're done here," he said.

"Then let's get to work. Pilate wants this wrapped up before sundown, on account of the Jews' holy day."

The centurion's men stood and immediately approached the execution stakes. They removed supports from the bases, hoisted the upright beams out of the earth, and stood back as the wooden posts slammed to the ground. Without ceremony, soldiers pried iron nails from pierced wrists and heels, dropping the long spikes into leather pouches for later use.

"Claim the body? Anyone?" The legionnaire at the first execution stake searched the crowd, then grabbed the dead man's arms and dragged him toward the steep slope that ran down to the ravine. After one last call he pressed his foot on the man's back, gave him an upward nudge, and sent him tumbling toward his eternal resting place.

The soldier who had worked on the third prisoner repeated the process, scanning the few remaining observers. "Anyone claim this one?" When the crowd recoiled, he dragged the dead man toward the precipice and shoved him over the edge.

Another soldier had just finished pulling spikes from the Nazarene. "Never killed a king before," he said, noting the inscription. He shifted, about to pick up the Nazarene's arms, when a voice stopped him.

"Wait!" A striking bearded man, immaculately dressed in the dark colors of the Judean elders, walked through the gloom with a scroll in his hand. "Tribune," he said and bowed before me. "I come from Pilate. Please . . . heed this."

Lucius recognized the man. "You're the Arimathean. I saw you with the prefect."

"I am Joseph of Arimathea, yes." He handed me the scroll, then pressed his hands together and looked at me.

I skimmed the message. "You're placing the Nazarene in your own family tomb?"

"That's right."

I handed the paper back. "What was he to you?"

The Arimathean's eyes welled with tears. "Please—the Sabbath's almost upon us. I have maybe two hours. Please."

I glanced around. A handful of weeping women still lingered, but they hadn't come forward to claim the body. Apparently no one else wanted him. "He's yours."

The Arimathean bowed again, then hurried back down the slope where another Jew waited with a handcart.

"Nicodemus—please." The Arimathean gestured to the weeping women, and the second man walked toward them, speaking to them in a low voice as the Arimathean pushed his cart up the hill.

I turned to the waiting legionnaires. "Don't worry about the Nazarene—they will bury him. Go find your centurion; you are done here."

The grateful men tossed their tools into a leather bag and hurried off, one of them tugging the dead man's robe over his head to stave off the rising wind.

Joseph of Arimathea dragged his cart closer. On it he carried a water jug, some folded linen, and a large bag of spices. I could smell myrrh from where I stood. I watched, arms folded, as the Arimathean approached the body and lifted the crown of thorns from the Nazarene's head. Weeping, he removed it and slid it over his arm, freeing his hands to lift the body.

"Gently," the one called Nicodemus said, hurrying forward to help.

Leaving them to their task, I mounted my horse and waited for the Arimathean and his friend. I had promised Pilate that I would finish this matter, so I would see the Nazarene safely to his tomb.

The proud men of Rome's Tenth Legion did not quit before the task was done.

6

Rachel

With my water jug on my hip, I lingered at the well. A premature darkness had fallen over the city, and my nervous neighbors kept glancing at the sky as if it might open up at any moment. The women moved with furtive steps, startled easily, and held on to their veils as the wind sharpened and blew dust into our faces.

"Were you there?" I asked again, moving to question yet another neighbor. "Were you at Golgotha today?"

She threw me a sharp look. "Why would I be there?"

"The Nazarene." I lowered my voice as she glanced left and right. "The rabbi from Galilee."

She lowered her head while reaching for the well rope. "What do you know of him?"

Encouraged that she hadn't walked away or ignored my question, I stepped closer. "Not much. But I saw him on the road—he fell right in front of me. He looked at me, and though I do not know much about such things, I do not understand how a rabbi can end up on an execution stake. I followed him to the place of the skull, but left when he sent his mother away."

"His mother was there?" The woman's hand trembled on the rope. "Mary?"

I nodded. "I believe that is her name. There was another Mary who didn't leave—and a man who led the rabbi's mother away. She was so wracked with grief that I helped him guide her down the hill. She trembled so terribly I thought she might faint."

The woman gripped an edge of her veil and held it taut against the wind, her brows constricting as she closed her eyes. "I know of her. She's related to a cousin who lives in Bethlehem. She always said something like this would happen."

"Surely she didn't mean crucifixion—"

"Not that exactly. But a prophet told her that a sword would one day pierce her heart." The woman shook her head and thrust the bucket toward me, spilling water onto my tunic. "If I were you, I would not speak of the Nazarene again. He has caused enough grief for his family. They all think he was crazy."

I took the bucket, but water was the last thing on my mind. "Did you know the rabbi? What could he have done to deserve death?"

She shook her head as she hoisted her water jug. "What do any of them do? Threaten Rome. Disturb the peace or challenge the Pharisees. Or maybe he dared to mock a Roman soldier. Whatever he did, he should have known better." She glanced at the dark sky again, then started for home, leaving me alone.

I pushed the bucket over the edge of the well and waited, listening for the answering splash.

7

Clavius

Dusk had gone blue and congealed with mist by the time Titus and I made our way to the officers' baths at the fortress. After stepping into the steamy pool area, I found I was not alone. Pilate had also come to enjoy the warm waters.

"Clavius!" Relief rang in his greeting. "Come and soak this horrible day away." To his attendant he added, "Fill his cup, and keep it filled."

I handed my robe to Titus and waded into the warm pool, then sank to an underwater bench and accepted the proffered cup. "Are the baths at the praetorium not to your liking?"

Pilate made a face. "There's only one problem with staying

at Herod's old palace—Antipas and his retinue are also in residence. Plenty of room for us to conduct business, but only one decent bath."

"And you probably prefer to be around Romans."

"Who wouldn't? So here I am, soaking away the cares of this horrible day." He drew a deep breath and sank beneath the water for a moment before reappearing, spouting like some pale, pink sea creature. "What do you desire, Tribune?" he asked, apparently feeling magnanimous. "A meal? Massage? A girl?"

I leaned against the wall and exhaled slowly. "Just this."

"You're still young," Pilate said, a note of envy in his voice. "A night's rest and you'll rise ready to do it all again."

When I raised a hand in protest, Pilate laughed. "Your service is valued, Tribune. I rely upon it, especially since we have lost Gaius Aelius. I ask pardon if today I seemed . . . vexed."

I smiled. "No matter."

Pilate sipped from his cup, wiped his chin with his forearm. "Is the Nazarene entombed?"

"I helped push the stone against it myself—huge rock." I sipped too. "The Nazarene had many admirers."

"Let's hope all that admiration is buried with him. Still have to clean up a few scraps." He lifted his cup again, then froze. "A strange episode. Don't think I've ever seen a death so welcomed—even by him. As if he *wanted* to be sacrificed."

"They're fanatics," I said. "Yahweh deranges them."

"Yes, 'no other gods' and all that. Lately I pray only to Minerva, for wisdom. You?"

"Mars," I answered, then dryly added, "and I am ever mindful of Dis. I find myself assisting him more often than I would like."

Pilate chuckled. "Of course you would pray to the gods of war and the underworld. Hopefully one of them hears us—I could use a little divine help." He gulped noisily and then thrust his cup toward his attendant. "Zealots, priests, wives, emperors—nothing I do is ever enough for them. I'm not a prefect, I'm a juggler. But one does what one must to keep them all happy."

I closed my eyes and gestured to Titus, who stood behind me. "I don't envy the mantle you wear, Prefect."

Pilate snorted. "Spare me—this is your path too."

I looked up, surprised by his insight.

"Your ambition, Clavius, is noticed." As Titus began to scrape the strigil over my back and shoulders, Pilate gave me a watchful smile. "Where do you hope your career leads?"

I considered my answer carefully. At thirty-eight I had to serve five more years before I could retire from the military. I hoped to step aside with glory and honor enough to serve in the Senate, but one could not openly admit such ambitions without risk of seeming audacious. My family, after all, was of the equestrian class, so I could not assume I would win a senatorial seat. If I did well and managed to avoid offending the emperor or any of his underlings, I might be appointed prefect or procurator of some pleasant province. In time I might possess authority equal to or greater than Pontius Pilate's.

I smiled. "Where? Rome, of course."

"And after that?"

I shrugged. "Position. Power."

"Which brings you?"

"Wealth. A good family. Fine horses. Someday a place in the country."

"Where you'll find . . . ?"

"An end to travail." I flattened my smile. "A day without death."

Pilate's mouth twisted. "All that for peace? Is there no other way?"

"Would that there were."

"Indeed." He released a hollow, mocking laugh that bounced between the walls of the nearly empty room. "Well, I'm off. Back to the praetorium and then to bed. Tomorrow promises further punishment."

He stepped out of the water and waited while his attendant wrapped him in a towel, then he turned. "The Nazarene, did you find him . . . different?"

I lifted a brow. "I found him dead."

Pilate smiled again. "So you did. Peace, Tribune. Good night."

8

Rachel

Sitting alone at my small table, I lit the two Shabbat candles, then covered my eyes to pray the blessing:

Barukh atah Adonai Eloheinu melekh ha'olam asher kid'shanu b'mitzvotav v'tzivanu l'hadlik ner shel shabbat.

Blessed are you, Lord our God, Ruler of the Universe, who has sanctified us with commandments and commanded us to light Shabbat candles.

When I lowered my hands and opened my eyes, some part of me hoped he would be sitting across from me, but I beheld only an empty chair. A chair that had been empty for more than two years.

I broke a sheet of matzah and bit into a small piece, analyzing the flavor, taste, and texture as I chewed slowly. Aaron had always liked my bread, though he never said so. But he could eat an entire braided *challah* at one meal and later wake in the night wanting more. His desire had given me the courage to open a booth in the marketplace, a booth that had become my livelihood since his death.

I picked up a small piece of dried fish and nibbled at it, then plucked a fine bone from my tongue and set it on the table. Aaron used to eat the bones, crunching them between his teeth, but I had never been able to accept the idea that humans should eat like dogs. Bones should be removed, I told him, soups should be sipped, and water should be strained before drinking.

But he had not listened to me. He laughed off my concerns and kept eating the way he'd always eaten, even though I warned that he might die from a bone caught in his throat.

I was wrong about that. It wasn't a fish that killed him, but a horse.

I had just returned from the marketplace when a Roman officer appeared on my doorstep to give me the news. I had been so intimidated by the decorations on his molded breastplate and the metallic clack of his sword belt that for a moment I could not grasp the news he brought: my husband was outside in a cart, killed by a skittish Roman stallion that had reared and struck Aaron's head.

My husband's parents rushed to the house as soon as they heard the news. Women from the neighborhood took Aaron's body from the cart and laid him on my table. They bathed him and tucked fragrant herbs among the linens they used to create his shroud. He had to be buried before sunset, so, still stunned, I mindlessly followed the funeral procession to the cemetery, where my in-laws and a few neighbors placed my husband in his grave.

Afterward, when I returned to my small, empty home, after Aaron's parents and younger brother told me good-bye with wailing and tears, I looked out my window and saw the Roman standing across the street. He did not attempt to speak to me, nor did he approach the house. But over the next several weeks I saw him many times, his expression as intense and burning as the sun upon my skin.

Pity moved my neighbors to patronize my booth, so I returned to baking. Working at night to avoid the hottest hours of the day, I baked challah and matzah and loaves of rye and fine wheat. I baked pomegranate cakes and small pies flavored with nuts. I enlarged my stone oven and carved out a small window at the back of the house to release the heat. I moved a bed to the roof and slept under the stars while my living loaves fermented and doubled and sputtered into delicious dough. Then I baked them.

And while I did the work of two or three women, my heart lay cold within my chest, silent and still. When women at the well asked how I was doing, I offered them pomegranate cake.

How could I explain that it was difficult to miss a man who never seemed very present in the first place? We had been married five years, and I could not recall ever having an in-depth discussion on any topic. Aaron was dutiful, always coming home at the end of the day, and he never struck me. But neither did he share the thoughts that filled his head or the memories that had shaped his heart. He rose before sunrise every morning, said his prayers, and went to the woodcutter's shop; at the end of the day he came home, ate dinner, and went to bed. And on the rare occasions when he reached for me, his touches were abrupt and quick, leaving my heart unsatisfied and my womb empty.

Once, after days of struggling to work up my courage, I asked if he found me unpleasant. He said no. I asked if I'd done something to make him unhappy. He shook his head.

When he died I was sorry for his loss, but I cannot say I mourned him. The house was emptier without him, though no quieter.

One day, more than ten months after Aaron's death, the Roman stood across the counter and offered three denarii—more than Aaron would have earned in a week as a woodcutter—for a cake filled with dried figs. Was his overgenerous offer prompted by pity?

Impolite words flew out of my mouth. "Was it your horse then?"

He blinked as color flooded his face. "No," he answered, his eyes grave. "But the rider was under my command."

I sold him the cake with no further comment, and he returned every day to make the same purchase at the same price.

I served many Gentiles at my booth—Greeks, Romans, Samaritans, and even the occasional Egyptian visitor. Word of my cakes and breads spread throughout Jerusalem, and as my neighbors noted the uptick in Gentile customers, their patronage declined.

One day as I wrapped the Roman's bread in parchment, a breeze blew through the market and caught the wrapper. It fluttered away, so I left my booth to chase it.

I was unaware that the Roman had also left the booth until I reached for the parchment and found his hand next to mine. For a moment time seemed to stop. Then I lifted my second finger and let it brush his. I lifted my gaze and found him studying me.

"Why are you here?" I whispered.

"Because . . ." he said, and I had never heard so many possibilities in one breathless word.

That night, after the sun had set and only shadows stirred in the darkness, I heard a knock and knew who it was.

My heart thudded noisily within me as I went to the door, and he said nothing when I opened it. I stepped aside to let him in, and when he stood in the flickering circle of lamplight, my first inclination—a gesture born of long habit—was to point to the stool where Aaron used to sit after returning from work.

The Roman obeyed silently, holding his helmet against his hip as I knelt and began to unlace his sandals. He made a small sound of protest deep in his throat, but I shook my head, silencing his objection. I removed the sandals, pulled a basin to my side, and filled it with water from my pitcher. I picked up his bare foot and used clean linen to wash away the grit of the day. His feet were callused, but neat, and tidy enough to have been tended by a slave. His calves were trim and muscular, probably from all the riding soldiers had to do, and I commanded my eyes to look no higher. I did not yet know what sort of dance I—we—were doing.

I did not dare look at his face as I worked, afraid of what I might read in his eyes, or he in mine.

When I had finished, I remained kneeling before him, my eyes downcast as a thousand thoughts raced through my head. I should never have let him inside. I had a reputation to consider. I had in-laws and neighbors who lived nearby and might have seen this man approach the house. Most of my people abhorred the Romans, because as an occupying force they made few efforts to understand that we were a chosen people who did not *want* to be assimilated. Yet here was a Roman in my home, an officer, the very man who had brought devastating news to this house. . . .

I shivered as his hand brushed my hair, skimmed my neck, and gently lifted my chin until our gazes locked. He bent and pressed his lips to mine, and even though a voice in my head shrieked protestations, I raised my hands to his shoulders and allowed myself to be pulled into his arms.

Later, as we lay on my bed, I stared at the stars and knew I had entered a dark territory from which I could never return. My husband's parents would never forgive me for this; the community would shun me if they knew. The priests would not allow me to enter the Temple, and if I were ever caught in this Roman's arms, I could face death by stoning.

But this man . . . I closed my eyes, reliving the memory of him in the marketplace. An aura of melancholy had clung to him, an air of quiet desperation, and I couldn't help feeling drawn to him. Something in me understood his despair and I wanted to heal him, to make him smile.

Another part of me, I had to admit, longed for the loving warmth of a man's touch. I had been lonely for so long . . . and Aaron had never been tender toward me.

The Roman stirred, and I braced myself for the conversation to come. He rolled onto his side, propped his head with his hand, and watched me for a long moment. His free hand tiptoed over my belly and caught my hip, pulling me closer.

"Why?" I looked at him, curiosity making me brave. "Why a Judean woman when you could have any sort of—"

"I didn't want just any woman."

I studied his tanned face, then timidly placed a fingertip on a scar that ran along his jawline. "Did it hurt?"

The corner of his mouth twitched in what looked like the beginning of a smile. "Not until after the battle."

That twitch—the first sign that he might possess a sense of humor—cheered me. "I don't even know your name."

There it was again—the same movement, this time involving both corners of his mouth. "Is it so important? It is a mouthful of words."

"So much?" I smiled despite his clear reluctance to share information that would mark him as more than an anonymous Roman. "I am only Rachel."

"You should not belittle yourself." His hand rose to brush my cheek. "You would stand out in any crowd."

I looked away as a blush burned my skin. I was not accustomed to compliments. Aaron had been a man of plain speech when he spoke at all. "Do not flatter me, sir. I am a simple woman, and tonight I have behaved badly, in a way completely foreign to my nature—"

"I hope you are mistaken." A muscle clenched along his jaw, and his gaze drifted to a place I didn't want to imagine. "The soldiers of Rome take whatever females they can find, and I've taken my share over the years. But I find no joy in lying with a hysterical woman, or one who lifts her skirts for money. Women like you . . . are as rare as dragons' teeth."

That was the first of many nights I shared with the Roman, who eventually gave me his name: Clavius Aquila Valerius Niger. Mindful of my reputation, he was careful to avoid being seen. The task was easier than I had imagined, because he could simply play the part of a soldier on patrol, a role guaranteed to send any late-night loiterers running for the safety of their homes.

I knew I shouldn't let him in, yet I could not—would not—

turn him away. He had become a listening ear, a source of alternative viewpoints, and a reason to live.

And when I lay in his arms, I felt cherished. Though my arranged marriage had never been deep or profound, I held no illusions about the Roman. For one day he would leave Jerusalem, and probably take my heart with him.

But when he held me, I felt beautiful, precious, wanted. And for now, that was enough.

9

Clavius

The night watch had assumed their posts by the time Titus and I left the baths. "Will you be ready for bed soon?" Titus asked.

"I think I'll walk a bit," I answered. "Clear my mind before sleep."

"Very good. I'll make things ready for you."

He hurried away while I climbed the stairs and stepped onto the rampart, home to a glittering view that never failed to calm me. Leaning on the stones of the short wall, looking out on hundreds of shining lights to the north and east, I could almost believe that Rome had civilized this part of the world.

The sun had set while I was in the bath, but I never tired of watching one day move into the next. As the sun lowered to mark the beginning of another Sabbath, Jerusalem pulled itself in like a turtle. Now the bustling city lay quiet, its cobblestone streets empty save for foreigners and the occasional hurried straggler. When the sun dipped below the horizon, darkness rose, first filling the alleys between dried brick buildings, then sliding up pillars and walls as shadows carpeted the pavement and crept upward to join the black velvet of a star-studded sky. Small lamps and candles had been lit in each home before sunset to avoid the prohibition against lighting a fire on the Sabbath. The women in those homes had uttered a Sabbath prayer before sharing a meal with her family.

I could not look out on Jerusalem's lights without thinking of Rachel. When she taught me about the Sabbath ritual, I found it difficult to ignore the yearning in her voice. She wanted to sit with *me* at her Sabbath meal; she wanted to include me in her blessing.

If only I could tell her how often I had since felt the same yearning—not because I believed in her demanding Yahweh, but because I believed in her.

Rome, my sworn mistress, was always right, but she wasn't always *good*. Rachel was.

"Tribune?" Titus's voice cut through the heavy silence. "If you wish to write your sister before retiring tonight—"

"I do," I told Titus, "but I'll write in my own hand. Tomorrow you may post my reply. Send it through the same legionnaire who posted it for my sister."

"Yes, sir."

"To bed with you then."

When he had gone, I went back to my quarters and began to write.

Dearest Adorabella—

How happy I was to hear your news! Titus read your letter to me, and the grin on his face was as wide as the great sea. He is, I daresay, apt to be more excited about your news than your husband, whom I recall as a rather somber fellow. I hope you are content with him. I hope you are content with life. You deserve happiness, if anyone does.

Do you remember how we used to play in the courtyard? How I wanted to be a physician and you wanted to be a mother? My wish was unsuited to me, but yours, dear Adorabella, suits you perfectly. May the gods bless you and grant you a safe delivery. I hope to meet my niece or nephew before I am in my dotage—and now I am jesting. If all goes well, I hope to return to Rome when I retire. Your child will be just the right age to sit and listen to my stories of war.

I do look forward to returning home. Judea is not a pleasant post, as the people here are uncommonly clannish and stubborn. They refuse to adapt to the Roman way of life and cling to their own gods and traditions—one god, actually, who has reportedly delivered them from slavery in the past. They seem intent on goading him to deliver them from Rome, so they sacrifice and refuse all manner of Roman innovations that might make their lives easier and more civilized. They are particularly repelled by our Roman gods, though I cannot understand why. Our gods are much less demanding than the one they serve.

Today I executed a man who supposedly worked miracles. At dinner tonight I talked to legionnaires who were familiar with the story. According to the rumors, this messiah, a Nazarene, fed thousands from a few loaves and fishes. He healed lame men, opened the eyes of the blind, and raised a dead man who had been four days in the tomb. Can you imagine what a military commander this messiah would make? His army would not need to carry food or medical supplies. Any man who died by the sword would be raised by a word, and forward they would march, conquering all as they went.

Unfortunately, this warrior messiah proved to be exceptionally meek and disappointingly mortal. I heard that he did not raise a word in his defense, nor did he resist the prefect who questioned him. And he died early—much sooner than the thieves who hung with him in the place of execution.

Most ironic of all, the religious leaders of his own people were the ones who pressured the prefect into ordering his execution. Have I not already mentioned that the Jews refuse all sorts of things that would make their lives easier? I have never encountered a more stubborn and stiff-necked people.

As I said, this is not a civilized place. How I long for Rome, and to see you of course. I miss you.

Yet I must not allow you to believe I am the most miserable brother on earth. I have met a woman—not the sort I could marry, unfortunately—but in her way she reminds me of you. Her eyes brim with life, and her actions are gentle and good. When I first saw her, something within me trembled to think that such a lovely and fragile being could exist in this infernal place, and you would laugh if you saw how your fearsome brother is reduced to mildness in her presence.

Not that anyone else would notice. But you would, for you know me so well. As I know you.

Be strong, dear sister, and take care of my niece or nephew until I am able to come home again. I will offer daily prayers to Lucina on your behalf.

> *Much love to you and yours,*
> *Clavius*

10

Clavius

Dawn came up in streaks and slashes over the walls of the fortress. Stepping into the rising warmth, I sipped from a cup of water and watched the brightening sky with approval. Time had appeased whichever gods had been displeased yesterday, so surely this day would be better than the one before.

I turned to the small niche in the wall where I made my daily offerings. A clay statue of Mars stood within, along with a small cup of wine and a spray of laurel leaves. I pressed my forehead to the wall above the niche and said my morning prayers: "O Mars, faithful warrior, I crave your face and favor will bless the lion and the Roman people, visiting fear and dread on our foes. And with this offering, your devoted servant seeks divine obligation to further his pursuits that I may prosper and honor you eternally. Father Mars, I pray and beseech you that you be gracious and merciful to me, my family, and my men. Ward off and remove sickness, seen and unseen, destruction and ruin, and permit my endeavors to flourish and come to good issue. To you, Father Mars, I utter this prayer and do you reverence . . ."

The sound of somber music distracted me from prayer. Turning, I saw an all-too-familiar sight. As pipers played a melancholy tune, soldiers brought in the dead officers from our encounter with the zealots outside the city. Legionnaires, many of them wounded, stepped out of the barracks as my fallen comrades entered the open courtyard in a wagon, laid out for us to do them honor. At the end of the procession a narrow cart carried a body covered with a scarlet banner embroidered with the emblem of *Legio X Fretensis*, the Tenth Legion. Legionnaires lifted the body off the cart and placed it in the center of the courtyard.

Aware that scores of men were waiting, I went downstairs and strode across the courtyard until I reached the covered shroud. After kneeling beside it, I loosened the drawstring at the top, pulling until the opening revealed the blue face of Gaius Aelius, of praetorian rank and a valued commander of our legion. A slash, hastily sewn shut by one of the physicians, marred what used to be a distinguished face.

"A coin for the ferryman, Gaius Aelius," I said, inserting two coins into his mouth. "Journey well, sir." I stood and saluted while the men cheered the bravery of the Tenth Legion.

Bareheaded and unshaven, I led the procession out of the courtyard, through the city gate, and into the Roman cemetery, a path lined with steles and simple mounded graves. The funeral pyres of lesser soldiers were already burning there, filling the air with smoke and drifting ashes.

I watched in respectful silence as legionnaires laid the body of Gaius Aelius atop his own pyre, then set it alight as his comrades bore silent witness. Crackling in fiendish glee, flames rose to consume the body and send Aelius to Dis, caretaker of the infernal regions of the underworld.

The flames were still roaring when I spotted Pilate's messenger near the cemetery gate.

———◈———

I approached the prefect through an open portico and found him bent over a table covered with scrolls and maps. I offered a perfunctory salute. "Salve, Prefect."

Pilate's eyes narrowed as he turned and sniffed. "You smell of meat—a feast?"

"A funeral."

Pilate grimaced and then gestured to someone I couldn't see. "There's your solution—burn him. In public."

"Cremation is not our way."

I stepped into the room and discovered Caiaphas, the Jews' high priest and leader of their Sanhedrin, a seventy-one member court composed of priests, elders, and rabbis. The high priest was instantly recognizable in his distinctive long white garment, covered by a shorter blue tunic trimmed with scarlet, purple, and blue fringe. The black-robed members of the Sanhedrin were also recognizable, for most of them were Pharisees who disdained jewelry in favor of an overt display of fringe and phylacteries—capsules of holy scripture written on parchment—tied to their heads and arms. Religiosity on full display.

I turned from their sanctimonious faces and waited on Pilate.

"Cremation may not be your way," he remarked, his mouth dipping in a wry frown, "but neither is work on the Sabbath, yet here you are."

Caiaphas ignored the jibe and acknowledged me with a nod. "Tribune."

"Burn who?" I asked, ready to get to the heart of the matter.

Again Pilate frowned. "The crucified Nazarene."

I looked from Pilate to the high priest. Cremation was the Roman way, definitely not favored by the Jews. "Why burn him?"

"Because he's business unfinished," Caiaphas answered with a scowl.

"The man is dead, Caiaphas," Pilate said. "His followers are hiding. He's no longer a threat to your monopoly on piety."

"But still a threat, Prefect." The high priest turned to me. "While alive, that deceiver said he would rise again after three days—he foretold it. We request the sepulcher be sealed until the third day has passed lest his disciples come by night, steal him away, and claim he has risen from death. That would cause more unrest in this city than all his blasphemies combined."

Pilate looked at me for confirmation. I inclined my head in a subtle nod. I probably had a more intimate knowledge of the Jews than he did, and I knew they believed that a soul lingered near the body for three days before departing for Sheol. I could see why the priests were concerned, and understood why the Nazarene's followers might believe the ridiculous claim. After all, if the Nazarene had previously raised the dead, why couldn't he resurrect himself?

But rumors were as plentiful as rats in this part of the world, and I had never met any man, Roman or Jew, who could defeat the absolute power of death.

"You have a guard," I reminded Caiaphas. "Secure the tomb yourself."

Pilate folded his hands. "My words exactly."

"Let me explain *again* that we need a Roman seal," Caiaphas said, speaking as if we were idiots. "This must be seen as the impartial will of the prefect."

"And not your own," Pilate added, a corner of his mouth twisting.

The high priest spread his hands to include all the Pharisees who had accompanied him. "We seek only what Caesar seeks: peace in Jerusalem, peace in Judea . . . a peace you will lose if this man's body vanishes."

Ah, there it was again. The subtle threat of blackmail in the form of a letter to Tiberius Caesar.

Both Caiaphas and Pilate looked at me.

"Hence my summoning," I replied, my voice dry.

Pilate grimaced and waved me away. "Just see to it."

Groaning inwardly, I saluted him and nodded at the group of Judean elders. And as I walked away from that particular flock of black crows, I thought of Rachel and realized again how much she was risking by opening her home to me.

That sanctimonious group wouldn't hesitate to tear her apart.

11

Rachel

My people could eat no leavened bread until the end of the seven-day feast, and no bread at all until tomorrow. But after the priest waved the firstfruits of the grain harvest before Adonai, they would be hungry, and they would want bread.

I had been up since sunrise, loading dung patties into my oven and setting the fire. Sweat now streamed from my brow and trickled down my back, but the fire was finally hot enough for baking.

I measured flour into my bowl, then carefully poured in a measure of cold water from the Pool of Siloam.

Perspiration—any excess water—was my enemy. All of the five major grains—wheat, spelt, barley, oats, and rye—began to ferment when combined with water, and fermentation caused dough to rise if it was allowed to rest. The dough could be mixed only for the time it took to sing a stanza from Isaiah, and not a breath more lest the ingredients begin to foam.

Words my father had taught me came back to me as I sang and stirred.

> "We all, like sheep, went astray; we turned, each one, to
>   his own way;
> yet Adonai laid on him the guilt of all of us.
> Though mistreated, he was submissive—he did not
>   open his mouth.
> Like a lamb led to be slaughtered, like a sheep silent be-
>   fore its shearers, he did not open his mouth.
> After forcible arrest and sentencing, he was taken away;
> and none of his generation protested his being cut off
>   from the land of the living
> for the crimes of my people, who deserved the punish-
>   ment themselves.
> He was given a grave among the wicked; in his death he
>   was with a rich man."

With the mixing done, I tossed my dough onto my linen-covered board and kneaded it, leaning my weight on my hands, flattening the dough to a thin layer. Once I had rolled it into a rectangular shape, I draped it over the spiked rolling pin and carried it to the oven, where I placed it on the serrated cooking stone. Then I sat back and watched the dough crisp, turning it with a wooden paddle once the bottom had developed brown stripes. I removed it, set it on the table to cool, and went back to my board to make another sheet of matzah.

While I worked, my thoughts returned to the crucified Nazarene. After talking to several people in my neighborhood, I learned that the mere mention of his name—Yeshua—tended to elicit one of two reactions. People were either glad the Roman governor had killed him or extremely sorry that the Nazarene was dead.

"I saw him first when I went to see John the Baptizer," one tearful woman told me. "Yeshua was there and asked to be put under the water. John refused, saying that Yeshua had no sin to repent of, but Yeshua insisted. So John lowered him beneath the waters, and when he came out, we heard a rumbling from heaven. John said, 'Look, here is the Lamb of God who takes away the sins of the world!'"

My neighbor wiped her wet cheeks and looked at me. "What do you suppose he meant by that?"

I had no answers for her, but as I pounded my dough, a new flood of memories from previous Passover feasts came back to me.

My father, whose big, booming voice always seemed to fill our house, had placed a great deal of emphasis on the unleavened bread. "Unleavened bread is the only bread permitted during Passover," he would tell me, shaking his finger at me as Mother poured cold water into the flour. "It is the bread of affliction, because we were thrust out of Egypt."

Mother could not let the dough rest, so she worked quickly. "There are special rules for baking the bread," Father would say, his wide eyes rolling toward the hot oven in the corner of the house. "The bread must be striped and pierced. Bread that is not striped and pierced—"

"Is not suitable for Passover," I would answer, smiling at him.

After the sacrificial lamb had roasted and the bread baked, Father would open our door and let the invited guests enter.

The door remained open during the feast, symbolizing our willingness to welcome anyone who wanted to come.

Once our table had filled with more than ten friends and neighbors, my father began the Passover meal by reciting the *kiddush*, a benediction, over the first cup of wine. Then we would wash our hands and dip parsley into salt water and eat it. The green vegetable, Father explained, symbolized the hyssop which was dipped into the lamb's blood and applied to the lintels and doorposts of our forefathers' homes in Egypt.

Next, Father would pray over three unleavened loaves of bread, break the middle one, and eat the smaller piece. He wrapped the larger one in a piece of linen and hid it while I covered my eyes, determined not to peek.

Next came the four questions, and no matter how many people sat at our table, Father always directed the questions at me. "Why is this night different from all other nights?" he would ask.

"On all other nights we may eat leavened or unleavened bread, but on this night only unleavened. Why is that?"

"On all other nights we can eat all manner of herbs, on this night only those which are bitter. Why is that?"

"On all other nights we do not dip even once, but on this night, twice. Why is that?"

"On all other nights we can eat any kind of lamb in any way, and any kind of meat in any way, but on this night it is the Paschal lamb that is roasted. Why is that?"

Then I would recite the answer: "We were all slaves to Pharaoh in Egypt. If God had not delivered our ancestors with a strong hand, with an outstretched arm, we would still be slaves in the land of Egypt. This is why this night is different. Wherefore, even if we were all wise men, it would still be our duty to recount the story of the Passover or the coming forth from Egypt."

As I listened along with the other guests, Father would tell the story of how God brought Israel out of Egypt. And when he had finished, I and any other children present would be allowed to search for the missing second piece of matzah. Often I would find it tucked beneath my father's chair, or in an empty pitcher on the table. But whenever I found it, my father always praised me highly, even as he unwrapped the matzah and passed it around for everyone to break off a piece to eat.

We would end the evening by singing hymns of praise, usually the Great Hallel.

> "Give thanks to Adonai, for he is good,
> For his grace continues forever.
> Give thanks to the God of gods,
> For his grace continues forever.
> Give thanks to the Lord of lords,
> For his grace continues forever. . . ."

I shut off the flow of memories as my internal clock signaled that the time of kneading had ended. In one quick move I ran my spiked rolling pin over the thin dough, piercing it, then draped the dough over the pin and crossed to the oven. After spreading it on the serrated stone, I stood back and listened to the moisture within the dough sizzle . . . and again considered the Nazarene.

Though I had no way of knowing for certain, I suspected he had shared a Passover Seder Thursday night with his followers. Yet he was crucified yesterday, apparently in the same hour the priests blew the shofar and offered the special Passover sacrifice in the Temple compound.

He had not protested or cursed while hanging on the execution stake. He told his friend to care for his mother, and another time he lifted his gaze and said, "Father, forgive them; they don't understand what they are doing."

What . . . what if John the Baptizer had been thinking of Passover when he referred to the Nazarene as the Lamb of God?

I had seen the Nazarene's back . . . it was striped. And in the act of crucifixion, his wrists and feet had been pierced.

I sank to my stool as my knees began to tremble. Not for me, because I willingly bore my sin and my shame. No, I trembled at the thought of the Nazarene on the stake, and the knowledge that my Roman lover had been among the men who crucified him.

12

Clavius

Joseph of Arimathea had constructed an expensive tomb for his family in a cemetery filled with expensive tombs. Located just outside the city walls, in a leafy garden with several flowering trees, the wealthy man's burial chamber had never been used until yesterday. Lucius, several Pharisees, and half a dozen legionnaires met me at the spot, and together we Romans rolled away the stone to confirm that the Nazarene's body still lay inside.

I bent to thrust my head into the space and immediately noticed the body had not begun to smell. Given the heat and the general messiness associated with crucifixion, however, the inevitable stench would develop soon enough. I called for a torch and lifted it in order to survey the crypt. The cavernous space was larger than most tombs, with a stone slab for the body and several niches in the wall to hold ossuaries, where the bones would rest in a stone box after the body had decayed. Such was the common practice in Palestine, as family members shared a tomb. A year or so after death, an individual's decayed remains would be placed in a decorated container and stored, leaving the slab for more recently deceased family members.

This Arimathean must have felt a strong kinship with the Nazarene, if he was willing to count a convicted criminal as part of his family.

I moved a step forward and held my torch above the body. It had been quickly encased in a linen shroud. Blood stained the fabric at the man's head, hands, and feet, rusty stains that would grow darker in time.

If the Nazarene's disciples could see what I saw, they would not doubt the finality of death.

I backed out of the tomb and addressed one of the somber priests who lingered nearby. "Satisfy yourself, if you must, before we seal it."

The priest stepped into the tomb, then hastily backed out and nodded.

"Seal it." I gestured to my men, who braced themselves and rolled the huge circular stone back into place. Once the opening was tightly covered, a legionnaire wove ropes between iron hasps driven into the stone and the tomb opening. When the ropes had been secured, Lucius spread wet clay over the knots, then pressed Pilate's seal into the soft earth.

I chose two soldiers to stand guard overnight. I could tell they weren't happy to have the extra duty, but they didn't dare complain.

I looked at the taller man. "No one touches these seals before sunset tomorrow—understood?"

They nodded.

"Once the sun has set on the morrow, report to the priests at the Temple." They nodded again, but not before I saw a flash of apprehension cross the second guard's face. "Where's your centurion, soldier?"

The second guard stiffened. "At the fort, sir. He's not himself . . . not since yesterday."

"Are you pained by his absence?"

"No, sir. No."

The first guard spoke up. "It's just . . . we were to have the night off."

"I'll have rations sent."

I took the reins of my horse from Lucius and turned the beast as Joseph of Arimathea came forward and reverently placed his hand on the secured stone. Behind him, a few of the Pharisees hissed their disapproval, but Joseph paid them no mind.

"He deserved a pit like the other two." A Pharisee spat the words at Joseph, then backed away when I stepped forward with my hand on the hilt of my sword. The man glared at me, turned and murmured something to the others. A moment later they scurried off like dark beetles.

I waited until Joseph moved away from the tomb before addressing him. "You're part of the Sanhedrin too, are you not?"

Joseph nodded without looking up.

"Your brothers despised this man, and yet you mourn him."

Joseph hesitated, glanced back at the sealed stone. "He was . . . unique among men."

"Was he a king?"

For the first time, Joseph looked directly at me. "You test me, Tribune."

I blew out a breath and shook my head. "What was he called—by the people who knew him?"

Joseph's eyes glittered in the light of the setting sun. "Some called him Rabbi, some called him the Light of the World, and some called him the Bread of Life. But most people called him Yeshua."

With my task completed, I rode slowly through sunset's slanting rays, hoping I might find a Greek or Roman merchant who would sell me a statue of Lucina, goddess of childbirth. Wrapped in my cloak I rode like a shadow accompanied only by the steady clip-clop of my horse's hooves. Occasionally, voices drifted out from behind shuttered windows.

"Where's your dead rabbi's magic now? He was never the one. Not a son of David."

"Like bleating sheep they scattered, without even putting up a fight."

"Why do you ignore us, Adonai? Why have you been silent for so long?"

"Grass will grow on your cheeks and still the messiah will not have come. . . ."

Giving up on the idea of finding an idol so near the Temple, I left my horse at an inn and slipped through the shadows to a house I knew well. A house I only dared visit after dark.

13

Rachel

I heard his knock, as gentle as always, and hurried to the door, drawing him in with an eagerness that brought a smile to his weary face.

"I am glad you are here," I said, barring the door behind him as he sat on the stool. "I have been longing to talk to you."

Gone was the awkwardness with which I used to greet him. I smiled, as always, but hurried to untie the laces of his sandals and spilled half the water I meant to pour into my basin. "I've been thinking"—I pulled one foot free of its shoe—"about the Nazarene."

"Wait." Clavius looked at me, placing a finger beneath my chin and tipping my face toward his. "No kiss?"

"What was I thinking?" I threw both arms around his neck and kissed him as long as my patience would allow, then pulled away and went back to washing his feet. Realizing, belatedly, that the subject of crucifixion might be troubling for him, I took a deep breath and forced myself to calm down.

I untied his second shoe and lowered his foot into the basin. A good woman should always honor her husband—man—and inquire about his health and well-being.

"How are you?" I asked, glancing up as I splashed sand from his feet.

My question—and the eagerness he undoubtedly saw behind it—lifted lines of weariness around his eyes. "Tired," he said, leaning against the wall, "but I always feel more rested the moment I walk into your house."

"What has exhausted you?" I asked, doing my best to give him my full attention. "I hope there were no more revolts in the city."

"No revolts, only politics." He sat while I unfolded a linen square to dry his feet. "And grief from the leaders of your Temple."

I heard the subtle emphasis, *your* Temple, and wanted to reply that I had nothing to do with the religious leaders, but perhaps I did. If Isaiah spoke truly, perhaps the Nazarene had been sent for my people, the people who did not recognize their own sacrificial lamb.

When I lowered the towel, he caught my hands and stood, lifting me. With his arms around me, he bent his head to graze my neck, breathing in the scent of my hair.

"I was fortunate," he whispered. He straightened and planted a kiss on the spot where his lips naturally touched my forehead. "I've just come from the Nazarene's tomb, and I feared I would smell like death."

"His tomb?" I pulled away to study his face. "I understood he was a poor man."

"He may have been, but he had wealthy friends." Clavius shook his head. "He died with the wicked, but was buried with the rich. I should be so favored by the gods."

I backed away, my breath catching in my throat. "I have a song," I said, taking his hand, "I want to sing to you."

I gave him honey water and porridge. I fed him matzah, honeyed figs, and cheese until he could eat no more. When he was satisfied and content, I pulled him down to the pillows and sat across from him. He leaned forward as if he would kiss me, but I pressed gently on his chest and told him I wanted to talk.

I never ceased to marvel that this man *listened*. "All right," he said, stretching out on the rug and propping his head on his bent arm. "Tell me what's on your mind. But if you want to talk about bread and cakes, be forewarned—I might have to interrupt and kiss you."

I frowned. "Whatever for?"

A slow smile spread across his face. "Because even the aroma of bread reminds me of you."

An unexpected tremor of desire ran through me, but I pushed it aside. "My father," I began, "taught me the words of the prophets after every Shabbat dinner."

I closed my eyes and sang the song from Isaiah. When I opened my eyes again, Clavius was watching me with frank longing on his face.

"Well?" I asked.

He slid closer. "I'm not sure I understand what you are asking."

"Yeshua . . . Could he be the one Isaiah spoke of?"

Clavius kissed the top of my knee, then looked up. "How could anyone know what will happen in the future?"

I blew out a breath, frustrated by the logical Roman mind. "Don't your people have oracles?"

He shrugged. "Certainly."

"And I know you have gods. So surely you must believe that a god could confide something important to an oracle."

He made a *tsk*ing sound with his tongue and held up a warning finger. "Who knows? Our gods are not all-powerful."

I stared at him, baffled. "Then what are they?"

"Give attention." With his finger he drew on the carpet the zigzag shape of a staircase. "On the bottom step," he said, "are the animals. They have life and limited power, but they are beneath man, agreed?"

I nodded.

"On the next step are men—and women, I suppose. We are higher than the animals, but not as powerful as gods."

I nodded again, more slowly this time.

"On the top step are the gods. They are more than men, but definitely not all-powerful. They make mistakes. They argue and fight. They are prone to jealousy and are sometimes forgetful. That is why we must remind them to honor our sacrifices and our many prayers."

I stared at the carpet, confused. "I have heard that your former emperor Julius Caesar has been made a god."

"True." The Roman nodded soberly. "Caesar Augustus, of course, was known as the son of a god, even though he was adopted by Caesar in his will. The current emperor, Tiberius, will no doubt be elevated to divinity as well, if he hasn't already."

"The distance, then, between man and god—"

"Is not great," he finished. "Only a step up, as it were. You might say the gods are superhuman." He reached out and tugged on a hank of my hair. "Isn't that how people described Yeshua the Nazarene?"

"No." The answer slipped from my tongue before I could form a proper response.

Clavius lifted a brow. "If he wasn't the son of a god, then what *was* he?"

I lifted my hands, confused and unprepared. "First, our God—"

"Yahweh?"

"We call him Adonai," I said, "because His name is too holy to pronounce. He does not sin. He does not lie. He does not commit evil of any kind."

"Sounds rather stern," he remarked. "Our gods are a livelier lot."

I shook my head. "Our God is one; He is complete and perfect. He created the universe, He controls and maintains the world, and He orders all things. He knows we are not perfect, but He wants us to be a holy people. That is why we sacrifice at the Temple—not to motivate Him to answer our prayers, but to pay a blood penalty for our sins."

"Quite a racket." Clavius's eyes narrowed. "Your priests must have an enormous appetite for lamb and beef, if you sacrifice for every flaw in your human nature."

"And you never pay a penalty? If you lie or steal or sleep with another man's wife—"

"We pay for our foolishness with consequences on earth. If a man is caught stealing, his hand is chopped off. A woman who lies, if discovered, will be ostracized by her friends. And there is no wrong in sleeping with another man's wife so long as the man is discreet about it."

I stared at him, my head swirling with confusion. I had heard of course that the Romans were nothing like us, but I had no idea our cultures were so far apart. I had been carrying a load of sin and shame for sleeping with a man not my husband, while Clavius's conscience remained untroubled.

"We are so very d-different," I stammered. "In my world, this—what we—"

"I know." He sat up and moved closer, drawing me into the circle of his arms. "I know I have placed you in danger. That is why I'm careful where you're concerned."

I leaned into him, resting my head on his chest and listening to the strong, steady beat of his heart. Just as I was about to surrender entirely, a thought occurred to me.

"Clavius"—I pulled away to look in his eyes—"in your culture, who is above the gods? If a storm wipes out a city, or a rainstorm ends a drought, who sent them? Not even a superhuman can control the weather and the stars."

His eyes narrowed for a moment, and a muscle worked in his jaw. "The fates," he said simply. "And they are so far above us that they are unreachable."

I tapped his chin with my finger. "That's not the fates," I told him. "That's Adonai. And He is never unreachable."

14

Clavius

On an open rooftop protected by waist-high walls, I lay on my back in Rachel's bed. She rested beside me, her hair a silken river on my bare chest, her hand over my heart.

"But what sort of god demands that a man mutilate himself?" I asked the air, taking care to keep my voice low. "Can you explain that?"

"It's our covenant with Adonai," Rachel answered, her breath warming my ear. Her eyes took on a distant look as she quoted, "'For the life of the creature is in the blood, and I have given it to you on the altar to make atonement for your lives; for it is the blood that makes atonement because of the life.'"

"Still, the very thought . . ." I looked around, eyed my own hands and feet, and shook my head. Rachel smiled and lightly touched the scab on my lower lip. "Who circumcised your lip?"

"A zealot. Two days ago."

"And what did it cost him?"

I remained silent for a long moment, remembering the instant I thrust my sword into the man's chest. "His price . . . has nothing to do with you."

She sat up and pinned me in a long scrutiny. "You know what happens to Judean widows found with Romans who slay other Jews? They would stone me."

"I would stop them."

"Until you leave Jerusalem—then what will become of me?"

I returned her look, drinking in the beauty of her dark eyes, her flowing hair, that perfect oval face . . .

She had surprised me with her talk of prophecies and burials and sacrificial lambs, but I didn't mind indulging her in conversation. In Rachel's company I had learned many useful things about the Jews. I could not resent her religious beliefs, no matter how bizarre they seemed, because those beliefs had made her the woman she was. Because I loved her, I would listen to anything she wanted to say.

Sitting up, I removed the garnet amulet from my neck and slipped it over her head. "Mars has protected me for years. Now he protects you."

Sighing, she pulled the amulet off and dropped it into the space between us. "Mars cares nothing for me. I was hoping . . . to hear some promising word from you."

I trailed my hand down the side of her warm throat. "Rachel, you ask for assurances I cannot give. A Roman soldier cannot marry until he retires, and I have five years of service remaining. I cannot change my circumstances or alter who I am."

"Speak the truth, please—you cannot marry me because I'm only a plaything."

"You are anything *but* a plaything." I hesitated. "You wish to stop this? Should I no longer visit you?"

"I wish . . . we weren't enemies." She held her hand over mine, squeezed it, and left the bed, moving to a spot that overlooked the city. "I wish," she said, her voice floating on the breeze, "Rome had never come here and you were of my tribe. I wish HaShem would deliver what He has promised us. I wish people could change into what they ought to be." She glanced over her shoulder at me. "What do you wish, Clavius?"

I lay back down and rolled onto my side. "That you would all stop seeking messiahs. And that you would come back to bed."

She gave me a resigned smile and strolled back to me. "I think," she said, climbing in and pressing a gentle kiss to my cheek, "that I am nothing but your secret, and you are nothing but mine. And that's all we will ever be."

"Then let that be enough." I pulled her to me, more than willing to lose myself in her arms once again.

15

Clavius

SUNDAY, ANTE MERIDIEM

I slept later than usual the next morning, a fact I realized when I stepped out of my quarters and found the sky already flaming with orange and pink. I drained a cup of water and leaned against a pillar as a pair of guards opened the gates to the barracks. A man waited there, a fellow I recognized instantly: Pilate's messenger.

"Tribune," the man called, spotting me on the rampart. "The prefect—"

I raised my hand, cutting him off, then went inside to find Titus and finish dressing.

When I reached the praetorium, the prefect was pacing, his mouth curled as if he wanted to spit. Spotting me, Pilate showed his teeth in an expression that was not a smile. "He's *gone!*"

I blinked. My mind filled with possibilities, but I selected the most logical. "The Nazarene?"

"Of course the Nazarene. Who else would I mean? His tomb is empty!"

I locked my hands behind my back. "Who brought this news—the guards?"

Pilate's face crumpled with misery. "The guards—*your* guards—are also missing. Some simpleton reported it! Who in Hades did you put on the detail? When you find them, have them flogged—to death."

I remained silent and allowed the prefect to rage. Surely there had been some mistake. Every legionnaire knew that sleeping on watch and deserting a post were both punishable by death. The two I left at the tomb may not have been the Tenth Legion's brightest and best, but neither were they ignorant fools.

When Pilate finally fell silent, I cleared my throat. "Shall I investigate?"

"Oh, that would be helpful." The prefect's voice vibrated with scorn. "Just do it before Caiaphas and his pack of raving Pharisees show up here."

"Too late," a voice called from the hallway.

Pilate and I turned as Caiaphas strode into the room with his entourage. The high priest, however, was not exhibiting the confidence of a man who had been proved right. Indeed, something seemed to be distracting—*upsetting*—him.

The high priest looked first at me, then at Pilate. "Shall we dispense with lies? The guards have told me what happened."

Pilate lifted a brow. "They came to you?"

"Seeking sanctuary. They know the penalty for sleeping on duty, and they feared for their lives."

Pilate's features hardened in a stare of disapproval. "What did they tell you?"

"They related a tale that went exactly as I predicted." The high priest tucked his thumbs into his belt. "The heretic's disciples came in the night and stole his body. Already they are proclaiming that he has risen from the grave. That he lives."

Pilate clenched his jaw. "Will the people believe it?"

"The weak will," Caiaphas said. "Others will want to . . . so we must announce the theft. No sweeping this one under the rug."

"But will they believe *you*?" Pilate asked. "Everyone knows you wanted the man dead."

Annoyance struggled with anger on the priest's face as he glared at Pilate. "They will believe the guards," Caiaphas answered, "*if* you don't kill them first."

Snarling in disgust, Pilate walked to his balcony and looked out over the courtyard. "Endless, these trials."

"Proclaim it," Caiaphas insisted. "Before this rumor spreads."

When Pilate turned back to us, I could see his thoughts working behind his eyes. "It's not enough. Without a corpse to *prove* the Nazarene dead, we have a potential messiah on our hands. I want proof. Tiberius cannot arrive to unrest in Judea. The body must be found." He shot the priest a pointed look. "You will help?"

"Of course. But *proclaim* the news."

Pilate looked at me, the once polished and friendly veneer

peeled back to reveal the animosity underneath. "Was my confidence in you misplaced, Tribune? Perhaps you'd prefer a post in the palace of Dis? You will hunt down these disciples, each and every one. But first and most important, get me the corpse of this cursed Yeshua before it rots."

In any thorough investigation, the first step is to visit the scene of the crime. I returned to the Antonia only long enough to pick up Lucius, and then we rode straightway to the tomb.

No one in his right mind enjoyed a dressing down by his superior, but as Lucius and I rode toward the tomb where we had last seen the Nazarene, I had to admit that despite my displeasure in enduring Pilate's rebuke, I had enjoyed seeing the high priest discomfited. Caiaphas was usually so smug and secure. He commanded the people far more effectively than did Rome, and he knew it. Because he held the real power in Jerusalem, I suspected he considered Pilate his personal puppet.

This morning, however, even the high priest had been unsettled by the thought of a missing messiah. Which made me wonder . . . what had the guards told him before he scripted their story?

I glanced over at Lucius, who seemed unusually quiet as he sat astride his wide mount. "This will be a pleasant break," I told him. "Shouldn't have to spill much blood over a man who's already dead."

"You shy away from the sword?"

"That would be impossible." I pressed my knee to my stallion's flank, nudging him toward Lucius's mount. "The work of death—we do so much of it I sometimes feel like Dis's personal ambassador. Putting down rebellions, conducting executions, killing those who disturb or threaten the peace of Rome—everything we do involves a sword. A routine investigation will be a welcome change of pace."

Lucius's mouth twisted in a wry smile. "I thought the work of a soldier depended on his blade."

"At times, yes. But a man must be careful. You are a patrician, destined to become an officer. And a leader of men should not be brutish."

Lucius gave me a grudging nod. "Do you read Ovid, Tribune?"

"The exiled poet?" I laughed. "I have read him—in my youth, when I had time to read."

"'Fortune and love favor the brave'—that's Ovid."

"I'm familiar."

"So why should I hold back my inclinations? If a man's heart leads him to charge ahead and do the brave thing, should the heart not be obeyed?"

I shook my head. "'In war, the olive branch of peace is of use.' That's Ovid too."

Lucius tipped his face to the sun. "I would never have imagined you a scholar."

"Never underestimate your commander, Beneficiarii. And never question his judgment." I clucked my tongue, urging my stallion up the hill that led to the garden cemetery.

At first glance the scene at the tomb seemed to fit the scenario the priests had described. The stone had been rolled away, the ropes detached, the seal broken. Inside the tomb, the Nazarene's empty shroud lay abandoned on the stone slab while a square piece of linen lay on the floor, somewhat apart from the rest. I picked it up, shook it open, held it to the single beam of sunlight that came through the door—and blinked when I saw an image of the Nazarene's face.

How could that happen?

I thrust my head outside the tomb. "Bring me the Arimathean!"

Lucius looked to a legionnaire, who hurried off to find the tomb's owner.

I began to evaluate the evidence. I picked up the end of a rope and noticed the strands of the jagged end were of varying lengths—as if they had been torn apart, not cleanly cut. Yet who but Hercules could snap a new rope in two? And why would anyone *need* to snap a rope? A thief would only have to break the seal and undo the knots.

I looked around for further evidence. Across from the stone, beneath an olive tree, I spied the cloaks, shields, and pila of the two guards . . . along with an empty wineskin. I picked it up, poured the dregs into my palm, and tasted. Wine, of course, and cheap wine at that. Those two had not only deserted their post, they had been drinking on duty, another provocation for which they should be severely punished.

I turned at the sound of men approaching on the garden path. Joseph of Arimathea walked with one of my men, and his eyes went wide when he caught his first look at the open tomb. After stepping inside and seeing the empty shroud, his eyes appeared to be in danger of dropping out of his lined face. "Where has he gone?" he asked me, a note of accusation in his voice.

"You tell me."

I would have pressed him, but Joseph appeared genuinely stunned. He peered into the tomb again, stared at the ropes, held the square facecloth in his trembling hands. He turned to face me. "If you didn't move him, who did?"

"That's what I intend to discover."

"How?"

"Investigation." I pointed to the small square marked by the shadowy image. "Had the body been anointed?"

Joseph shook his head. "No time. We wrapped him with bits of myrrh and aloes, then left because of the approaching Sabbath. We intended to finish preparing him today."

I took the facecloth and showed it to Lucius. "That's what you see here—sweat and herbs." Taking custody of the linen square, I ushered everyone out of the tomb. "Let nothing be disturbed," I told Lucius. "Post a watch here. Then set men at all the city gates. Every conveyance leaving Jerusalem must be searched. Send men in plain clothes to mingle among the crowds. Arrest anyone claiming the Nazarene lives and bring them in for questioning. We will track down the source of these rumors."

"Yes, Tribune. By the way, sir—"

"What?"

"Yesterday I overheard one of the Italians talking with his fellows. Apparently a detachment of Pilate's men went with the Temple guard and the council members to arrest the Nazarene."

I lifted a brow at the news. "And?"

"They arrested him in a garden called Gethsemane. Ran into a bit of trouble when one of the Nazarene's men attacked a Temple guard, but apparently this Yeshua stopped the bleeding, so no real harm was done." Lucius tilted his head. "I thought the Nazarene's men were supposed to be peace-loving."

I blew out an exasperated breath. "If there's a point in this story—"

"It's a garden, sir, and the Nazarene used it often. If his men needed a place to hide the body, mightn't they take it to someplace familiar?"

"Ah, Beneficiarii." I gave him an approving smile. "You are

beginning to think like an officer. I'll visit this garden straight-away."

The young man's face brightened with pleasure. "Anything else, sir?"

"Assign a century to comb the city for bodies dead in the last week. Examine each for marks of the crucified."

Lucius blanched. "You mean . . . dig them up?"

"All of them." I pressed my lips together and pointed to Joseph. "Bring him to me presently. I'll return to my quarters after I've visited this garden called Gethsemane."

The garden of Gethsemane, which, appropriately enough, meant *olive press* in the local tongue, lay across the Kidron Valley at the foot of the Mount of Olives. I rode there on horseback and found myself enjoying the fresh air outside the city. The late morning was warm and burnished with sunlight, and my stallion seemed happy to canter freely. He picked his way through the brook at the lowest point of the valley, and before we knew it we had arrived at a walled garden filled with olive trees.

I dismounted and opened the gate to the garden. No one stopped me; indeed, I saw no one in the area. But a downward glance revealed soft earth that had been trampled by footprints. Since we'd had no rain in the last several days, the prints could have been made the night the chief priests and their men arrested Yeshua. Or they could be only hours old, made by disciples intent on hiding their master's body.

After searching more thoroughly I did not find tracks that might have been made by a wagon or handcart, unless those tracks had been smoothed away and trampled again.

Unwilling to risk losing my horse, I clicked my tongue and

led the stallion into the garden, where he walked over to browse the grass along the wall. The garden itself consisted of dozens of gnarled olive trees arranged in rows, their bushy canopies filled with thousands of oblong fruit. Harvest would not begin for several months, so this place should have been quiet and little used.

A path curved like a pointing finger through the trees, so I followed it. My pulse quickened when I spotted a rocky outcropping with an opening beneath it, but rather than leading to a possible tomb, it led to a cave that held the olive press for which the place had been named. Nothing unusual there, not even a workman. This place would be busy in the fall, but who required an olive press when the olives were still in the tree?

I searched the garden again, particularly at the rear, where thicker trees created a dense shade. Several boulders littered the ground here, but while they might have provided a seat or table for anyone who wanted to linger, I saw no suitable place for a tomb. I searched the ground for mounded earth or any signs of digging and found nothing.

Lucius's suggestion had been a good one, but I found no corpse hidden among the trees.

I did, however, find blood. In a far corner, on a limestone boulder situated between two gnarled trees, I saw what appeared to be drops of blood. I searched the ground for signs of spatter or the sort of puddle that might result from a serious wound, but found nothing of the sort. Just drops of blood on a boulder in a solitary corner with no obvious explanation.

I had nearly reached the gate when an old man entered, and from his alarmed expression I gathered that he was surprised to find the garden occupied. I lifted my hand, hoping to assure him that my intentions were peaceable, and he bowed in an overenthusiastic greeting. "No trouble brewing here, no trouble at all," he said.

"Do you own this garden?" I asked.

He spread his hands. "Everyone owns this garden."

"Do you operate the olive press?"

Again with the bobbing.

"Would you happen to know if several men came here early this morning? They would have been pushing a handcart or a wagon . . . or they might have been leading a donkey."

He shook his head rapidly. "No one came. We've had no trouble here."

"I suppose you had no trouble when the Nazarene was arrested either."

"Ah." His brows lifted. "I saw that. I was here because sometimes I sleep back by the press to keep an eye on things. Those men come here often, but that night most of them stayed outside." He pointed beyond the gate in the wall. "Four men came inside, and three slept there"—he pointed to an open area next to the path—"while the teacher went farther into the garden. I heard him."

My nerves tightened. Had the Nazarene had some sort of secret meeting before his arrest? "What did you hear?"

The man's smile vanished. "Weeping. Anguish. Then he came out to meet the mob that arrived with torches and weapons. The other men, the ones sleeping outside, they also came in."

"You saw the arrest? When the Temple guard arrived with Roman soldiers?"

The man dipped his head in a sober nod. "Aye. Pharisees too. One man, big smile, opened his arms and walked to the rabbi, then kissed him on both cheeks. The teacher said, 'Who do you want?' and one of the Pharisees said, "Yeshua from Nazareth."'

"He freely admitted who he was?"

"Aye. The rabbi said, 'I am.' And when he said that, they stepped back from him and fell to the ground. So he asked again, 'Who do you want?' They said, 'Yeshua,' and he said, 'I told you, I am, so let these others go.' They couldn't run, you see, on account of the wall."

"They fell to the ground?" I looked at the old man, convinced he was mistaken. Roman soldiers did not surrender ground unless overcome by a superior fighting force, and they never would have given way to a group of Galilean fishermen. "Surely you mean that someone stumbled."

"They *all* fell," the old man insisted, "as if a giant hand had knocked them over. No sooner had they gotten up than one of the rabbi's men drew his sword and struck Melekh, a servant of the high priest. Took off his ear, as clean as you please. But the rabbi picked up the ear, put it back on Melekh's head, and told his man to put the sword away. He said his father had given him a cup, so he would drink it."

I stared at the ground, my mind spinning with bewilderment. The situation the old man described was so unbelievable I didn't know how to respond. The man was clearly mad, so I ought to simply go—

"After that," the old man said, shrugging, "they bound the teacher's hands and led him away. The rabbi's men, well . . ."

"What of them?"

"They ran." The old man spat the words as if they were stones. "One ran so fast he left his robe behind when it got caught on a branch. Another climbed a tree to leap over the wall. But the plucky one with the sword"—the old man grinned, displaying a row of missing front teeth—"he followed them."

I rubbed my jaw in grim pleasure. So . . . the Nazarene's

disciples weren't as meek and timid as we'd heard. If one had used a sword and followed Yeshua after his arrest, perhaps others were gathering their courage for an assault even now.

This assignment might not be as bloodless as I imagined.

I thanked the old man for his help, then mounted my horse and rode back to the city.

16

Rachel

To acknowledge Adonai's claim on the land and His people, the priest lifted the bound sheaf of barley and waved it above the altar. With the sheaf, other priests offered sacrifices of a year-old unblemished lamb, a grain offering of fine flour mixed with oil, and a drink offering of a quarter of a hin of wine, for these were required on the day after the Sabbath during the Feast of Unleavened Bread.

Standing with others of my community in the court of the Temple, I lifted my voice with them as we praised Adonai for bringing us a bountiful harvest. As the songs of praise continued, I edged toward the side of the court in order to make a quick exit. My booth at the marketplace stood empty, but I had already laid out sheets of matzah, some dipped in salt, some sprinkled with honey, and covered them with linen. As soon as the Temple ceremony ended, we would be free to eat bread and grain products from the newly harvested fields, as long as they contained no leaven.

I slipped away from the Temple and hurried along the street on my way to the booth. My nearest neighbor, Leah, a seller of purple, had already uncovered her wares, and she leaned over to eye my matzot. "I have been waiting," she said, giving me a broad smile. "I never realize how much I enjoy bread until I'm told I can't have it."

"Here." I handed her a sheet of matzah and grinned when she broke off a crisp corner. "Thank you, Rachel! If I can ever do you a favor—"

"I don't know that I'll ever be able to afford to wear purple," I told her, "but I can always use someone to test my breads."

Within minutes a flood of customers arrived from the Temple, and for the next several hours I stayed busy wrapping and dispensing matzot. The first day of the week was nearly always busy, as women came to the market to buy what they'd been unable to purchase on the Sabbath. After going without fresh bread products, they were eager to bring matzah back to their dining tables.

I had just given small pieces of matzah to a pair of children when I noticed the crowd parting like the Red Sea. I looked down the alley and saw Romans approaching on horseback. My breath caught in my throat when I recognized Clavius as the first rider. Beside him rode a young man I'd never seen in Clavius's company before. My lover's expression was restrained, even blank, but the young Roman wore an imperious look as he guided his horse through the crowded marketplace.

I tried not to look at him but felt Clavius's gaze brush me as he passed. Public acknowledgment would not benefit either of us, so I understood why he did not speak. His young companion, however, had not yet learned how to maintain custody of his eyes, and the bold look he gave me was enough to sear my cheeks.

And Clavius thought he could protect me?

"Impudent bullies," a nearby woman hissed.

"Shh," her companion warned. The second woman waited until the parade of Romans had passed before she approached my booth.

"Matzot?" I asked.

She shook her head and leaned closer. "Two days ago I spoke to you at the well—do you remember?"

I nodded, finally recalling her face. She was one of the women I had asked about Yeshua.

"Well . . ." She drew her lips together in a restrained smile. "I have heard from one of the women who was at Golgotha—the Nazarene lives! This morning they went to the tomb to anoint his body, but he was gone."

I blinked. "Gone?"

"Not only that, but they saw an angel!" Tears filled the woman's eyes, an overflow of joy. "The angel told them to tell the disciples that their teacher had been raised from the dead. He will meet them in Galilee."

A thousand thoughts swirled in my head. What had the prophet Isaiah said? *"If he would present himself as a guilt offering . . . He would see his offspring, and he will prolong his days . . . and at his hand Adonai's desire will be accomplished."*

"He exposed himself to death," I whispered, lifting my gaze to meet the woman's, "while bearing the sins of many."

She caught my hand and squeezed it. "Why can't everyone see it? Our Passover lamb—the man who takes away the sin of the world—died and rose on the day the priest presented the firstfruits of the harvest! What are the firstfruits, if not new life?"

New life . . . The words touched a raw spot in my heart. More than anything I wanted to bring a new life into the world, but Aaron and I had never conceived a child, and I dared not conceive one with Clavius. Still, my heart yearned to hold a baby.

"I want to know more." With both hands I clung to her arm. "I don't understand all this, but I'm desperate to learn more."

She leaned even closer. "I have a friend who is one of Yeshua's disciples. I will send him to you when it is safe. He can answer your questions better than I can."

"The third house on Straight Street," I whispered. "I will leave a lamp burning in the window."

17

Clavius

Written in both Greek and Latin, mounted on thirteen entrances of the low parapet that marked the boundary between the expansive Court of the Gentiles and the Court of Israel, the declaration was simple and bold: *No foreigner is to enter within the forecourt and the balustrade around the sanctuary. Whoever is caught will have himself to blame for his subsequent death.*

Exhibiting a patience I did not feel, I carried my helmet under my arm and waited for Caiaphas's man to return with my missing guard. Since they would not allow any Gentile to venture beyond the open quadrangle, they must have stashed the guard at the high priest's palace or a nearby property. I had left Lucius on the street, hoping he would spot Caiaphas's safe house.

Finally I saw the Levite. Beside him, walking with a lowered head, was one of the legionnaires I'd last seen at the Nazarene's tomb.

They stopped before me, but the guard would not lift his head.

The Levite nodded. "Here's your man."

I shifted my attention to the soldier, who barely acknowledged me. "Tribune."

I turned to the Levite. "I said I wanted to speak to him in private."

The Levite smirked and retreated about ten paces. I turned my back to him and peered at the guard. "Where is your fellow?"

The guard shook his head. "He doesn't wish to speak."

"Truly? He had no trouble avowing the theft of the Nazarene's body."

"He's afraid . . . as am I."

"You should be—you disgraced the Tenth Legion. And sleeping on watch means death."

The guard took a half step back.

"Fortunately for you," I went on, "the prefect has spared your lives. You can both return to the barracks."

The guard warily raised his head, drops of sweat running over his pale forehead. "Unpunished?"

"If you bare yourself honestly about what happened."

The man's gaze dropped like a stone. "We were . . . while sleeping, we were attacked in the night by the Nazarene's rabid disciples. They stole his body and bade us say he is risen."

I let out an exasperated breath. "Rabid, you say? How many attacked you?"

"Eight, ten—I'm not sure."

"All armed?"

"Yes."

"And you saw this while sleeping?"

"No. I—we—awoke as they were cutting the ropes."

"*Cutting* them?"

"Aye. Then they . . . they rolled away the stone and took his body and ran."

"While you watched?"

"No. Yes. Well . . . they held us at spear point."

"How many held you?"

"Five . . . six."

"Leaving two to roll the stone and take the corpse?"

"I think."

"And they bade you say he is risen?"

Clearly agitated, the guard bobbed his head.

I stepped closer and spoke directly into his ear. "Strange. If I were a body thief, I would have smothered any witnesses and claimed Yahweh struck you down."

The guard's forehead knit in puzzlement, and he began to stammer, "I . . . we—"

"Have you been told to say these things, soldier?"

The guard shook his lowered head.

"Were you drinking last night?"

"No."

From beneath my paludamentum I pulled out the empty wineskin.

Surprise siphoned blood from the man's face as he stared at the evidence dangling from my hand.

"What else is a lie?" I whispered.

Without saying anything, the guard pivoted on the ball of

his foot and scurried away, the Levite following like a protective shadow.

But not before shooting me a warning look.

———◆———

I rode slowly back to the barracks, taking the pulse of the city through my eyes and ears.

At one intersection I stopped my horse and watched my legionnaires search a funeral procession. The deceased man's family and friends stood nearby, some weeping, some fuming, as the soldiers ripped open the shroud to inspect the body. Behind them, other legionnaires searched ordinary wagons, upending baskets of pomegranates and shifting jugs of olive oil as they struggled to reach any container large enough to hold a human body, entire or in pieces. The locals were not happy about these invasions, but they should have counted themselves fortunate. If we did not find the Nazarene's corpse among the living inhabitants of Jerusalem, we would begin to unearth the dead in cemeteries.

By the time I reached the Antonia, Joseph of Arimathea was waiting in my quarters. Titus had made him comfortable, giving him water and allowing him to sit. I dismissed Titus and asked the old man to forgive my tardiness. When we were alone, I leaned against my desk and folded my arms. "Who took the body, Joseph?"

He met my gaze without flinching. "I don't know."

"If you did, would you tell me?"

The man's brows flickered. "What difference would it make? It would not bring him back . . . not really."

I uncrossed my arms and tried a different tack. "They say you're an honest man . . . are you also a follower of Yeshua?"

When he did not answer immediately, I assured him with a smile. "Truth will not prove fatal today."

Joseph lifted his shoulders in a barely discernible shrug. "I hardly knew him. Still, I was moved by what he said and taught, and I felt he didn't deserve such a death. But I cannot say I was an open follower."

"Who is?"

For the first time, Joseph smiled. "They don't deserve such a death either."

"They ripped open your tomb to steal a corpse to promote a lie that threatens Rome and the Sanhedrin. *That* sort of activity merits protection?"

"Whoever did it, they were not Yeshua's followers . . . not the true believers. They are heartbroken."

"They're zealots."

Joseph shrugged again. "If you say so."

I shook my head and moved to the window. I looked down on legionnaires training with wooden swords and weighted shields. "Some are saying he is risen to lead Israel against Rome. They call him the messiah. Do you believe that?"

"Messiah." Joseph breathed the word. "*Anointed one.* Our holy Scriptures use the word to describe the divinely chosen kings of Israel; the high priest; Cyrus, king of Persia; and a coming prince. Which messiah would you have him be?"

"I don't care. What matters is what you and your people believe about him."

Joseph stared at the floor for a moment. A small smile flitted through his beard. "I believe," he said, "that if he yet lived, Yeshua would embrace you as a brother . . . even as you slew him. Does that fit with your notion of what a messiah would do?"

I leaned against the wall, frustrated by the man's refusal to give me a direct answer. He did not behave like a man guarding a secret, but his behavior was unnatural. By all rights he should be furious with whoever had desecrated his family tomb and irritated with me for questioning him. So why was he behaving as though this crime was of no importance?

"Joseph . . ." I shook my head. "You may go."

He stood, bowed with great dignity, and moved toward the door.

"Wait."

He paused.

"I will try other means . . . before I'm forced to break you."

The older man turned, resolution evident in his eyes. "One thing I have withheld from you, Tribune, and I now confess it. You asked me if Yeshua was a king."

He opened his cloak and gently pulled out a circlet of thorny acacia branches. "I now return his crown."

After my evening meal I sat at my desk and examined the evidence I'd removed from the tomb: a section of frazzled rope that had definitely not been cut by a blade, the facecloth imprinted with the image of the Nazarene, and a few pieces of clay from the broken seal. Evidence always pointed to the truth, but in this case, truth contradicted the evidence.

Lucius rapped on my door, entered, and saluted.

"Progress?" I asked, still staring at the jagged ends of the rope.

"Six arrests today. Four claim that the Nazarene lives. All second- and third-hand reports, but the rumors are spreading."

"Any disciples?"

"Not yet." He cleared his throat. "Sir, if I may—"

"Speak freely."

"Herod Antipas is still in Jerusalem, and I've heard he was obsessed with the Nazarene. It might be worth our while to pay him a visit."

I shifted my gaze to my young beneficiarii, who was clearly intent on being useful. "What would motivate Antipas to steal the Nazarene's body?"

Lucius shifted uneasily. "I don't know, sir. But surely it's better to leave no stone unturned. The prefect will expect us to do a thorough job."

I tipped my head back and studied my aide more closely. The youth reeked of ambition, and he had Pilate's ear. If I didn't follow through with his suggestions, no matter how inane, he might tell Pilate that I had not done all I could to find the missing messiah.

The religious leaders weren't the only ones familiar with the weapon of blackmail.

"We will visit Herod Antipas tomorrow." I picked up the piece of shredded rope and ran my fingertip over the uneven ends. "But for now, Pilate has sent word that one of the Nazarene's men was an informer. Find him."

18

Clavius

MONDAY, ANTE MERIDIEM

After breaking our fast and saying our prayers, Lucius and I mounted our horses and rode across the city to the praetorium, temporary home to Pontius Pilate and Herod Antipas, son of the late Herod the Great. The former Herod had built the impressive complex, and although the egos of both Pilate and Herod were large enough to make the palace feel cramped, in reality the edifice was more than spacious enough to house them and their separate retinues.

We dismounted, handed our horses to a groom at the stable, and walked to the southern end of the building, where Herod was celebrating the Hebrew feast. Herod made a show of keeping the Judean law, but he was an Idumean, and the Idumeans had been forced to convert to Judaism when they migrated to southern Judah generations before. Herod Antipas might be a Jew on the outside, but I doubted that his heart had been circumcised.

"What do you know about Herod?" I asked Lucius as we walked to the great hall.

Lucius gave me a sharp glance. "I know he's a tetrarch who wants to be king. And I heard he killed a Judean prophet a couple of years back."

"John the Baptizer, who was popular with the common people. Did you know that John was cousin to the Nazarene?"

Lucius's brows shot up. "I did not."

"It pays to keep an ear to the ground. After the Baptizer's death, many thought the Nazarene might launch some sort of campaign against Antipas, but it never happened. Now it's too late for revenge."

The guards outside the door saluted at our approach, and I nodded in acknowledgment. "I would like to speak with the tetrarch at once."

One of the legionnaires nodded and darted through the doorway while I glanced at his fellow. These men were from the Italian cohort and billeted at the praetorium, so I'd never met them.

"Where are you stationed?" I asked. "Caesarea or Tiberius?"

"Tiberius, sir." The guard remained at attention, his eyes focused on some distant point.

"Do you know when you'll be returning to your barracks?"

"After the feast, sir. In a few more days."

The door opened at that moment, and the first guard reappeared. "The tetrarch will see you now."

Herod Antipas had made himself at home in his late father's palace. The room we entered was long and narrow, lit by clerestory windows beneath the roofline. Sumptuous chairs and couches lined the walls, and several tables groaned under trays of rich food. Servants hovered near the trays, making certain they never emptied, and dozens of beautiful women lounged on the couches, languidly nibbling at pastries and munching on dried figs.

Herod stood before one of the trays, picking his way through assorted dainties—none of which, I noticed, appeared to be made of unleavened bread.

"Tribune!" Herod greeted me with a broad smile. "Can I interest you in a fig roll?"

I saluted him, then removed my helmet and attempted to smile. I wanted him to be at ease, though my gut tightened at the mere sight of the man. Roman rulers tended to be a disciplined lot; most of them had come up through the military and knew the importance of moderation in all things. But this Antipas—with his haughty gestures, curled hair, and heavy robes dripping with gold accents and chains—was not Roman.

"Greetings, Tetrarch. I have come on behalf of the prefect. It—"

"My newest best friend?" If anything, the man's smile widened. "How can I help?"

"We've come about a matter concerning the Nazarene crucified four days ago. Yeshua of Nazareth."

A smug look crept over the man's features, almost an expression of gloating. "I sent him away with a gift, a royal robe. Seemed the least I could do for a man who would be king over my territory."

"The body has been missing since yesterday, Tetrarch. I have been charged with finding it."

Antipas's satisfied expression gave way to sudden shock—and from the vulnerable look in his eye, I would have sworn this was the first time he'd heard the news.

"Why—" his chin quivered—"have you come to me?"

I drew a breath, about to explain that we wanted to alert him because the thieves were most likely citizens of his jurisdiction, but Antipas leapt to a different conclusion.

"Protection!" He gasped. "I must have protection. While that man said nothing the entire time he stood before me, I knew what he was thinking. He blames me for murdering his kinsman. He faults me for marrying my brother's wife. And if not even a grave can hold him—"

"Peace, Tetrarch." I held out a hand to soothe him. "The body has undoubtedly been hidden, and we will find it. I myself saw the spear enter his side, where blood and water flowed. He is quite dead, I assure you."

Antipas wore a distracted, inward look, as though thinking hard about something else. He nodded rapidly, then moved to the gilded chair at the front of the room. "You are certain he is dead?"

"I would stake my own life on it."

"The Baptizer had no power over death," Herod said, his words running together in a continual stream, "so why should I concern myself with the other man? He is nothing, for what comes out of Nazareth but fishermen, carpenters, and brick-makers? He was a simpleton, really, unable to speak a word before my splendid glory, unable even to defend the charges against him. I'd been hoping for so much more, yet he did nothing noteworthy in my presence. No healings, no feedings, not even something simple like making it rain indoors. If he was a god, if he was *half* what they said he was, he would surely have done something to impress me, for who wouldn't want me on his side? But he couldn't speak. Wouldn't speak. So I let Pilate deal with him."

Antipas looked at me, then drew a deep, quivering breath. "Thank my friend Pilate for bringing me this news," he said, clinging to the armrests of his throne. "And know that if I hear anything, or if in my territory I discover the scoundrels who stole the body, I will most certainly render a certain and harsh justice. Pilate need not worry about my cooperation."

I saluted him, as did Lucius, and together we turned and walked out of the great hall. And as we made our way to the stable, Lucius glanced at me. "Coward."

I nodded. "Scared spitless, and why? Superstition."

19

Rachel

I closed the door behind me, then checked my basket—a dozen fresh eggs, an omer of freshly ground wheat, a bottle of olive oil, and honey—everything I needed to bake challah. Because we were still in the week of Unleavened Bread I wouldn't eat the loaves, but perhaps Adonai would allow me to bake and sell them.

Humming happily, I spread my purchases on the table and pulled out the clay bowl that had been my mother's. I brought little with me when I married save for my mother's mixing bowl and measures. These items had only become more precious with time, for not only did they remind me of my family, but they had also proved invaluable in my survival. What bread maker could bake without a sturdy bowl and accurate measures?

I pulled out the covered cup of wet dough I'd stored on the shelf beneath my table. One whiff assured me the dough had begun to ferment and would be enough to spread leaven throughout a new loaf. I added honey to the mixture and set it aside to continue the fermentation process.

After sweeping the floor, braiding my hair, and exchanging my linen tunic for something more suited to a workday, I returned to the foaming dough and reserved a small portion to serve as a starter for future loaves. I continued mixing, adding eggs, olive oil, more honey, and a bit of salt. I stirred the dough until it formed a ball at the bottom of my bowl. I dumped the ball onto my covered board and kneaded it, pounding, smoothing, and folding until the dough was smooth and pliable beneath my fingers. After allowing the dough to rise and double, I shaped it into a short log and cut the log into six identical pieces.

After rubbing the pieces between my floured hands until they had formed long ropes—as a child, I had always called them worms—I arranged them on my floured board. As I worked I could see myself as a little girl, standing at the side of the table, my eyes level with my mother's flour-covered hands. She would lay out the six long pieces like a peacock's tail, then braid the pieces so quickly that my eyes couldn't follow her hands. I begged her to teach me, and she tried, but at that age all I heard was "this piece to the left, then the right down the middle, then that piece to the right, and the left piece down the middle."

After both my mother and father died of a catarrh, I did learn how to braid a six-strand challah, but only when my aunt explained the symbolism behind the six layers. "This piece," she said, touching each strand as she explained her method, "is the father, and this the mother, and this the child. See how they all exchange places and wrap around each other?"

"What about the other pieces?" I asked.

My aunt smiled. "This one is David, and this the prophet Elijah, and this is Moses. They all move left and right, then return to the middle, which is the love of HaShem."

With my aunt's voice ringing in my head, I braided the loaf on my floured board and then took in the beautiful result beneath my hands. I would bake this one and serve it to Clavius if he visited tonight. But first, the finishing touches.

I dipped a soft brush into a beaten raw egg and painted the top of the braid. I then covered the challah with a linen cloth and set it on the table to rise. I had just picked up my mixing bowl when I heard voices outside. I paused, straining to listen, and screamed when my door flew open, the result of a Roman soldier's swift kick.

A legionnaire stood at my door, sword in hand, and his eyes flashed with distaste as he glared at me. "Rachel the baker?"

I nodded, my throat too tight for words.

"You must come with me."

"What—why—?"

"Come at once or be dragged out, woman."

I stood tense and quivering as a thousand thoughts flew through my mind. Clavius had betrayed me—or someone had betrayed Clavius. Someone had accused me to the priests, who had sent Romans . . .

No. If the religious rulers wanted to accuse me of fornication, they wouldn't involve the Romans. I alone would bear the blame for my sin.

I drew myself up, swallowed to bring my heart down from my throat, and wiped my hands on a towel.

"At once!" the soldier repeated, pointing toward the street with his sword.

I nodded and moved forward, my heart congealing to a small lump of terror.

20

Clavius

The tombs were not as ornate as those in the cemetery where Joseph of Arimathea had laid the Nazarene, but there were dozens of them, and they were but a stone's throw from the Temple. Standing at the cemetery gate, Lucius and I could lift our gazes and see Jerusalem's eastern wall and, immediately behind that structure, the golden ornaments on the Temple's roofline.

"Those tombs," one of Caiaphas's assistants told us when we stopped by the high priest's palace to ask if the Jews had any special or sacred cemeteries, "are reserved for the Levites who devote their older years to Temple service. When a man reaches fifty, he no longer participates in the lottery that determines who will offer sacrifices, yet many of our older men are widowers and want to continue serving Adonai. So we welcome them to do small tasks at the Temple, we give them a place to live in Jerusalem, and we care for their daily needs. When they die, they are buried in the tombs carved into the Temple Mount."

"Would we find tombs of former high priests there?"

The assistant smiled. "No. The high priests would be buried in private tombs, one of those overlooking the Kidron Valley."

"So the other place is dedicated to poor priests," I summarized.

The assistant held up his hand. "And some women. When a widow wishes to spend the rest of her life serving in the Temple, we accommodate her as well."

As we mounted to ride away, Caiaphas's assistant remarked that we'd find the more recent tombs at the front of the cemetery, the older ones in back.

"I don't know why I didn't think of this sooner," I said while Lucius held the gate open. "If you wished to honor your rabbi, why not hide his body in a cemetery dedicated to that purpose?"

Lucius followed me, then braced his hands on his hips and looked around. "Clearly, the place is not often visited."

Unlike the wealthier cemeteries we had ridden past, this place featured no trees, flowers, or fountains. Nothing of nature but dust, dirt, and rock within the short stone walls.

The man-made objects, however, indicated some regard for the beings entombed within the brick walls. Several of the crypts were quite large and handsomely ornamented, constructed with intricate designs in the stonework. No graven images and no paintings, but still, various touches of beauty.

"You start over there," I said, pointing to the crypts on the west side. "I'll work from the east."

The first crypt I approached had been sealed with mortared stone, and the mortar remained intact. I considered chipping away at the opening with my sword, then decided to leave it. These rocks had not been disturbed in some time. The second tomb looked much like the first, only its mortar had begun to wear away—by the erosion of wind, no doubt, because those rocks had not been disturbed either.

The third tomb I approached had been carved into the limestone of the Temple Mount and not sealed by stones. An iron gate hung aslant on rusty hinges, the tomb open for anyone who wished to enter.

I knelt at the entrance and searched the sands for signs of recent footprints. The sand was not smooth, but rounded and pitched. Whether it had been disturbed by human steps, an irregular wind, or wandering animals, I could not tell.

I saw Lucius testing the seal of another crypt. He was occupied, so I left him alone.

Aware that snakes often sought the cool shadows of crypts, I pulled my sword and eased through the opening. The crypt was a typical locular tomb, with an open space in the center and several smaller compartments carved into the three remaining walls. The builder had cut out a basin in the center area, a space that allowed a visitor to stand to his full height.

I straightened my spine and inhaled deeply, parsing the smells of the place—nothing but the scents of dust and hot, dry earth. Despite the open entrance, the air had a stale quality, as if it had not been regularly circulated.

No light came into the crypt except through the low rectangular opening, and my eyes needed a few moments to adjust before I could see clearly. No body lay on the limestone slab in the center, and all of the compartments held ossuaries . . . except the last two. The ossuaries of those two had been pulled out of their compartments and spilled, but the bones of the deceased were missing.

I sighed. Not only did this tomb not hold the missing messiah, it had been visited by tomb robbers. But what sort of tomb robbers would rob a place as poor as this?

"Tribune?" Lucius thrust his head into the tomb and smiled in apparent relief. "I could see nothing amiss on the other side of the cemetery."

I motioned to the spilled ossuaries on the floor. "What make you of this, Beneficiarii?"

He came forward, stepped into the basin, and stood erect. His brows lowered. "My first thought is thieves. But who would steal human bones, and why only from two graves?"

I folded my arms and stepped back, giving him more room to observe as his eyes grew accustomed to the low light. "The gate was open when I approached."

"I saw that," he said, "but an iron gate is prone to rust and go awry. Perhaps some animal has committed this mischief . . . a wild dog, perhaps?"

"Could a wild dog pull a heavy stone box from its crypt?"

His mouth twisted. "Not a dog, then, unless it had fingers. A person. Someone given to the black arts?"

I nodded. "My first thought. But then I looked down."

Lucius followed my gaze and stared at the sand, which had blown into the crypt and covered the stone floor. My sandal prints ended at the basin where we stood, but beyond us, the otherwise smooth sand had been marred by a jumble of unshod feet and toes leading from the back of the tomb toward the exit.

Lucius's eyes went wide. "That . . . makes no sense." He looked up at me. "Have you an answer?"

I studied the floor a moment more. "None."

Lucius looked again at the ossuaries, then smiled. "The earthquake. It shook these boxes from their resting places."

"I could almost believe that . . . but since when have earthquakes evidenced toes and feet?"

Lucius and I returned to the hill of Golgotha, which was again populated with criminals on execution stakes. Ignoring the men who writhed in agony, we walked to the ledge where bodies were routinely discarded. Before venturing into the valley below, we tied squares of linen over our mouths and noses. This would be a disagreeable job, but when Rome commanded, we obeyed.

Moving carefully over the rocky slope, we made our way down to the trench filled with bloating bodies, scattered skeletons, and swarms of biting flies. Fortunately we were only interested in the corpses at the top of the pile. The body thieves, I realized, might have been clever enough to hide the Nazarene's body in plain sight.

I pointed to a likely dark-haired candidate. "Turn him over . . . no." I pointed to another. "How old is that one?"

The legionnaire tilted his head to consider. "At least a week, I'd say."

I backed away, searching for a breath of untainted air. Beside me, Lucius was gagging on the stench. He leaned over and lost his breakfast in the shade of a scrawny acacia tree.

I pointed to another cluster of bodies. "And those?"

"The thieves he died with."

"In two days they'll be unrecognizable," I remarked, beginning my uphill climb. I turned to check on my young assistant. "Brace yourself, Beneficiarii. Wait until you see combat."

Later that morning I dismounted at a cemetery outside the city walls, a place for Jews who couldn't afford expensive family tombs. Lucius had ridden ahead with legionnaires and orders to exhume any fresh grave, and thus far they had dug up four possible candidates.

Their efforts had not been appreciated. "Defiler!" one woman hissed.

"No false messiahs here!" a wizened older man cried, his face flushing in indignation. "Leave us, pagans!"

We ignored the insults and pressed forward. As my men opened shrouds for me to examine the bodies, Lucius pointed out the particulars: "One hand is missing here, but see the hole in the other? His beard looks as though portions have been pulled out."

"Not him," I said, moving on. "The legs are broken."

Lucius gestured for the guard to close the shroud. "That's why we need your eyes, Tribune. Consider this one—the grave is recent and shallow."

"No." I looked away. "That is not the Nazarene."

The sun had nearly reached its zenith by the time we entered another Judean cemetery where legionnaires had pulled bodies from hillside niches.

I squinted at the first gray face, far too swollen for me to identify with certainty. "No, I don't think so."

The legionnaire waved flies away from his face. "Sorry, sir. I never saw the Nazarene alive."

"You did well, soldier—the grave looks hasty and hidden. Good job, despite the result."

Over by the horses, Lucius was speaking to a messenger. He waved for my attention as he hurried over. "Tribune! The informer's been found."

We found the informer—one of the Nazarene's disciples, a man known as Judas of Kriot—in an abandoned field. An old Judean man pointed the way, and after scrambling over yet another rocky slope, we stared up at the man we'd come to see.

Or what was left of him.

I studied the dark face, bloated above the noose. "How long?"

Lucius spoke through the cloth he held over his nose and mouth. "Three days, at least." He jerked his thumb toward the old man who had reported the body. "The farmer said it was suicide."

"How would he know?"

"This Judas betrayed the Nazarene. Handed him over to the priests for thirty pieces of silver."

I turned away from the swaying corpse. "Bury him before your next informant hears of this. This was revenge, carried out by angry disciples." I shook my head. "The ones who are supposedly heartbroken."

We had found the informer . . . but no answers.

I began to climb the hill while Lucius scrambled up the tree. Judas of Kriot trembled as Lucius sawed the rope with his gladius. Then the body fell, the swollen skin bursting and spilling its contents into the field.

While Lucius retched, I squared my shoulders and moved

toward the horses. I had dared to hope that this assignment might result in a day without death, but that dream continued to elude me.

The scent of death clings to a man. Even after washing, the odor lingers in fabric, on wood, upon flesh. A soldier may learn how to endure it, but I don't believe anyone can become so inured that he is no longer repulsed by it.

After returning to my quarters, I washed my hands, arms, and face in a basin, then sat at my desk and sniffed at my palms. Even though I had not handled a single corpse, my flesh still reeked. I reached for the chicory plant growing near the window and rubbed a twig between my hands to cut the odor.

Titus came in to collect the wet linen, paused to sniff, and gave me a sympathetic smile. "Rough morning?"

"Bad enough."

Lucius knocked on the door, then entered and saluted. "Two score questioned. I've retained eight you should examine further. One, I suspect, could be a disciple." He paused to swallow a queasy belch. "Forgive me, Tribune."

Titus broke off a twig and handed it to Lucius.

"Take the chicory," I said. "In time, the stomach learns to handle these things. Now, on to the matter at hand." I steeled myself for the task ahead. "Bring them in one by one."

Titus cleared my desk of everything but parchment and a pen, then left the room. Lucius brought in the first man, an un-smiling fellow whose left eye was marked by a purpling bruise.

"I didn't say Yeshua still lives," he began, tension in every line of his body. "I said his lies still do."

"Lies?" I said.

"That weakness is blessed. That sin is somehow forgiven . . . because of him! That Adonai, *our* God, loves everyone."

A thunderous scowl darkened the man's brow, so I returned it in full measure. "Not a follower then?"

The man snorted in derision. "If I knew them or their hiding place, I'd give them up in a moment. Fools."

"So easily? I've heard reports of disciples denying Yeshua to save themselves. Is that you—a lying coward?"

The man pressed his lips together, seething with anger and . . . what? Shame, perhaps?

"I'm glad the Nazarene is dead," he finally said. "He was another disappointment—not what we deserve."

"What then do you deserve? A vengeful messiah? Is that what you long for?"

The man practically growled. "Your words, Tribune, not mine."

"I see how you feel, and he"—I nodded at Lucius, who stood near the door—"knows where you live. We'll be watching. Now get out."

The man blinked, then stood and left the room.

I looked at Lucius. "Next."

I was staring out the window when the next suspect shuffled in, so I was surprised when I turned and saw an old woman sitting before me. Even more surprising were her milky white eyes, the eyes of a blind woman.

I gave Lucius a skeptical look as he handed me the report. Did he really believe this woman had anything useful to offer?

I glanced back at the woman, who was trembling in the chair. "Why do you tremble?"

Her head turned as she followed the sound of my voice. "You are Roman."

"Good guess." I made an effort to soften my tone. "You were heard shouting that Yeshua lives." I glanced down at the report. "*Joyously*, it says here. Why would you do that? You didn't *see* him."

"I heard Him. On the street."

"You heard a report from passersby?"

A soft smile lit her face. "No—I heard *Him*."

"Yeshua?"

"Yesterday. On the road." Her lined mouth curved with confidence. "I know voices. I recognize them as easily as you would recognize a face."

"I have no doubt. Are you a follower of the Nazarene—" I checked the report—"Miriam, or just a follower of a follower?"

The woman tilted her head, and her smile broadened, putting color in her cheeks. Her trembling stopped. "He loved me, an old woman. He lifted me up."

"Lifted you?"

"If you knew Him, you'd understand."

I studied her more closely. Years of criminal interrogations had sharpened my sensibilities, and I could usually spot a liar within five minutes. But I saw no guile in this woman's countenance, only naïve devotion.

"I have heard," I said slowly, "that the Nazarene healed people, yet you are still blind. Did he refuse to heal you?"

"Oh." She released a nervous laugh. "Who am I to ask for such a thing? I see very well, just not with my eyes."

I set Lucius's report aside. "Go," I told her, "and stop spreading rumors that men are lifted from death."

The old woman nodded, and Lucius stepped forward to guide her through the doorway. But before leaving, she turned her face toward me. "Don't you want to know what He said?"

I lifted a brow. "Of course."

"He said a grain of wheat that falls to the earth and dies produces much fruit." Her face glowed with confidence. "You're too late to stop the harvest."

Lucius tugged on her arm to escort her from the room.

I leaned back in my chair. While the followers of Yeshua Barabbas were violent men with weapons, those who followed the Nazarene seemed to be armed only with perplexing notions and baffling predictions. Why did Pilate and the priests view them as such a threat?

On the other hand, one of the disciples *did* draw a sword and attempt to lop off a servant's ear. And someone strung up Judas of Kriot.

Despite their foolish talk, the Nazarene's men might be just as reckless and violent as every other would-be messiah's.

The short man sitting across from me hunched over his round tummy and looked up with narrowed eyes. "What have I done now?"

I looked at the report. "That remains to be seen . . . Shammah?"

"That's the name."

"Well then." I crossed my arms and made an attempt at hospitality. "You were waiting a while—can I get you anything? I could send my slave for water."

The little man glanced uneasily at Titus, who hovered near the doorway like a disapproving shadow. "I just want to be done and on my way."

"Very well." I glanced at the report again. "It says here that you operate a booth near the city gate."

"What of it?"

"Several days ago, on the first day of the week, a man from Nazareth entered Jerusalem with his followers. Apparently he made somewhat of a grand entrance, complete with a young donkey, a cheering crowd, and people waving palm branches."

A flush began to creep up the man's neck. "I still don't know what I'm doing here."

"You sell palm branches, do you not?"

"Sometimes."

"But you sold several dozen that day. I hear the Nazarene's entrance turned into quite a spectacle." I stared at the man as a sudden thought struck. "Have you ever traveled to Rome?"

He snorted. "Me? No."

"Perhaps you've heard, then, of the triumphs regularly staged for victorious generals. In a campaign that kills at least five thousand of the enemy, an extravagant spectacle is held in the streets of Rome. The conqueror enters the city through a gate, of course, usually riding a white horse, while the people cheer his name and wave palm branches."

The man's face flushed to the color of my cloak. "There's no law against selling palm branches! And I have never seen such a thing as you described."

"Perhaps someone else planned the demonstration. How did you happen to have so many palm branches on hand? And what did you tell the people to shout when they waved those branches?"

"I—we—told my servants to cut more when we heard the Nazarene was coming. And we didn't tell anyone to shout. They just did it."

"What were they saying?"

The man folded his arms. "I don't remember."

"Think harder."

His forehead creased with the effort. "Um . . . they were shouting 'Hosanna, son of David.'"

"*Hosanna*—that's a Greek word, is it not?"

"So?"

"The common people of Jerusalem speak Hebrew or Aramaic. So I'll ask again—what were your people shouting?"

The man drew a deep breath and glanced toward the door. The door stood open, but if he bolted, he would encounter at least a dozen legionnaires before reaching the gate.

"*Hoshiya na*," he murmured.

"Thank you for adding more Hebrew to my vocabulary. Perhaps you would be good enough to share the phrase's meaning?"

The man pressed his lips together, then defiantly met my gaze. "It means *Deliver us.*"

"Interesting." I made a note on the report. "So you were handing out palm fronds to people and urging them to shout 'Deliver us.' But I'm curious—from whom or what did you want to be delivered?"

"I wasn't urging nobody to do nothing," he snapped, rising from his chair. "They were shouting on their own. And if you don't know who they wanted to be delivered from, you should get out of this fortress more often."

Titus stepped forward, ready to grab the man who now hovered over my desk, but I held up my hand to warn the slave off. "Deliver us from Rome," I said, writing on the report. "Son of David—is the Nazarene son to a man called David?"

Shammah stepped back and looked at me as if I were an idiot. I'd had legionnaires whipped for less.

"His father was Joseph, but he's a son of David, all right."

"David . . . of Nazareth?"

"King David of Jerusalem." Shammah narrowed his eyes.

"Conqueror of Jerusalem, the sweet singer of Israel, and the man to whom Adonai promised an eternal throne."

I lowered my pen. "But Jerusalem has no throne. The city is part of the empire."

"Jerusalem will have a king again," Shammah insisted. "All Israel will bow before a son of David who will sit on the royal throne and reign—"

"I've grasped the general idea," I said. "And this Nazarene, apparently, was descended from King David?"

Shammah nodded. "And he entered the city on the tenth day of Nisan."

I paused. "Your Hebrew calendar, of course. Why is that date significant?"

The man smiled, no doubt happy to be in possession of knowledge I lacked. "It's selection day. Everyone comes to Jerusalem to pick out their Passover lamb. You can barely move through the press of people near the Temple. Add to that the shepherds, the livestock, the money changers—"

"I've seen it." I nodded, filing the information away for future reference. "You knew then there would be a mob. And so did the Nazarene."

"There's always a crowd during Passover week. But definitely more people on selection day and Passover."

"Good for business, right? Please take your seat and tell me— did you go hear the prophet after his triumphal entry? Did you cheer for him when he overturned tables at the Temple? Did you conspire with the Nazarene and his followers and *plan* to cause a scene? Did he want to be arrested? Did he sacrifice his life in an act of martyrdom?"

The little man slumped forward in his chair, his hands over his ears. When I finished running down the list of places where the Nazarene had been seen before his arrest, Shammah looked at me with bleary eyes. "All I know," he said, "is that people were calling him the son of David and talking about the prophet Zechariah and his writings."

"Which writings?"

Shammah closed his eyes. "'Rejoice greatly, O people of Zion! Shout in triumph, O people of Jerusalem! Look, your king is coming to you. He is righteous and victorious, yet he is humble, riding on a donkey—even on a donkey's colt.'"

"You saw the Nazarene as a king?"

"Not me, the prophet did. And so did all the people who were waving palm branches. We've been waiting for a king to deliver us for a long, long time."

With so many stories and legends to goad the masses, no wonder Judea was a hotbed of insurrection. I met the weary man's gaze. "I'm sorry, Shammah, but the Nazarene was no king. And if he intended to be a martyr, he wasn't the first. He'll be forgotten by the time the next one comes along."

The palm seller looked at me. "Is that it then? I can go?"

I nodded.

After Titus left the room, I breathed deeply, enjoying the silence. The next time I visited Rachel, I'd have to ask her about these prophets and past kings . . . if I could remember such trivial details.

I looked up at the sound of footsteps in the hallway. Lucius brought in the next suspect, and shock ran through me when a woman came through the doorway.

Rachel—appearing as if my thoughts had summoned her.

She was wearing a simple tunic that bore traces of flour.

She wore no veil, which was unusual for any Judean woman in public, and she had pulled her hair back in a loose braid. Clearly, she'd been taken without warning.

Lucius led her to the chair, where she reluctantly sat. She looked at me, her brown eyes sparking beneath her brows. I could tell she was not happy to find herself at the Antonia.

I struggled to maintain control of my reaction, yet heat flooded my face. I looked at Lucius, searching his eyes for any sign of deviousness, but his expression revealed nothing.

"Your name?" I took Lucius's report and avoided her gaze.

"Rachel."

"And you live where?"

"Jerusalem."

"Why have you been brought here?"

She tilted her head toward Lucius. "Ask him."

Lucius stiffened. "Sir, a neighbor reports a suspicious figure visiting her often in the night—almost certainly a zealot. She is clearly not what she seems, for she wears *this* around her neck."

The amulet of Mars dangled from his fingers, the necklace I'd given Rachel two nights before.

Lucius dropped it onto my desk. "Probably stripped from our dead."

I shifted, my head spinning with conflicting thoughts. Lucius could not have gathered more evidence against me if he'd set out to have me disgraced. But I didn't think he'd been in Jerusalem long enough to learn my habits . . . or my secrets.

I girded up my courage and looked squarely at Rachel, who did not flinch. "A Judean woman honoring Roman gods?"

"It was a gift," she said. "I have . . . a friend. He visits from time to time." She shrugged. "I wear it to honor the giver, not the god. Whereas you"—her eyes darted to my hand—"wear a tribune's ring. Does that mean you worship Rome?"

"Of course not."

She crossed her legs, unconsciously revealing that her sandaled foot trembled as if she'd suddenly developed palsy. "How odd, then, that Rome comes before everything in a soldier's life. Before family, marriage . . . even righteousness. You must do what Rome tells you, no matter what the consequence. Am I right?"

"You should watch yourself." Lucius stepped forward and looked at Rachel with cold and piercing eyes. "You are speaking to a tribune of Rome."

Rachel exhaled, but kept her lips pressed together.

"Thank you, Beneficiarii, but I think I can handle this." I straightened and adjusted my demeanor. "We are searching for whoever stole the body of Yeshua the Nazarene. If you had nothing to do with that crime, you will be released. Did you know him?"

"No."

"Were you one of his followers?"

"No."

"Anyone in your family, perhaps a husband—"

"I'm a widow. Is that a crime?"

"How do you support yourself?"

"I bake bread to sell in the marketplace. I was preparing loaves when your man burst into my house and dragged me away."

I ignored her complaint. "You make enough to survive?"

"I live a simple life. My needs are few."

"This friend you mentioned—is he a disciple of the Nazarene?"

She chuckled. "I hardly think so."

"What does he do?"

"I'm not sure anymore." She glanced around my quarters, pointedly taking in my pilum and gladius, my narrow bed, the embroidered standard of my cohort. "Something tells me he's a brute."

"You don't trust him?"

She tilted her head. "To a point."

"With your life?"

"I'd like to think I could."

"Surely he feels the same."

From the corner of my eye, I saw Lucius's brow arch. Our conversation had left him behind; would it arouse his curiosity? If I were to become more than the de facto commander of the Augustan cohort, I would have to be more cautious. Perhaps I should curtail my after-hours visits. While Rome had no problem with legionnaires visiting prostitutes and bawdy houses, my superiors would not want to hear that I'd developed a relationship with a Judean.

"Clearly you have concerns about this man," I said, "so why see him?"

The corner of her mouth twitched. "I doubt you'd understand."

"Because he's a zealot? A follower of the dead Nazarene?"

"Because he doesn't return love. I don't know if he can."

I blinked and lifted my hands in genuine frustration. I stood, walked to the window, then turned to face my assistant. "I see no offense here, Lucius. Indiscretion, perhaps, but no crime . . . against Roman law at least."

Lucius didn't move. "Sir, should we not get the man's name?"

I ignored him. "Take care not to be seen with zealots, Rachel of Jerusalem. And for your own safety, see no more of this so-called friend."

"That's it?" Her voice was soft with disbelief. "We're finished here?"

I dipped my chin in a terse nod.

Tears welled in Rachel's eyes as she stood. "I suppose I should be grateful."

She swept past Lucius and walked away, her head high. I glanced at my confused beneficiarii. "Next?"

Lucius shook his head and hurried to escort Rachel out of the fortress.

In his absence, I wiped my mouth with the back of my hand and wondered what I had just done. Some logical part of my brain knew my relationship with Rachel was ill-advised . . . for her, and for my career. In Rome, a man could use a female slave or a woman of lower class for his own pleasure, but love and marriage would be out of the question. I ought to give her up, but I couldn't. After a full day of dealing with brutality and death, she alone reminded me that I was a man, a man with the potential for goodness. She was light in a world of darkness. She was laughter in a barracks of raucous shouting. She was rest and consolation, and I couldn't imagine being without her.

I looked up when Lucius returned with a bearded fellow in a sweat-stained tunic. The man paced nervously before dropping into the chair.

"What can you tell us?" I asked, forgoing the preliminaries. "What have you heard about the Nazarene called Yeshua?"

"Nothing really," the man said, fidgeting. "But I overhead something in a tavern. A fellow at another table was talking."

"Fellow or *follower*?"

"I have no idea, I swear! I didn't know the man."

I lifted my hand in an effort to quell the suspect's panic. "What did this fellow say?"

"Something . . . something about Yeshua being seen alive."

"Did he imply that he'd seen Yeshua, or was he merely passing on a story?"

"Don't know. Couldn't tell."

"At the tavern, was there any reaction to his news?"

The suspect snorted. "He was laughed at, then given a good pounding. He left after, and I don't think he will be telling that story again."

I sighed and pointed to the door. The suspect leapt to his feet and froze, his eyes as wide as platters. "Am I . . . can I go?"

"Go."

As the man hurried away, I stood to stretch, wearied by sitting in one place for too long. I looked at Lucius and warned him off. "Time for a break."

"But this next one, Tribune, I believe—"

"Good. Bring him in and let him wait."

21

Clavius

Monday, post meridiem

I stepped out of my quarters and walked along the rampart for a breath of fresh air and an opportunity to clear my thoughts. The designers of the Antonia Fortress had constructed four towers, one at each corner of the fort, to allow us to survey the city with a glance. The tower at the southeast corner rose higher than the others, allowing us to look into the Temple and surveil all but the most sacred chambers in that holy place.

I stood at the crenelated wall of the rampart and looked into the Court of the Gentiles, but no obvious trouble stirred there. The money changers and those who sold animals for sacrifice were dismantling their booths and animal pens, and the smoke of the daily sacrifices had long since dispersed. I crossed the rampart and looked into the courtyard of the Antonia, where two centurions were grilling legionnaires about their task to locate the missing messiah. Beyond the fortress, in the west, the sun was streaking the sky with orange and red and purple as darkness lowered like the lid of a coffin.

Why couldn't that troublesome Nazarene manage to stay put?

I turned back to my task, but paused at the niche that housed my statue of Mars. I pressed my head to the wall and prayed with all my might: "I pray not to thee today, divine Mars, but to the god of the Hebrews—Yahweh. Hear me. Take back your favor in defense of these criminals I seek. I pray, I beseech, I ask your indulgence, that you withdraw and desert these people and their Yeshua, and that you relinquish them to me. Come then to favor Rome by crossing over to me and be propitious to me. If you make this happen with clear and recognizable signs, I vow to erect temples for you and initiate games in your honor."

I pulled three gold coins from my drawstring purse and set them inside the niche, then, as an afterthought, I knocked the statue of Mars onto its side. If Yahweh was as holy and all-powerful as the Jews insisted, let him come to my aid. I cared not who helped me so long as someone led me to the missing Nazarene.

When I stepped back into my chamber, I found Lucius waiting alone. "We're losing daylight," I said, pinching the bridge of my nose. "I thought you had another suspect?"

"I do. But you wanted a break."

"I've taken it. What follows this interview?"

Lucius grimaced. "More bodies."

I gestured toward the door. "Let's have another suspect then."

Lucius hesitated before handing over his report. "This next one is unusual."

"How so?"

"He's a member of the Judean council, yet he was with Joseph the Arimathean the day of the crucifixion, and was reportedly carrying seventy-five pounds of burial spices."

"I remember."

"Doesn't that seem odd to you? We brought him in because he was clearly a supporter of the Nazarene, but why bring ointment for the body if you planned to steal it later?"

I pointed to my nose. "Because you might not want to be overcome by the odors of putrefaction as you hauled the body away on the third day. Now bring him in."

A moment later I was facing Nicodemus, a name I remembered hearing at the crucifixion. I had not personally spoken to the man, but he had seemed to be close to Joseph of Arimathea. As a member of the council, Pilate would want me to treat this one with respect.

How interesting. The Judean council had persuaded Pilate to crucify the Nazarene, yet here was a Pharisee, one of the most religious of them all.

Tall, thin, and dressed in the stern black-and-white garb of his sect, Nicodemus sat and looked around with curiosity. Clearly, he had never before been inside the Roman garrison.

"Thank you for coming in," I told him, though we both knew he'd had no choice. "As you might imagine, we're trying to locate the body of Yeshua the Nazarene."

"I suspected as much." The man leaned forward, one hand stroking his beard, the other resting on his walking stick. "I was greatly distressed when I heard the news. Distressed, but hopeful too."

"Why hopeful?"

His eyes sparkled. "Because He told me this would happen. I went to visit Him one night—"

"Too afraid of your fellow Pharisees to visit by day?"

Nicodemus chuffed. "I was not afraid—I simply couldn't get near Him by day because of the crowds. But I found the house where He was staying in Jerusalem, and I went to interview Him for myself. I knew the others feared Him, you see. I wanted to sound Him out, discover His intentions."

I leaned forward, certain that I would finally learn something useful. "What did he tell you?"

Nicodemus lifted his chin. "I told Him that His name had been mentioned at a council meeting. We knew He came from God as a teacher, because no one could do the miracles He did unless HaShem was with Him. After hearing this, He gave me the oddest reply. He said, 'I tell you truly, unless a person is born again from above, he cannot see the kingdom of God.'"

I slumped, my certainty bludgeoned by swift disappointment. "Another riddle. The Nazarene was full of them."

"That's what I thought." Nicodemus relaxed into a smile. "When I asked how a grown man could be born again, Yeshua said that unless a man was born of water and the Spirit . . . He put it this way: 'What is born of flesh is flesh, and what is born from the Spirit is spirit.' When I asked Him to explain again, He asked how I could be a teacher in Israel and not know these things." The Pharisee chuckled softly. "How indeed?"

"You said he spoke of his death," I pressed. "Go on."

Nicodemus's face bore an inward look. Whatever he had seen, he was seeing it again. "He looked at me and said, 'Just as Moses lifted up the serpent in the desert, so must the Son of Man be lifted up; so everyone who trusts in him may have eternal life. Because God loved the world so much that he gave his only and unique Son, so everyone who trusts in him may have eternal life, instead of being utterly destroyed. God did not send the Son into the world to judge the world, but rather so that through him the world might be saved.'"

"I'm not familiar with your legends. I've heard of Moses, but—"

"Our *history*"—Nicodemus gently emphasized the word—"includes the story of poisonous snakes that struck our people after we escaped bondage in Egypt. The snakes came because our forefathers complained against Adonai, and many of our people died from snakebite. As others lay dying, Adonai commanded Moses to create a bronze serpent and lift it high on a pole. Moses had the snake cast in bronze, then affixed a crossbar to a pole and attached the snake to the crossbar. When he lifted it and carried it through the camp, anyone who looked at the snake was healed."

"Impossible." I shook my head. "I am not a physician, but even I know that people aren't healed by looking at something. They must be purged, or bled, or drink potions made with aromatic herbs—"

"It wasn't the looking that healed them," Nicodemus said. "It was *faith* that made them look."

"Faith?" My tongue tripped over the word. Roman religion was based on knowledge.

"We have forgotten," Nicodemus continued, his face sinking into lines of sorrow. "We have been so busy striving to keep the law that we have forgotten what our nation is built on. It is this: 'And Abram believed Adonai, and Adonai counted him as righteous because of his faith.'"

Nicodemus's brow wrinkled. "I didn't understand at first.

But when I went with Joseph to Golgotha, when I stood at the base of the hill and looked up to see Yeshua lifted high on the execution stake, I understood. Yeshua is HaShem's provision for our sin. Anyone who looks to Him for healing, for eternal life, will receive it."

The room swelled with silence as I tried to make sense of what he was saying. Roman religion had nothing to do with the notions of faith or sin, and the idea that man had to tremble constantly before a holy god was decidedly un-Roman. We were educated, civilized, and not at all superstitious. Let the uncivilized peoples of the world quake before their gods in fear; we Romans were noble and free.

I cleared my throat. "Is faith the reason why you took the body on the third day? So others would see the empty tomb and believe in Yeshua's prediction?"

The Pharisee looked up, a sharp gleam in his eye, and shook his head. "I would have believed even if the tomb had not been empty. I saw His miracles. I finally understood what He meant about being born of the Spirit. So many times we think we are serving Adonai by keeping His law, but Yeshua helped me see that more than anything else, HaShem wants me to return His love. Now I obey His law because I love Him."

Nicodemus gripped his walking stick and met my gaze head on. "Last fall, when the council met to discuss what to do about Yeshua of Nazareth, many wanted to arrest Him. I pointed out that our Torah doesn't judge a man unless it first hears from him and knows what he's doing. My comment was not well received by the council, but they did not arrest Him then. The time was not right." He paused. "Apparently Passover was the appropriate time. When HaShem demands a sacrificial lamb."

I picked up my pen and wrote down Nicodemus's name. We

might need to call him back, though clearly this man had no reason to steal the body.

"Thank you," I said. "I trust we may call upon you later?"

"You may," he said, the beginning of a smile lifting the corner of his mouth. "But I do not think you will ever find Yeshua's body . . . unless you find Him first."

Another riddle. I called for Lucius and sent the Pharisee on his way.

A man accustomed to constant training and action does not take well to sitting in a chair, yet there was no help for it. Though the sun had long since disappeared from the sky, Lucius insisted that I make time for two more interviews.

"The man outside is Agathon, a Jew from Greece," he said, handing me his preliminary report. "The high priest asked that we interview him today. I'm afraid the fellow isn't happy about it."

"Why would Caiaphas single out a Greek?"

"Apparently—" Lucius consulted his notes—"this man and several of his friends had a private meeting with the Nazarene before Passover. Caiaphas wants us to question them before they return to Greece."

"And since when does Caiaphas give us orders?"

Lucius did not answer, nor could he. Sighing, I sank into my chair and nodded. "Bring him in."

Agathon, a thin man, appeared lost in his flowing toga. He sat in the chair, folded his hands, and looked at me with a congested expression on his face. "I do not understand why my friends and I have been detained in Jerusalem. We have done nothing wrong."

"If that is true, you will be released and sent on your way." I leaned back and folded my hands as well, mirroring his posture to put him at ease. "I understand you recently had a private meeting with the Nazarene called Yeshua."

The thin line of Agathon's mouth clamped tight for an instant. Then he nodded and said, "I am not sure you could call it *private*. Many people were present."

"What sort of people?"

The man shrugged. "A few of Yeshua's disciples. Some of the women."

"Did Yeshua or his disciples ask you for any particular favors?"

The man shook his head. "I don't understand."

"What did you talk about?"

"Mysteries. At the time we didn't understand a word, but now . . . things are becoming clearer."

"What things?"

"He told us that 'unless a grain of wheat falls to the ground and dies, it is only a grain of wheat. But if it dies, it produces a bountiful harvest. Even so, he who loves his life will lose it, but he who hates his life in this world will keep it safe.'"

"I've heard babbling children make more sense."

"He wasn't speaking of grain, Tribune, he was speaking of his life. When we heard that he'd been executed, we mourned. But yesterday, when we heard that he had risen, we understood."

"He has not risen; the tomb was robbed. Someone, probably the man's followers, stole the body during the night in order to commit a fraud against the populace. And against Rome."

"Why would they do that?" The Greek sat back in his chair, his brows arching. "Not for riches, surely. Not for fame or power. You seem like a pragmatic sort, Tribune, so tell me—for what earthly reason would the Nazarene's followers perpetuate such a lie?"

I drew back, aware that the Greek had suddenly become the inquisitor. "I ask the questions here."

"Certainly." Agathon pressed his hand to his chest in a gesture of mock humility. "But in order to test your hypothesis, you should consider all possible motivations. And I tell you the truth—Yeshua's followers are simple people. They do not aspire to greatness. They do not desire money. Any power they wield is given to them from above. So why would they lie?"

Pressing my lips together, I silently cursed the Greeks' damnable logic. "No one asked you to linger in Jerusalem to help steal the body?"

The Greek laughed. "Why would they do that?"

"Because you might smuggle it out of the city. Because you would take the story with you, leaving fewer wagging tongues in Jerusalem."

Agathon fingered his beard for a moment, then smiled. "No one asked us to steal his body. But you are right about one thing: we *will* take the story of Yeshua with us."

I crumpled the Greek's report and called for Lucius to lead him away.

Finally, Lucius brought in our last interview of the day, a shifty sort of fellow who kept glancing around as if he expected us to clap him in chains at any moment.

"You know what I seek," I said, wearily sinking into my chair.

The man nodded.

I examined my nails. "Who told you the crucified Nazarene was alive?"

The man swallowed hard. "A friend . . . of a friend."

"A friend of Yeshua's? Perhaps a disciple?"

The man opened and closed his mouth, a picture of idiocy.

"Whatever you say," I warned, "make it the truth. This day has been longer than most, and my patience has nearly evaporated."

"This friend said he was told—the sighting was told of—by two women."

I lowered my hand and studied our suspect. This was new information.

"They went to the tomb," he continued, "before dawn on Sunday and found it empty. Later they met Yeshua on the road—alive. They spoke with him."

I glanced at Lucius, then focused more intently on our suspect. "Their names?"

The man hesitated.

"One way or another, we will have an answer."

"I know only one name," he said slowly. "She is a woman with a certain reputation. Mary of Magdala."

"Do you know where we can find this woman?"

He spread his hands. "Perhaps . . . if you will follow at a distance."

I stood and picked up my sword. "Lead us to this place."

As we went out, I snatched my coins from the altar niche.

⸻

While we hurried through Antonia's colonnade, Lucius gave me details of the information he'd gleaned from our last suspect. "She has not been back to the place where she was staying in days. She was last witnessed going out the morning his body was stolen—early, before sunrise, and not seen since."

"Where does she work?"

"She doesn't—well, not anymore. For the last three years she's been part of a group of women who have supported the Nazarene in his travels. They found lodging where they could, prepared meals, those sorts of things. Before that, she was a madwoman making her living on the streets, known best in Magdala."

"I don't know that place."

"It's a town near the Sea of Tiberias. Known for fabrics, dyes, and fish."

I glanced over my shoulder and counted. We had six legionnaires wearing plain cloaks over their uniforms—a good number. But . . .

"You're bringing no one who can identify her?"

Lucius's face went blank. "How . . . who would that be?"

I made an abrupt left turn and opened the door to the barracks of the enlisted men. One by one they stopped what they were doing and stared, alarmed by the unexpected intrusion.

"Any of you," I called, "know the woman Mary of Magdala?"

Silence reigned for a moment as the soldiers looked at each other. Finally, one hand rose, then another and another . . .

"Bring one of them," I told Lucius, stepping back into the hallway. "And be quick about it."

Any military man is familiar with the notion of hurrying in order to wait. We hurried to reach the inn Mary of Magdala was known to frequent, then crouched in shadows, leaning against casks and wagons, walls and fences. We murmured in low voices and chuckled softly, all the while keeping ourselves alert for any woman traveling alone, any woman who walked with furtive steps.

As we waited I fell into easy conversation with Lucius. Feeling confident now that we had a solid lead, I relaxed enough to talk of battles gone by. I told him about my early days in the cavalry after I'd spent a year training with the Tenth Legion and finally commanded a battalion in my first battle.

"They had outflanked us," I said, studying the street, "so we had to withdraw—a fighting retreat. Some dozen of our men were captured and dragged up into the hills. That night, down in the valley, we heard them screaming and looked up to see them impaled on the ridges—in full view so we could watch them suffer." I shifted my gaze to young Lucius. "That's why you offer no quarter, not ever. Your enemy will use your mercy against you."

Lucius was about to say something, but a sound from the tavern alerted me. I lifted my hand, signaling the others, and watched a man stagger out of the inn, his arm around a stumbling, drunken woman.

I looked at the legionnaire we had grabbed from the barracks. "That one?"

He peered past me, then shook his head.

Just then another woman appeared in the night—she wore a dark cloak pulled tight against her head. She looked up and down the street before moving through a splash of torchlight and walking toward the inn.

"That's her," the legionnaire said. "I'd know that face anywhere."

My men sprang into position, and we charged forward, crossing the street and barreling through the tavern doorway. Several people, mostly foreigners, had been dining in the front room; they scattered like rats as we entered. My men ignored them, but overturned tables and toppled chairs in a search for the mysterious Mary.

"There!" Lucius pointed to a shadow racing toward the rear of the building.

I signaled for three men to follow through the building while Lucius and I ran outside and circled the inn. Pressing ourselves flat against the shadowed wall, we spied her on the window ledge and saw her jump to the ground—and into our custody.

As I gripped her arm, I couldn't resist a grin. "Shalom, Mary."

22

Clavius

Tuesday dawn

After Titus brought me a late meal of bread, figs, and cheese, I returned to my quarters, where Lucius had been guarding Mary of Magdala. An oil lamp burned, gilding her face in a golden glow as the first pale hints of sunrise appeared on the horizon.

Lucius stood and saluted when I entered, then came forward to whisper in my ear, "'The silent countenance often speaks.'"

"Ovid?"

He nodded. "This one says volumes with her eyes."

"And what do her eyes say?"

Lucius pursed his lips and shook his head. "I don't know."

"Then let's use words, shall we?" I nodded at Lucius, dismissing him, and sat behind my desk. "I trust you were comfortable here."

She lifted one shoulder in a shrug. "I am fine."

"You must have a penchant for wandering in the hours before sunrise. This morning we found you at an inn. Sunday morning you were at the Nazarene's tomb before sunrise."

A small smile lifted her mouth. "If I was wandering in darkness, how could I be seen?"

I raised a brow. Score one for the madwoman. I pulled a sheet of parchment from a drawer, dipped my pen in ink, and held it above the paper. "You're a harlot."

"No more."

"What now then?"

Her smile broadened, lighting her eyes. "Forgiven. Healed."

I lowered my pen. "By whom, Yeshua? Only gods can change the past."

Mary said nothing, but studied the brightening sky outside the window.

"Why did you run from us?"

"Instinct."

I tried another approach. "If you are retired from your former occupation, what business did you have at the inn?"

"I was . . . delivering news."

"Good, deliver some. I'm eager to hear it."

She glanced at me, then returned her gaze to the window. "You're not ready to receive it."

I crossed my arms and stared at the woman. Mary of Magdala was no longer young, but mature. White streaks ran through her dark hair, and lines bracketed her nose and mouth. Yet clear traces of beauty remained in her face and form. I could see why she might be tempted to make her living on the street, especially if she had no husband or family to support her.

"Married?"

"Once."

"What became of your husband?"

Something flared in her eyes, then retreated as she looked away. "Romans killed him."

"Was he a criminal?"

"He was a father . . . who dared to step between an insolent son and a Roman sword."

She reached up to brush a trace of wetness from her cheek— a tear?—and I felt a pang of recognition at the gesture. "I've seen you before."

"My other life?"

"Yeshua's execution. You were there with other women. Were any of them at the tomb, prowling through the darkness with you?"

She rewarded me with another glance. "If you knew what happened there . . . all your cares would cease."

"Then enlighten me."

She tilted her head as if considering, but then shifted her attention back to the window. "It is beyond explanation. Especially for a man like you."

My hand crumpled the parchment beneath it. "Spare me the riddles and superstitious babble. Where did you take Yeshua?"

Finally, she looked me in the eyes. Her countenance shimmered with light from the window as she whispered, "He's right here."

Her admission was dredged from a place beyond logic and reason. How could anyone say such a thing?

I lifted my hands in frustration. "Where? Is he is a sprite? A goblin? Alive again somehow? That's your news, isn't it?"

"Open your heart," she said, lifting her hand to pat the skin above her chest, "and see for yourself."

We stared at each other across a sudden silence. I sank back in my chair and drew a deep breath. "I look at you and see nothing but delusion," I said. "I could have the information I want pulled from you. Or I could put you to death"—I snapped my fingers—"like that."

She lowered her chin. "It doesn't matter."

"So you want to be a martyr."

"Not especially."

"Then give me the others . . . and I'll give you your freedom."

"That's how Rome deals with human lives, isn't it? You trade them like coin." She chuckled. "No, thank you. I'm already free."

I pushed away from the desk, flexing my fingers until the urge to choke her had passed. I propped my elbows on the tabletop and looked at her over my tented hands. "Is every disciple like you?"

"No." She laughed again. "Some doubt. Some were weak. Some resent that He favored a woman." Her smile woke a dimple in her cheek. "He came to me first. Of all people, He came to *me*."

Ah. I was finally beginning to understand. "You were lovers."

"Not like that." Her smile flickered. "Yet His is the greatest love I've ever known."

Sensing I had found a weak spot, I rose and bent in front of her, my hands on my knees, my eyes level with hers. "You use present tense, Mary, but he's dead."

"No, He lives."

"Truly? Then share him. Show me the messiah—alive or dead—and show me those who follow him."

When she lifted her eyes to meet mine, they were more focused, as if a film of uncertainty or suspicion had been peeled away. "You look for something you'll never find, Tribune. You are looking for something that passes away . . . when you *could* see something eternal."

I shook my head in frustration. The sun had come up while we talked, flooding the room with light. I straightened and blew out the lamp, then stepped into the hall and summoned Lucius. "She's still a madwoman," I told him. "Refuses to talk sense."

"Perhaps a witch?" Lucius offered. "Should I have her stoned, sir? At least locked up?"

I glanced over my shoulder, where Mary sat unmovable by the window. "Just . . . let her go."

"Sir?"

"Release her. The woman's touched." I tapped the side of my head.

Lucius looked at me with sympathy. "Two nights without sleep, Tribune. You will soon be seeing things yourself."

I exhaled a breath and stepped back into my quarters. I turned over the hourglass on my desk. "When that empties," I told my beneficiarii, "send Titus to wake me."

When he had escorted the woman from Magdala away, I stretched out on my bed and fell into a deep sleep.

Wrapped in a blanket of heat and exhaustion, I dreamed. I was thrust into a black storm-tossed sea, struggling to remain afloat despite my weighty armor, laboring to keep my lungs filled with air. Inexplicably, in the midst of the roiling sea, an execution stake stood without wavering. Lightning split the thunderclouds, casting light on the wooden beams and leaving the image of the stake imprinted on my pupils even when

I closed my eyes. I flailed about, thrashing helplessly, unable to resist the waves that carried me ever nearer to the man who hung on the crossed beams.

Why wouldn't the gods let me drown? Considering all the people I had escorted to Dis, I had expected a quicker journey to the infernal regions.

Lightning shattered the surface of the churning water, brightening swells so large they looked like the rolling hills outside Rome. I tried to swim, but got nowhere. I tried to drown, but the current propelled me upward so I could not die.

I was caught in a swirling vortex centered on the strangely unyielding execution stake.

It was the Nazarene's. I could see the inscription above his head, the wound at his ribs, the blood at his wrists and heels.

The swells lifted me toward him and dropped me, raised me to the level of his feet and released me, thrust me, finally, to the point where I met him face-to-face. Against my will, at close range I beheld the thorn-pierced forehead, the swollen nose, and the eyes! They opened, stared into me, looked *through* me to the basest part of my soul. He saw, he *knew* everything I had ever said, done, or thought. Then the wave relinquished me to the dizzying churn of black waters and gray-flecked foam—

I woke, breathless and drenched in sweat.

A moment later, Titus entered, blinking in surprise to find me awake and sitting up. "Tribune, your sand has run out—Pilate has summoned you again."

23

Clavius

TUESDAY, ANTE MERIDIEM

The prefect was not happy.

"You're *digging up* the dead?" Pilate's nostrils flared with fury.

"No stone unturned, Prefect."

"But . . . a Hebrew cemetery?"

I folded my hands. "It seemed logical. He's a Jew—and deceased."

The prefect jabbed a finger toward the city outside the window. "Do you not realize the wrath incurred?"

"Another day or two and wrath won't matter. Nature will have taken its course."

Pilate glared at me with burning, reproachful eyes, then turned away, probably overwhelmed by the impossibility of our task. "Caesar's spies will hear of all this," he said, his voice low and trembling.

I nodded. "An unfortunate dilemma."

"For both of us, Tribune." He gave me a sharp look, his mouth compressed into a line. "That common Nazarene, that *carpenter*, will *not* be the ruin of me, do you hear? I want his body lying over there!" He pointed at the pavement where the Nazarene had stood when condemned to die. "By tonight, do you understand?"

I saluted, and Lucius and I hurried out of the room. On our way out I hissed in Lucius's ear, "The disciples are the key. Find them, and we find him."

"We have another informant," Lucius said. "This one came forward voluntarily. I interviewed him while you were resting."

"Where is he?"

"Waiting at the fortress."

I quickened my pace. "Let us hope this one is not given to riddles."

Lucius and I made it only as far as the vestibule before a guard stopped us. The legionnaire, one of the Italian cohort that traveled with Pilate, jerked his head toward an old woman who stood half hidden behind a marble pillar. "She would have a word with you, Tribune."

"I've no time for conversations with slaves—"

The guard put out his hand, holding me in place. "She is handmaid to Procula, the prefect's wife."

I took a deep breath. Though in the strictest sense I did not serve Pilate's wife, any man with half a brain knew that he ignored the wives of commanding officers at his own peril. I left Lucius in the vestibule and went to the old woman.

"How may I be of service?" I asked.

"My mistress"—she pointed down a corridor—"would have a word with you."

"Lead on."

I followed the handmaid down a polished hallway and paused outside a pair of carved doors. "Wait here." The old woman slipped into the room, returning a moment later to let me in.

I had never been in the private rooms of Herod's former palace, and I was taken aback by the opulence of the chamber. Several patterned columns supported a ceiling of carved tiles accented with what looked like gold leaf. An elevated bed occupied the center of the room, but the lady who wanted to talk to me was draped over an upholstered couch as a slave applied her cosmetics. Procula's elaborately curled hair hung from a jeweled clasp at the back of her head, and an intricately beaded necklace covered the bare skin of her neck and chest.

An image of Rachel flitted before my eyes—she who wore no jewelry and favored an uncomplicated arrangement of hair. Both women were beautiful, but while Procula's highly adorned appearance would be much praised in Rome, I preferred Rachel's simple loveliness.

The old woman dipped before her mistress and gestured to me. "I have brought the Tribune, mistress."

Procula took a moment to consult her reflection in a looking brass, then dismissed the slave with a flick of her hand.

"Tribune." She rose from the sofa in one fluid motion and approached. "Will you walk with me on the balcony? I've something to discuss with you."

I took a step, but then hesitated. "I would not want to offend your husband . . ."

A sad smile curved her lips. "My husband is not likely to be enjoying the fresh air this morning. And I will not keep you long."

We walked toward the balcony, away from the slaves tending to her wardrobe and cosmetics tray. "Five nights ago," she began, keeping her voice low as we strolled, "before my husband had ever seen the Nazarene they call Yeshua, I went to bed early with a headache. I dreamed, and in my vision I saw my husband standing on the pavement in the center of the courtyard while this man, a Jew, sat in the governor's seat. I was alarmed, of course. Why would any Jew be sitting in judgment over a Roman prefect? And then I heard the judge speak.

"'You, Pontius Pilate'"—the lady closed her eyes as she recalled the dream—"'are guilty of acquitting criminals and condemning the innocent. For this you will be condemned and forever be known as an equivocator and a coward. But do not despair, for even this fulfills the plan of God. Even as the evil one bruised a man's heel, Adonai will bruise your head.'"

She stopped and looked at me, her gray eyes filled with distress. "When I woke, I had no idea what the dream meant, but I wrote down the details in case I needed to remember. Caesar's wife, Calpurnia, dreamed of Caesar's murder the day before he was stabbed to death in the Senate. Caesar heeded her warning until one of the conspirators told him the other senators would mock him for listening to his wife. So he went to the Senate and fulfilled his wife's dream."

Her painted face took on a mournful look. "The next morning, when my handmaid told me that Pilate was sitting in judgment on a Jew from Nazareth, I knew my dream was about to be fulfilled. I sent Pilate a message, warning him to have nothing to do with that just man, and perhaps he would have listened, but the shouts of the people overpowered the voice of his conscience. Pilate fears only one thing, and they knew it. They threatened him with the emperor's scorn, and thus cowed him into silence."

A sudden thought occurred to me. Could Pilate's wife have had anything to do with Yeshua's disappearance? The idea seemed farfetched, yet she might have been motivated by love for her husband. If the Nazarene lived, after all, her husband could not be guilty of executing an innocent man.

I watched her, grateful that her maid had caught me before I left the building. Pilate would be highly offended if I summoned his wife for questioning, but since the lady had presented herself . . .

I motioned toward a bench in the shade. "Would you like to sit? Now that I've heard your story, I would like to know more."

She sat while I stood in front of her, trying to decide on the best approach. I opted for directness. "Mistress, why did you tell me this story?"

"I told you the story because I want you to do your best to preserve Pilate's reputation in all this. His success as governor depends entirely on your success in handling this affair."

"Did you, by chance, employ men to remove the Nazarene's body from its tomb?"

She blinked rapidly. "Did I . . . ? No! I know nothing about any theft."

I clasped my hands behind my back. "After all, your husband could avoid trouble with Rome if he did *not* kill an innocent man. If the Nazarene was merely injured, for instance, and somehow managed to escape death . . . wouldn't that bode well for your husband?"

Her eyes blazed at me in an extraordinary expression of alarm. "Not dead? I have been assured that the Nazarene most assuredly is dead. Unless *you* have been lying to the prefect!"

"I do not lie," I assured her.

"Then I find your suggestion ludicrous and insulting. My husband might be an equivocator, Tribune, but he is not a liar. If he made the wrong decision—and by all the gods it appears that he did—he will stand before the emperor and accept his due. He is a man of honor."

"Of course." I bowed slightly. "Forgive my impertinent supposition. As an inquisitor, however, it is my duty to make unpleasant and even illogical suppositions in order to discover the truth."

She lifted her chin. "Be that as it may, I do not think I will mention this to my husband. He has worries enough of his own."

I thanked her for her time and walked away, exhaling a deep breath as I went. I would have enjoyed finding the source of our problem here in Pilate's quarters, even though Pilate might have had me killed rather than expose his wife as a conspirator.

But the lady's alarm had been real, and her umbrage undeniable.

I would have to look elsewhere for my body thieves. Fortunately, Lucius had an informant waiting at the Antonia.

————◆————

Back at the Antonia Fortress, I tossed a small pouch onto the floor at the informant's feet. "For your help."

The bearded man blinked at me, then bent and picked up the pouch, opened it, and stared at the silver coins.

"There's more if you assist us further."

The man said nothing.

"You will continue, won't you? I'm sure you wouldn't want word of your cooperation to get out."

The man hesitated. "What do you mean by *assist*?"

"We have a few questions." I shifted in my chair and gave him a perfunctory smile. "The Nazarene's disciples—how many are there? What are their names? Their plans? Their weapons caches? Where do they gather? Who leads them now? And most important, where are they hiding his corpse?"

The man held the pouch in his palm as if weighing it before tucking it into his belt. "I'll learn all I can and let you know." He started to leave, but then stopped in the doorway and looked back over his shoulder. "There were seventy, but the inner circle was twelve. Eleven now. All hiding—I know not where."

"Do you have names?"

The man held up a finger. "I can give you one of the seventy. Cleopas. Come, and I'll lead you to him."

Lucius and I followed him out of the fortress.

Remaining a discreet distance behind the man, we trailed him through the narrow streets of Jerusalem. Attempting to look like casual observers, we strolled through markets and courtyards, cobblestone streets and dirt passageways, alleys populated with sheep and humans and dogs. Finally our informant paused before a house with peeling paint. He caught my eye and nodded, then drifted away.

Lucius and I pulled our swords and forced the door. Inside the crowded house, a startled family was sitting on a carpet to share the midday meal. The woman screamed when she saw us, but I ignored her and waved my sword between the bearded men. "Who's Cleopas?"

A wide-eyed fellow with curly hair lowered his cup. "I am he."

Another man at the table immediately leapt up and backed away, pointing to Cleopas as if he were a bad smell.

"These friends," Cleopas continued, apparently unconcerned by his friend's sudden shift in loyalty, "are newly met. They offered a place at their table . . . it's not them you seek."

"You have spoken the truth," I acknowledged. "As long as you come quietly."

I sat behind my desk, Lucius at one side and Titus at the other, as Cleopas sat in a chair and grinned like a simpleton.

"Well?" I asked.

"Why am I smiling?"

"That was the question."

"I suppose—" he stifled a giggle—"I suppose it is because I know something you don't."

I clenched my jaw and struggled to be patient. "And what would that be?"

The man's grin expanded as he stood and thrust his hands into the air. "Yeshua is alive!" He bounced like a lively child. "Alive!"

The man danced around the chair, shouted excitedly a few times, and dropped back into his seat, momentarily breathless.

Titus gaped in amazement, and I could feel Lucius's gaze on me, but I did not look away from our suspect. Earlier, someone had referred to the Nazarene's disciples as *rabid*. I was beginning to understand why.

"What do you hope to win by spreading this fantasy?" I asked, keeping my voice calm and level.

Cleopas leaned forward. "With my own eyes, Tribune—I saw Him. I walked with Him on the road that leads to Emmaus. He spoke to me. He broke bread in my house and *ate* it with me and my companion. Unbelievable, but true. He's as alive as you and me."

"Then conjure him up—right now—or show me the body he must have shed like a snakeskin."

Cleopas drew back. "God is not at my beck and call."

"God? Yahweh manifests himself through a crazy, poor, dead Jew?"

The grin flashed through his beard again. "So it appears."

"And what does this rebirth mean?"

The man's mouth dropped open. "Why—eternal life! For everyone who believes."

I cast Lucius a sidelong look of utter disbelief. "Marvelous recruiting tool. Much better than salt."

Titus laughed, and Cleopas grinned like a dog with a bone. "And that's not all."

"There's more?"

"Many more." I didn't think it was possible, but the man's grin broadened. "Others," he said, lowering his voice to a near whisper, "who were dead and buried are now alive and walking the streets of Jerusalem."

A scream of frustration rattled at the back of my throat. How was I supposed to make any progress when I kept interviewing crazy people? "You expect me to believe—?"

"Actually—" he laughed—"I *don't* expect you to believe. I don't expect anyone to believe it, but it's true. On the first day of the week, when Yeshua rose from death, He brought other righteous believers with Him! They came out of their graves and went into Jerusalem, where many people have seen them. They are reunited with their families and rejoicing even now."

I brought my hands to my forehead and massaged my throbbing temples. I expected Cleopas to start gibbering at any moment, but he simply sat there, smiling like a simpleton.

From beneath my hand I shot Lucius a stern look of displeasure, then turned back to the suspect. "The time for foolishness is done. Forget those you claim are resurrected. I want to know how many disciples remain in Jerusalem. How many are you?"

Cleopas lifted his hand as if to count on his fingers, then clenched his fists and opened them several times. "Well, we are only a few for now—and our only weapon is love—but this changes everything."

"Really? What will change? What are your intentions?"

The man's face went blank with shock. "Intentions? Do you jest? We intend to tell the world! What else would we do?" He shook his head when I did not share his hilarity. "Why do you fear Yeshua? Your empire means *nothing* to Him." He waved his arm as if clearing my desk. "'Render unto Caesar what is Caesar's.' Ha! That is what He taught us. What do you want then? More taxes? My death? Have it all."

"I want," I said, easing into his fantasy, "what Caesar wants, and the emperor wants to know where your confederates hide. I want to see the Nazarene's corpse. Immediately."

"What you really want," Cleopas said, beaming, "is God's love. But perhaps you fear it too much."

I leaned back and tapped the edge of my desk, then smiled. "Ever seen a man crucified, Cleopas?"

His bright expression dimmed a degree. "No."

"That's correct, for I don't remember seeing you there. Probably because you were hiding, right?"

Cleopas blanched at the words.

"Shall I tell you what you missed?" When he didn't answer, I stood and pressed on, circling Cleopas as I spoke. "Yeshua was already deep in the throes of agony when he arrived at Golgotha. The flesh had been whipped from his back, the heavy crossbar had crushed him for a mile, the thorny crown had sent blood running down his face. Then imagine having *this*"—I picked up an iron spike from my desk and threw it at Cleopas's feet—"driven through your wrists. Feel it. Then that same spike driven through your feet. Your *feet*, Cleopas, can you imagine? That is what you hang from—spikes. Rubbing against bone. You have to decide what's worse, the agony *here*—" I leaned forward to pinch the tendons at his wrist—"or *here*." I aimed a sharp kick at his anklebone. "You must choose which torture your own weight will inflict, hands or heels, constantly. Then you discover you can't breathe and realize you will never breathe easy again, and that every breath for the rest of your horrific life will be like sucking air through wet fur.

"Yeshua was lucky. He only hung like that for six hours. Most take days to die, gasping for someone to kill them. If he still felt anything at the end, he surely felt the spear thrust up under his ribs to pierce his heart and lungs. Sometimes we have to bury them with the nails still—"

"Enough!" Breathing heavily, Cleopas held his head between his hands, covering his ears.

Leaning back against my desk, I clasped my hands. "Let's not speak any more of his body. By now it must look hideous. But one last time I will ask you—where are the other disciples? I will not ask again."

Cleopas lifted his head, pain and regret flickering in his eyes.

"Tell me and you're free to go."

"Do you"—Cleopas lowered his voice—"give me your word on that?"

"I do. Where are they?"

Cleopas stood and slowly approached as if to whisper in my ear. From the corner of my eye I saw Lucius straighten, his hand moving to his sword, but I did not believe this fool capable of attacking a soldier of Rome.

Cleopas bent toward me. "The disciples—" he suddenly straightened—"are everywhere!"

He then tipped his head back and roared with laughter.

———⊰❖⊱———

What could we do but release him? From the rampart I watched Lucius walk him to the fortress gate, then stand back as Cleopas waved cheerfully and disappeared into the crowd. Lucius did not respond, but signaled our paid informant, who slipped into the crowd and followed the fool.

I called for Titus and asked him to bring clean linen and chicory leaves.

24

Rachel

As the sun began to sink toward the west, I lowered the awning on my booth and slipped the few coins I had earned into my purse. I took my few remaining matzot and walked to the corner where Miriam, the blind woman, sold her straw brooms.

"Fresh matzah for you," I said, placing the bread on her lap. "Eat it in good health."

"May Adonai bless you, child." She turned her white eyes in my direction and smiled. "He has a special blessing for you today."

I turned away, a wry smile on my lips. I could have used a special blessing yesterday when that young Roman had dragged me to the Antonia to be interrogated. Clavius had not come to my house last night, and I felt certain the interview had ended our relationship. As we played our parts, our false selves had shone the light of truth on who and what we were: the brute and the hypocrite.

I could have gone home, but my feet followed the road that led to the Temple. Though the daily services had almost ended, I knew the courts would still be filled with people who sought a touch of glory before ending their day.

I crossed the Royal Portico, walked quickly through the Court of the Gentiles, and entered the Women's Court. There I stood, my hands uplifted, and tried to fashion words for Adonai. How could I, who was so impure and needy, come before such a holy God?

As I struggled to shape my thoughts, I overheard a woman who stood a few paces away.

"'But a branch will emerge from the trunk of Jesse,'" she was saying, "'a shoot will grow from his roots. The Spirit of Adonai will rest on him, the Spirit of wisdom and understanding, the Spirit of counsel and power, the Spirit of knowledge; he will be inspired by fearing Adonai.'"

I opened my eyes as the words came back to me. They were writings from Isaiah, which spoke of the coming Messiah, a descendant of David. Who was this woman, and why did she seem intent on attracting attention in the Women's Court?

I walked over and stood before her. She had closed her eyes, but her countenance seemed to radiate light. She wore a tunic of pure white, no shoes, and her long white hair flowed over her shoulders and down her back. Then her wide eyes opened, and she smiled at me.

"A blessing on you, child," she said, her voice warm and melodious.

This odd woman was fully human . . . and most certainly out of place. Proper women did not leave home without their heads covered, and when they went into the Court of the Women, their actions and voices remained quiet and reserved.

"I am sorry," I said, convinced that someone's elderly mother had wandered from her caretaker, "but I do not know your name."

She laughed, a delightful throaty sound. "I don't suppose you do. I am Anna Bat-P'nu'el, of the tribe of Asher. I used to come here every day, but have not stood in this court in more than thirty years."

I nodded out of politeness. "May I help you find your way home?"

The woman tipped her head back and laughed again. "I have no home, but the Levites let me sleep in a room not far from here. Isn't it wonderful? The child I once blessed has risen to be with His followers once more. And Adonai willed that I follow! So here I am, doing what I have always done, praising Adonai and the one who will restore Jerusalem to Israel."

"Shhh." Hearing her dangerous words, I took the old woman's arm and led her gently out of the Women's Court. When we reached the Court of the Gentiles, I pointed discreetly at one of the guards who stood at the edge of the portico. "We do not dare speak of such things openly. Just this week the Romans executed a rabbi who dared call himself king of the Jews."

The woman seemed preoccupied for a moment before her smile blossomed again, her eyes lighting with joy. "'He was wounded because of our crimes,'" she said, her eyes searching mine. "'Crushed because of our sins; the disciplining that makes us whole fell on him, and by his bruises we are healed.'"

"Words from Isaiah; I know them well." I slipped my arm

around her, determined to lead her away from the Temple, where she might be overheard. I had taken less than a dozen steps when a man called her name. "Anna! You're still here!"

I turned and saw an old man dressed in the same manner as the woman. He wore a spotless white robe, his feet were bare, and his thin white hair floated around his head. "And you are?" I asked, wondering if they had escaped from the same household.

"Simeon," he answered. "And I have returned to share the glorious news! I first saw Him when He was but a babe in his mother Mary's arms, but even then I knew I held Adonai's Yeshua, a light that will be the glory of Israel and bring revelation to the Gentiles. I blessed Mary and warned her that the boy would become a sign people would speak against—"

"They will speak against you too," I interrupted, wondering if in this situation it would be acceptable to grab an old man by the arm and lead him away. "These are dangerous times, and the very stones of this Temple have ears—"

"The earth will one day shout His name." Simeon lifted his voice, drawing the attention of everyone who still lingered in the courtyard. "'For he who sits in heaven laughs; Adonai looks at them in derision. Then in his anger he rebukes them and says, "I myself have installed my king on Zion, my holy mountain."'"

I caught his hand and gripped it hard. "Would you and Anna like to sup with me? I can bake something, and you can stay the night at my house."

"Thank you, but no." Quite firmly, Simeon freed his hand. "This is where we belong, daughter."

I looked at them—lost, confused, and in such danger that they would not last another day if they kept proclaiming their prophecies. But they did not listen to me and they were not my kin.

"If you will not come with me," I told them, "I will be on my way. But I must respectfully admonish you to temper your voice. Do not risk your lives to proclaim such dangerous tidings."

Anna looked at Simeon, and in their shared glance a compact was made and received. "Do not fret," Simeon said, his eyes sparking with life. "Now that He is risen, death holds no power over those who believe."

I nodded slowly and turned away, more than ready to put distance between myself and their brash words.

But I could not help admiring their fearlessness in the face of death.

25

Clavius

Long afternoon shadows stretched over the walls and streets of Jerusalem by the time I walked in front of a canvas-covered handcart destined for the praetorium. Passersby scattered like quail as we approached, repelled by the noxious reek.

Doing my best to ignore the stench, I led the way to Pilate's headquarters and instructed legionnaires to park the handcart and set its contents on the courtyard pavement.

The prefect did not take long to join us.

"Salve, Prefect." I saluted him and stepped aside so he could see what we had brought. "Observe." I pointed at the bloated corpse on the cobblestones. "Nail holes in the hands and feet.

● ● ● 191 ● ● ●

A wound in the side beneath the rib cage." I gestured to a nearby soldier, who made a face as he flipped the rigid body into a prone position. "The marks of scourging. And note—the legs are unbroken. There are even wounds along the hairline."

Standing as far away as possible, Pilate squinted beyond the perfumed cloth he held over his nose. "But the face, I cannot tell . . ."

"Nor can anyone else."

Understanding filled the prefect's eyes.

"At this point," I continued, "almost any corpse could be the Nazarene—so long as it bears the appropriate wounds."

Pilate slumped and exhaled a long sigh.

"Let it be so, Prefect," I urged him. "I see no better option. I will keep searching for those who took him. They are the real threat."

The prefect shook his head, then trudged to a pitcher on a stand and filled a cup with wine. He turned and sipped, staring thoughtfully at the corpse.

"Threat is a creature with many heads, Tribune, and I need you elsewhere now." When I lifted a brow, he stared upward and sniffed the heavens. "Trouble in Hebron. Trouble never sleeps."

But I was not ready to relinquish my quest—I needed answers. I moved closer to speak to Pilate alone. "Something yet needs unraveling with this situation. With your permission I'd like another week to pursue the matter."

Pilate gestured toward the south—toward Hebron—with his cup. "By next week there will be another messiah. And the week after that, another. Already the furor over Yeshua is fading, so next week I need you in Hebron."

He waited for my acquiescence, so reluctantly I nodded.

"You are dangerously clever," Pilate said, squinting at me with open suspicion. "Can I turn my back on you?"

"That is what I fear most, Prefect."

The prefect gave me a smile that was both admiring and cynical. "From the same cloth, Tribune. Indeed we are." He drained his cup, then looked toward the southern horizon. "I remember when I was like you—so sure, so . . . I forget what. But in the end, what does it really matter?"

I frowned. "Sir?"

Pilate waved his scented cloth toward the rancid body fouling his courtyard. "In a few years, that will be us."

I swallowed hard and saluted him, even as I was overcome by a wave of longing for Rachel.

By the time I reentered the gate of Antonia Fortress, the courtyard was bustling with activity. Despite the late hour, legionnaires were packing wagons and inspecting weapons. Centurions were supervising the loading of supply carts, and the stable master was busy shoeing a stallion.

I dismounted, led my horse to one of the livery attendants, then went upstairs and found Lucius. I gestured toward the nexus of activity and lifted a brow. "Why the commotion?"

Lucius squared his shoulders. "Rumor has it we are heading to Hebron, so I took the liberty of launching preparations, Tribune."

Truly? I removed my helmet and studied my young beneficiarii. The untested lad was not afraid to take the lead, even from his superior. He wore a look of eagerness I recognized from my younger days, and the realization did not altogether please me.

I handed my helmet to Titus. "Any news?"

Lucius spoke immediately. "Your tomb guards have been sighted, sir. They finally left their hiding place."

"Where?"

"A tavern in the western part of the city. It's rumored they have come into money."

I untied the linen scarf at my neck. "That's no surprise."

"I know you wish to triumph, sir," Lucius added. "I am certain things will come together in time."

I tossed the soiled linen to Titus and gave Lucius a curt nod. "Your ambition is noted."

I turned away, intending to change my reeking tunic and visit the bath before heading out again, but a glance at Titus's expression constrained me. "Thank you, Beneficiarii." I nodded. "That will be all."

When the young man had gone, Titus slumped in apparent relief. "Overactive young scamp. I grow weary just watching him."

"He is enthusiastic," I admitted. "And far too much like me." I turned back to my slave. "You have news?"

Smiling, Titus handed over a sealed scroll. "It arrived early this evening. Would you like me to read it?"

I broke the seal. "I would like you to light the lamp and let me read it. I crave a few moments of quiet and solitude."

Titus hurried to obey, backing out of the room and leaving me alone.

◆━◆━◆

I felt a small twinge of unease when I unrolled the parchment and did not recognize the handwriting. I had been expecting news from Adorabella, but this was a more masculine hand. A quick glance at the signature revealed the missive had been written by my sister's husband.

Dear Clavius:

I scarcely know how to write this letter, knowing of your love for your family and my honorable Adorabella, your sister, who is dead. She died while giving birth to our child. Sadly enough, our baby son died with her.

Despite many prayers and supplications to Juno, Lucina, and Jupiter, the gods did not favor us. As her labor dragged on for days, Adorabella knew what would happen. She begged me to write you and assure you that only death could stanch the affection she felt for her twin.

As for me, though I have no desire to flaunt my grief in the public forum, nor to exaggerate the cause I have for tears, would that I had some means to make it less! I am unaccustomed to such sorrow, having not walked with death as you have, nor having had it stare me in the face for so many years as you.

I write freely because I know you have found a way to harden your heart to death and grief, and in this moment I would freely exchange places with you. If you know of some remedy for this soul-crushing sorrow, please share it with me.

> *Your brother-in-law no more,*
> *Herminus*

Hard-hearted? Did he truly think of me as such?

I sat like a stone, absorbing the wrenching news in silence. Never had a single letter done more to rip at my heart and unseat my senses. Adorabella, my twin, my other self, had been snuffed out as completely as the light from an oil lamp. And to further amplify the horrific news, Herminus wrote as if I were an unthinking savage—as if my work for Rome had turned me into a monster that trudged heartlessly throughout the empire, mindlessly creating a river of blood with my sword.

Is this how everyone saw me? Did my brother-in-law think of me as an unfeeling *brute*?

The word opened a stream of memory, a wound I had all but forgotten in my determined focus on the task at hand. Rachel had called me a brute. She had sat in this very room, holding my protective amulet while her double-edged words struck at my heart. Did she think I came to her bed only because I yearned for a woman's warmth? Did she imagine that she meant nothing to me, that I was an animal who sought company only to indulge its basest instincts? Had I ever done or said or implied such a notion in her presence?

My mind bulged with questions, unasked and unanswered. They would have to wait, but they could not wait long.

Like Herminus, I had no desire to flaunt my grief, nor could I indulge myself by doing so. I would repress my feelings and focus on my duty, except when I lay on my bed and considered the breadth and length and scope of my life. Only then would I ponder the question of death . . . and wonder if my close association with it had stolen my hope for a life of significance.

Death. How a man met it defined his character, but I had little control over the circumstances. A soldier longed to die on the battlefield, yet many died in the barracks from sickness or wounds. A gladiator wanted to die in the arena, yet hundreds died in the *ludus*. Pilate said the Nazarene seemed to desire death on the execution stake, but why would any man want to be associated with that symbol of shame?

A woman who died in childbirth might welcome death, so

long as her child passed from her body into life. But my poor sister did not receive that mercy.

I lowered the scroll and left it lying on my desk. Titus would undoubtedly read it, poor fool, and then would carry the knowledge of Adorabella's death with him.

Powered by the unfeeling strength that comes from routine, I went to the baths, washed the reek of death from my skin, and dressed in a simple tunic and dark cloak. If we would soon be leaving for Hebron, I needed to say an important farewell.

Or perhaps I simply needed to see Rachel.

26

Rachel

I lit a lamp and placed it in the window on the first day of the week, and the second, but no disciple of Yeshua rapped on my door. I lit the lamp again on the third day, and shortly after returning from the Temple, I heard a sharp knock. Only one, but it was enough to draw me as if my feet had suddenly sprouted wings.

The bearded man had curly hair and entered quickly. He closed the door behind him, leaning against it as if to keep danger out. I watched with wide eyes, wondering if I had just welcomed a madman, but then the fellow smiled. "Matthew," he said, easing himself away from the door. "A friend of Lydia's.

She said I should come because you wanted to know more about Yeshua."

"I'm Rachel." My manners warred with my curiosity. "Can I get you something to drink? Would you like me to wash your feet?"

He waved my concerns away and walked casually to my small table. "No time for all that. What would you like to know?"

I gestured to a chair, which he took as I slid into the seat across from him. I laughed and confessed my nervousness. "This is most improper. You are a religious man, yet we are alone together in a house—"

He lifted his hand, cutting me off. "There is a time for everything, but this is not the time to observe social conventions. The Romans are searching for Yeshua's disciples, so I cannot stay long in any one place. So ask what you will, and I will do my best to answer."

I pressed my hands together and searched through my confused thoughts. "My uncle always said we should look for many messiahs," I began. "A royal messiah, a priestly messiah, and a messiah who would free us from Gentile rule. Was Yeshua one of those?"

"He *is* all of those things," Matthew said, smiling. "The Son of David died, but He lives now! We have seen Him and felt His wounds."

Son of David . . . The old woman at the Temple had spoken of a branch emerging from the trunk of Jesse, David's father. Could she . . . could all of this be connected in some way?

I stuttered in disbelief. "H-how can someone rise from the dead? And how can Yeshua be our deliverer? We are still under Roman rule."

"It is because Yeshua is the Son of God, the one who was,

and is, and is to come. He is the messenger of Adonai-Tzva'ot, the one the psalmist foretold. He is a descendant of David and heir to the throne. He is the one Zechariah spoke of when he wrote 'They will look to him, whom they have pierced. They will mourn for him as one mourns for an only son.'"

"How—what did he do to convince you of who he was?"

A grin flashed in the thicket of Matthew's curly beard. "You might say it began with the force of His personality. I was sitting in the market, in the booth for tax collections." A momentary look of horror must have crossed my face, because he laughed and pointed at me. "I know—horrible job, horrible Jews, those who work with Romans and handle dirty pagan money—and everyone knows we all skim far too much off the top to keep for ourselves. Anyway, I was sitting there, counting my denarii, when Yeshua came walking through the marketplace with His motley crew of followers. He saw me and said 'Follow me,' so I did. I followed Him through Capernaum, until He sat to teach a group that had gathered. I was so thrilled by what He said that I invited all my tax-collector friends to join us for dinner at my house. There we were, all grouped around the table—Yeshua, His disciples, the tax collectors, and me."

His voice grew wistful. "People actually gathered outside the house to protest, can you believe it? A couple of Pharisees and Torah teachers even threw stones at the window shutters. They couldn't believe that a teacher of Scripture would enter my house, much less share a platter with the likes of me and my friends. But Yeshua stood, opened the windows, and called out, 'The ones who need a doctor aren't the healthy, but the sick. I have not come to call those who think themselves righteous, but to call sinners to turn to God from their sins.'"

Matthew stared down at his hands. "After that, I knew I'd

follow Him anywhere He wanted to lead me. And while the Pharisees and that lot went on fasting and divining, we turned from our sins and celebrated because we had the bridegroom with us. Yeshua said the time would come when the bridegroom would be taken away, and when that time comes, we will fast. He is with us still, but probably not for much longer. We are ready now, I think, to bear witness to all we have seen."

He looked at me then, his dark eyes reflecting the light from the window lamp. "What about you, Rachel? Do you hear Him calling?"

I blinked. I didn't hear anything, and as far as turning from my sins . . . I didn't wish to surrender Clavius. He was more than a guilty pleasure; he was the only person who truly loved me. I had been brought up to believe that a Judean woman's purpose was to serve her family and bring new life into the world. Since I had failed miserably at those things, I found joy only in my secret love.

From some dark corner of my heart, I summoned a smile. "Thank you for coming to visit with me," I said, standing. "I will remember what you have said."

"Is that as far as you're willing to go?" Matthew's eyes searched my face. "You do not have to see Yeshua in order to believe in Him."

I lowered my gaze and moved to the door. "Thank you for coming."

"May the blessings of Adonai surround you, Rachel," Matthew said, pausing in the doorway. "And may He grant the peace you seek."

27

Clavius

TUESDAY EVENING

I did not get a horse from the stables, but instead walked through the shadows of familiar streets until I reached Rachel's small house. The glow of an oil lamp lit the single front window, yet as I waited for the street to clear, her door opened. A bearded man stepped out, a stranger, and he lingered for a moment as he shared words pitched for Rachel's ears alone.

An unexpected dart of jealousy made me wince. Who was he? What did he mean to Rachel, and why did I care? I had no claim on her, or she on me.

I drew a breath and exhaled it slowly, reining in my emotions.

The strange man moved off into the night, leaving Rachel alone in her doorway.

I stepped into a sliver of moonlight to catch her attention before she closed the door. A tiny flicker of surprise flitted across her face when she saw me, but she did not retreat. She waited, her arms loosely linked, until I stood in front of her.

"So," I said.

She lifted her gaze to study me. "How are you?" she asked. "Is that surprise I see on your face?"

"Nothing surprises me."

"Hurt, then? Jealousy? Disappointment? Or have you decided to ignore my guest in hope of an evening's pleasure?"

"I came to say good-bye," I said. "I leave for Hebron soon."

Her face emptied of expression and locked as a chilly silence fell between us.

"After our conversation at the fortress," she finally said, "I wondered if I would see you again. I hoped to, but we are too much oil and water. Yet that was the attraction, wasn't it?"

I gestured toward her departing lover. "Is he oil or water?"

The corner of her mouth twitched. "He is possibility. Hope for the future. I need hope . . . a purpose for my life."

"I see."

"I don't think you do." She shook her head. "Nothing touches you, Clavius. Nothing moves you, not even love. Don't you long for *anything*?"

She was wrong, of course. But she wasn't a Roman soldier and she hadn't been trained to shove personal feelings and ambitions into a dark and rarely accessed closet of the heart. And she wasn't raw because she had just lost her twin, her other self. I came here because I wanted to take Rachel in my arms and unload the burden of grief I carried. I wanted to unite with her and know that with her, at least, I could feel complete and *alive*.

But all that would be impossible now, because she had found someone else. Some other purpose.

"I do long for something," I told her, my voice sounding flat and lifeless in my own ears. "A wish even you should understand."

"And that is?"

"A day without death."

A wave of feeling rose within me and tumbled into a flood of words. "Every day, every hour I cause it, mourn it, investigate it, expect it. Death has become my life. Roman or Jew, it takes us all. Everything dies in the end. I long to be free of that, if only for a moment. I am not unfeeling, Rachel. Death is. And it continually strives to mold me in its likeness."

The corners of her mouth went tight as a sudden spasm of grief knit her brows. She reached out, took my rough hand, and lifted it to her cheek. Her eyes glittered with unshed tears as she pressed a kiss into my palm and . . . released me.

"Shalom, Tribune," she whispered. "I wish you peace."

I took a breath to respond, but knew I would never be able to speak past the boulder in my throat. So I lowered my chin in an abrupt nod, wrapped my cloak around me and stepped back, blending into the shadows as she closed her door.

———————

The garden cemetery lay quiet and still beneath a full moon. A Sabbath stillness reigned over the place, with only the churr of insects and rattle of palm leaves to disturb it.

I leaned against a block of limestone and thought of Rachel, who had just told me good-bye, and Adorabella, who had left me without a word. A suffocating sensation tightened my throat, and for a moment I wanted nothing more than to walk into the Arimathean's empty tomb, stretch out on the slab, and deliver my spirit to whatever god might be willing to take it. Grief was a tumor in my chest, taking up the space I needed to breathe. . . .

I gasped for air—focused on filling my lungs in a steady rhythm. Death was unavoidable, even for emperors and kings, and I knew its reality better than anyone. That truth had to be why the assignment to find the Nazarene's body had so consumed me. For his followers to perpetuate such a fraud—that death could be defeated—was unconscionable, beyond pardon. If they wanted to deny death and sell tickets to an eternal hereafter, let them taste of death themselves and *then* deny its bitter bite.

A curse fell from my lips as I looked around. I'm not sure why I went back to the garden tomb. Perhaps thoughts of Adorabella drew me here. If I were home in Rome, I would be standing by her funeral pyre, giving vent to my loss as a priest sent my sister to Dis and an eternity in the underworld. Or at least that was what they told us. But who really knew? Who had ever come back from Dis's domain? No one.

I sat on a rock in front of the Arimathean's tomb and stared into the yawning rectangle of the grave. Darkness pressed against the heavy sealing stone that still lay on its side, useless now that the tomb's occupant had vanished.

Was the stone an omen . . . or a metaphor? Would Pilate consider me just as useless because I had failed to find the missing messiah?

A thought reared its head as I sat in the silence—a thought that waved for my attention and then disappeared. What was it? What had I missed?

I stood and walked over to the tomb and ran my hands over the exterior surface of the limestone cavern. The mouth of the cave had been smoothed to ensure a proper fit with the circular cover stone, with iron hasps driven into the limestone to hold the ropes around the stone in place. Sections of rope still lay on the ground nearby, one piece dangling from a hasp at the entrance. I reached up and touched it, and felt my pulse quicken. I waited for a gray cloud to blow off the moon. When I could see clearly, I saw what my hand had felt: the iron hasp had been *twisted*.

No mere man could have twisted the iron with his bare hands or even using a tool. And why would he want to? I looked again at the cover stone, now washed in silver moonlight. If a group of disciples, even rabid ones, wanted to remove the body, they would break the seals, cut or untie the ropes, and roll the heavy stone four or five paces to the north or south. But this stone lay on its side at least ten paces from the tomb's entrance, almost as if it were a child's toy someone had knocked out of the way.

Something far stronger than a man's arm had done this. Something . . . beyond man. Perhaps something from beyond the grave.

The urge that had driven me to the tomb now had a sharper spur—I had to find the missing guard.

I had to know if death could be defeated.

———————

With a little extra money in his pocket, where would a soldier go? To a tavern, of course, preferably one near the Antonia, where he might run into a friend or two.

I slipped into the place quietly and stood in a corner while studying the men at the tables. The tavern was not nearly as busy as it might have been, because our cohort was preparing to leave for Hebron. But the Italian legionnaires, Pilate's men, were not going anywhere without the prefect, and several of them huddled around tables with cups of wine. In a far corner, partly hidden by sputtering shadows, I spied the man I sought.

Quietly, I slid onto the bench across from him. "Pricey wine for a legionary," I said, noting the full pitcher and the coins scattered on the table.

The man lifted his dazed eyes and belched, then slid an empty cup toward me. "Join me, Tribune?"

I pushed the cup back. "I'd rather have answers."

The guard shrugged and took another swallow from his drink.

"You've been hiding," I said. "How did you get the silver?"

The man shot a quick look at the tavern owner, who was eying us with concern. But I hadn't come to brawl.

"I got it," the guard said, slurring his words, "off a dead man."

"Of course. There are so many walking the streets these days."

The guard raised his hand in a defensive posture. "We . . . I am pardoned by the prefect. Pardoned. Nothing to be done to me. I said what they . . . what was proclaimed by the prefect."

He drained his cup in a sustained swallow, then refilled it.

"Say it again," I pressed.

"Why?"

"To see how your tale matches your mate's."

The guard wiped his mouth on his sleeve and frowned as if trying to remember a long-forgotten lesson. "We were . . . attacked in the night while sleeping . . . by the Nazarene's disciples."

"You forgot *rabid*."

"What?"

"The Nazarene's *rabid* disciples."

"Right. They stole his body—"

"The priests paid you to say this—why?"

". . . stole his body and bade us say he is—"

I slapped the cup from the man's hand. "How did the cover stone fall ten paces from the tomb? It took seven men—myself included—just to roll it over the opening. And the ropes were not cut; they were torn as if thread. The seals, melted like butter. The iron hasps, twisted by the force of—what?" I grabbed his arm. "Shall we go there so I can refresh your memory?"

"No!" Blood drained from the man's face, leaving him as pale as a corpse. "I'm not going back there. Ever."

"What are you hiding? Why does that place bother you so?"

The guard pressed the heels of his hands over his eyes as I reached across the table to grasp his tunic. "By the crust between Dis's toes, I'll tolerate no more lies! What happened to the Nazarene's body? How did they take him?"

Something in the guard snapped. He lowered his hands and stared, his throat moving in a convulsive swallow. "You forgot us! Forgot! We'd had no supper! That is why the wine made us sleepy!"

"What?"

Terror radiated from him like heat from a fire. "Yes, we slept! Up two days since the crucifixions and . . . and what could happen guarding a dead man? So we just closed our eyes in turns a bit until—"

"Until what?"

". . . until we were awakened . . . by this terrible . . . terrible . . . flash."

The man brought his hands up to his ears and stared past me at some appalling vision I could not see.

"The night was gone, and the air smelled burnt, the ropes . . . they just . . . exploded . . . and the stone flew like a leaf, and all at once the earth trembled and then . . ."

"What?"

The wide eyes swiveled and focused on me. "The sun rose in the tomb."

I leaned back, too astounded to speak.

"*It was the sun*—right in front of us! It was . . . everything! And a figure—a figure appeared. . . . I could not look at it because of the terrible light." Tears streamed from his wild eyes. "It wasn't a man . . . not . . . a man. It couldn't be. And there was a voice all around that I could not fathom . . . and one of them came out and *sat* on the stone, so we ran. We . . . we ran so far . . . so far . . . until we could think again . . . and so we went to tell the priests. Met 'em outside the Court of the Gentiles." The guard nodded, apparently remembering where he was. "Because that's what you bade us do."

I took a deep breath as my hunch solidified into certainty. "And Caiaphas paid for a different story."

The guard grabbed my arm. "Tribune, I have seen much in the emperor's service. Cannibals. Blue Celts in Gaul. Once I watched a sea monster bite a man in half. But never have I witnessed a moment so . . .." His hands fluttered as he struggled to find the words. He looked at me, his eyes pleading. "You're a tribune. Can you explain it to me?"

I stared into his desperate eyes and saw myself reflected in the wide black pupils. Could I explain it? No. But this man's mind could not accommodate the truth, so he needed an answer. I could not allow a soldier of Rome to lose his wits.

Nor could I sacrifice mine.

I picked up his cup and gently sloshed the wine within. "You were drunk. The wine you drank was tainted. What you saw was the dawn bursting upon the horizon."

"Truly?" The guard palmed tears from his cheeks. "Do you suppose? Perhaps it was tainted with opium? Frankincense? Perhaps his followers stole the Nazarene with magic, as the priests said. Perhaps our story *is* true."

I forced a shrug. "What else could it be?"

"I don't know." The man clasped his cup. "So I drink. Maybe I'll forget."

"Be well, soldier."

The guard's trembling hands reached for the pitcher, so I pushed it toward him and left him alone.

28

Clavius

Dawn came reluctantly, glowing dimly through an overcast sky. Coming from the tavern, I trudged through the gates of the fortress, crossed the courtyard, and climbed the stairs. I paused outside my chamber. Mars remained in his niche, but to my weary eyes he did not seem a fierce god of war, but rather a baked clay statue scarcely bigger than my palm. His smooth eyes saw nothing, his hands held no power, and his mouth had never touched the fruit and wine I left in his niche every morning.

I did not even attempt to pray.

In that moment the exercise of religion seemed an activity of supreme selfishness. We gave the gods something because we needed or wanted something else that lay outside our control. I had made sacrifices of fruit and wine for Adorabella's health and safety, and what happened? She died. Did I not give enough? Did I not suffer enough? Should I have cut my wrist and bled into a bowl to ensure her safety? Some people, desperate in their longing for something the fates had withheld, offered their own blood and even their lives.

What good were incantations? What did my sputtering repetitions and gifts, small or large, do for the gods who dwelled in heaven and under the earth? If I traveled to the place where they buried my sister's bones, if I left regular offerings of flowers or wine on her grave, would they bring her back to me? Would they raise her up to comfort her grieving husband? Could they give us her unborn child? If they would not and could not do what we asked, why did we bother to consult them?

My questions did not pertain to Romans alone. I had seen Pharisees, the most holy and religious of the Jews, tithing minuscule portions of salt and counting the number of steps they might take on a Saturday so as not to break their holy laws. Why did their god care if they took two steps too many? Would their houses collapse if they happened to eat a bite of pork? Would their god desert them or consign them to some horrible eternal fate? If not, why did they bind themselves with such inane restrictions? Why did they criticize and call for blood when one of their own deviated from their infernal rules?

Throughout my life, I had watched men and women—Romans, Greeks, Jews—live as though divine beings judged them from above and below. Yet this supernatural observation seemed to make little difference in the way people lived. Instead of being regarded as holy and worthy of reverence, deities served as friendly godlings they could occasionally bribe or even threaten to help them beat the odds. And though the Jews took great pride in being different from Romans, serving their one god instead of a pantheon, I could see no difference in the reality of their lives. They made offerings as we did. They spilled sacrificial blood as we did. They prayed and we prayed, and for what? To bend a god to our wills? If a supernatural being was so easily bent to the wills and whims of mortals, how could he be worthy of awe?

For the moment—perhaps for the rest of my life—I was done with gods. I would get myself through the coming day by relying on my comrades in the Tenth Legion for support. I had dedicated my mind, body, and soul to the army of Rome, and Rome, at least, had never failed me.

I had stepped inside my quarters, intending to snatch an hour or two of sleep, when Lucius came up behind me, practically quivering with news. His eyes were wide above his smile. "Tribune, we have them!"

Our paid informant had not stopped searching for Yeshua's disciples. As he threaded his way through a crowded Jerusalem street, I and half a dozen of my best men spread out and followed him, our uniforms covered by plain brown cloaks. We had followed the man past the Temple and were now in the western part of the city, a residential area where the houses overflowed with out-of-town guests who had traveled to Jerusalem for the Passover festival.

At last, the informant stopped, glanced over his shoulder and motioned to me. After peering around to be sure we had not wandered into a trap, I met him in an alley.

"The next street," he said, pointing westward. "The big house on the right—that's where I lost him."

"*Lost* him?"

"I believe that is where he went in."

"You're not certain?"

The informant swallowed hard. "It should be the home of John Mark, one of his followers. If it is, Yeshua ate the Passover in the upstairs room." When I frowned, more than a little suspicious of our sudden success, he hastened to add, "As we were walking, we passed two other disciples coming this way."

That was enough. I turned and gestured to my men. "You two—take the back. You—remain across the street. The rest of you come with me. I want at least two alive, so spare some. Go."

My men shed their disguising cloaks and pulled out their swords. I raced to the next street, found the large house on the right, and ran up the exterior stairs. The door was closed, so I kicked it open to find . . . nothing.

I stared at bare floorboards as cries of alarm rippled through the neighborhood. Our hasty approach had attracted attention. If the Nazarene's disciples were in the vicinity, they would take flight—

I ran down the steps and found the men I'd left in the street. "You four—down this side. Check every house, every upper room. You two—the other side. I'll block the end and work back this way."

Alone, I sprinted up the street as a group of young boys scrambled at my approach. After reaching the end of the block, I looked for signs of flight. People sliding out of windows, scurrying through the alleys between buildings, clambering across rooftops.

From the corner of my eye I saw a woman open a door and close it just as quickly. An instant later, my sleep-starved brain supplied her name: Mary of Magdala.

I did not hesitate, but ran up the outdoor staircase, never once taking my eyes off the door she had opened. When I reached the top, I drew my gladius and tried the handle . . . locked.

Irritated, I kicked at the door, breaking loose the hasp. I assumed a fighting stance and used my sword to push the door open . . .

A beam of sunlight from the open doorway spread over the faces in the crowded room. I saw Mary and two other women I had not seen before, several men I did not know, and one I did—Yeshua.

I stood outside on the landing as if rooted to the floor. The man whose dead eyes had stared blankly now looked at me with interest as his mouth curved in an enigmatic smile. The other men were grinning like children who knew a secret.

I shivered with a chill that was not from the air and slowly backed away from the doorway, retreating down the first few steps. What sort of magic was at work here? Had I finally lost my mind? Or had one of Yeshua's followers bewitched me?

"Tribune! Anything?"

Lucius's voice woke me from my stupor. I looked down and saw him on the street, frustration carved into his features.

"Nothing here," I called, my voice flat and lifeless. "Stand down. Return to the barracks."

"Sir?"

"Stand down."

"But they could be—"

"Go!" I spat the word with ferocity. "Look for me to return shortly." Knowing that my behavior seemed odd, I painted on a mask of indifference. "I'm . . . going to have a word with someone. I'll meet you later."

Lucius nodded. "Sir." Reluctantly, he saluted and walked

away to join his fellows. An instant later I heard him tell the others to return to the Antonia Fortress.

------◆------

When I went back to the doorway, still clutching my sword, the tableau inside had barely changed. A few wary glances took my measure, but most of the people in the room focused their attention on the sunlit figure who sat with them. A second, more careful look assured me that this man looked exactly like Yeshua. The face, the hair, the beard were the same. But it couldn't be. The would-be messiah we crucified would have wounds.

Some distant part of my mind registered the sound of footsteps on the stairs, but not until someone blew past me and knelt at Yeshua's feet did I fully realize that another man had joined us. His greeting consisted of an inexpressible cry of joy, and as others welcomed him—Thomas, his name—Yeshua stood and clasped him in a warm embrace. Then, with the tenderness of a father with a child, Yeshua lifted the sleeves of his robe, showing Thomas the scars at his wrists.

My sword fell to the floor with a clatter.

Without taking my eyes off the sobbing disciple in Yeshua's arms, I slid down the wall and squatted, content to be an observer in this unimaginable drama. The sounds of the room faded to a dull buzz as living images competed with vibrant memories.

Yeshua stroked Thomas's head, and my eyes superimposed iron spikes over those wounded wrists. I winced as Yeshua guided Thomas's trembling fingers into those same wounds. Then Yeshua opened his robe and placed his disciple's reluctant hand on the purple scar left by a Roman pilum.

As Thomas fell to his knees, crying, "My Lord and my God!" Yeshua turned, and I stared into the eyes that had haunted me but now brimmed with life and joy.

I slid closer to another disciple, who was leaning against the wall. "How?" I asked. "How can this be? How can a man travel to the underworld and return again?"

The man shrugged, but my question did not diminish his smile.

I had to be viewing an apparition. A spirit. I had heard of spectral beings, had even heard legionnaires speak of seeing them while on duty, yet no one had ever claimed to have seen one in daylight. And never had any man testified of an apparition that could be touched and handled.

While I pondered the mystery, Mary and the other women passed trays of roasted fish, matzot, and cheese. The disciples took and ate, and then, as I watched, Yeshua picked up a thin piece of bread and ate it, then drank from a cup. He ate. He drank . . . like a living man. This was no ghost.

I lowered my gaze for a split second, and when I lifted it again, Yeshua had vanished. Yet not for me only, because all the disciples were glancing around and wondering where their teacher had gone.

The man next to me smiled. "He does this," he said casually. Then he stood, and the other disciples gave him their full attention. No wonder, for the man was over six feet tall, big enough to be a member of the Roman infantry.

"Is He coming back?" another disciple asked.

The big man said, "How would I know?"

"What now, Peter?" A quiet fellow near the window turned trusting eyes on the man next to me. "What do we do?"

"Galilee." The unexpected sound of a woman's voice caused

every head to turn toward Mary of Magdala, who was standing with her arms around the other two women's waists. "When Salome, Miriam, and I saw the stranger in the garden, he told us to tell you that Yeshua would go before you to Galilee. There you will see Him, just as He said."

"But," another man protested, "we have already seen Him."

"In Galilee you will see Him again," Mary said, her eyes dancing. "But you should take care to avoid"—she freed her hand and pointed at me—"them."

Peter nodded. "We go home to Galilee, then."

The men began to pack their belongings, the women as well. While I sat, still overwhelmed, Peter picked up my fallen gladius and looked at me. "Yeshua allowed you to see Him for a reason."

"No doubt," Mary said, watching me.

Peter crouched and held out my sword in his open palms. "Tribune, could you betray this?" With a small smile he placed the gladius at my feet, then tied on his cloak and led the others out of the room.

I alone remained behind, staring into emptiness, as his question echoed in my mind.

29

Rachel

The morning after I told Clavius good-bye forever, I stood in my booth and wearily regarded my store of braided challah. After closing the door on Clavius, I had not baked matzah, but had fallen on my bed and watered my pillow with tears. I had never seen such a hard look in Clavius's eyes, nor heard such an edge in his voice. The man who stood on my threshold last night was a stranger to me, a man I would never invite into my bed or my heart.

Seeing that side of him, however, helped me understand why he had sought refuge in my home. Clavius was not yet the unfeeling brute he seemed in those moments, though perhaps in time he would be . . . unless he learned how to protect his heart from the brutality his work demanded. How was that accomplished? I had no idea.

I was sinking into a sea of despair when a man I did not know stopped and dipped his head beneath the awning. "I am Nathanael, and Matthew is a friend," he said, leaning over the display. "He thought you might like to go with us to Galilee."

I stared wordlessly at him, my heart pounding.

"We have other women along," he added. "But we are leaving today. If the idea suits you, come with me."

I froze, my limbs paralyzed by indecision. Who made such decisions on the spur of the moment? Who left their work, their goods, and trotted off in the hope of learning more about Yeshua?

Matthew had. Others had as well. Why couldn't I?

A bubble of irrational laughter rose in my chest as I tossed my remaining loaves into a cloth, then gathered up the corners and slung it over my shoulder. After all, travelers had to eat.

"Lead the way." I clutched at the slender sprig of hope Nathanael offered and followed him through the marketplace.

30

Clavius

WEDNESDAY, POST MERIDIEM

What to do? As voices from passersby and squealing children rose from the street and echoed in the upper room, I watched dust motes dance in a shaft of sunlight and considered the life I had always known as good and true.

By my father's order I had entered the army at age eighteen. I trained and worked and sweated and fought, all for the glory of the Roman Empire. I took the *sacramentum*, or military oath, after my time of probation and renewed my vow every year thereafter. Out of loyalty to Rome, I endured starvation and wounds, heat and cold, and hours in the saddle. I forswore marriage and love and a family of my own, all because I vowed never to desert, to enthusiastically perform whatever the emperor commanded, and never to shrink from death on behalf of the Roman state. I worshiped the Roman gods because every good Roman did. And when I became a tribune, I led my men to do the same things.

Last night, I walked away from Rachel . . . for Rome.

I did everything for Rome, because Rome was always right. The empire was civilization, culture, and morality. It elevated mankind and ordered the lower, less capable classes. It brought mechanical marvels and running water and modern medicine to primitive cities that had never known such advances. Rome was the light of the world, and I had gratefully sworn to use my body, my energies, and my talents to uphold her standard.

And what had Rome given me in return? A sense of belonging, a soldier's pay, and a job that dealt in death. The hope of a peaceful retirement, if I survived twenty-five years of near-constant violence. The promise of death without trial if I disobeyed or deserted the colors.

Could I turn my back on Rome to learn more about Yeshua? I had thought Cleopas a madman when he said that eternal life would now be possible for anyone who believed, but since then I had seen Yeshua alive again. What wouldn't I give to know more about eternal life!

Yet Pilate wanted me in Hebron, and I had never disobeyed an order. Lucius had been preparing for the trip, so my men were probably ready to move out. They might even be waiting on me. I should leave this place immediately.

And yet the question hovered like a miasma at the back of my mind—what if Rome was wrong? What if I had given my life to a cause that would vanish like smoke in the wind? What if a single, all-powerful god *did* exist, and Yeshua was the key to understanding him?

What if Cleopas had told the truth, and not only had Yeshua risen from death, but others as well? What if they were with their families now, enjoying an astonishing victory over death?

I pushed myself off the floor and looked around the room for parchment and pen. Lucius would soon come looking for me, and he'd begin his search here. I would not leave him guessing as to my intentions.

After finding what I sought in an old desk, I sat on the floor and scratched out a hasty letter:

> *To Prefect Pontius Pilate, greetings:*
>
> *Do not seek me. Do not follow or wonder about my intent. Persecute no one on my behalf.*
>
> *I have seen two things that cannot reconcile: a man dead without question, and that same man alive again. I pursue him—the Nazarene—to discover the truth. If death can be defeated, I would learn how, and why.*
>
> *My slave, Titus, is to wait one week for my return. If I have not returned in seven days, let this letter serve as his manumission document. I relinquish all claim to him and declare he is a free man and bound neither to me nor to the army of Rome.*
>
> *—Clavius Aquila Valerius Niger,*
> *Tribune Cohortis of the Tenth Legion*

Finally, to eliminate all doubt, I poured wax from a candle on the bottom of the parchment and impressed the wax with my signet ring.

Pilate would have to make other arrangements for Hebron.

I could not set my mind to another assignment until I had plumbed the depths of this mystery.

——————◆◆——————

I did not know how Yeshua's disciples were traveling north—the area surrounding the Sea of Tiberias, *Galilee* to the Jews, was a large region consisting of several small towns—but Nazareth was three days' journey from Jerusalem. Yeshua's disciples might not have known much about marching over long distances, but since most Jews made the journey from their homes to Jerusalem at least twice a year, I was certain they would know the best route to take. I planned to follow them, and not only for personal reasons. If they rendezvoused with Yeshua somewhere along the route, I wanted to see where he had been hiding.

I did not return to the Antonia, but instead began to shadow Peter after spotting him at a nearby marketplace, where he and the others were picking up supplies for the trip. To my surprise, a group of women were traveling with the disciples. When I paused at a merchant's booth to inquire about the women, the merchant's wife readily identified them as those who had always traveled with Yeshua. "They are his supporters," the merchant's wife told me. "Who do you think takes care of that lot? The women, that's who." The talkative woman, who apparently hadn't noticed that I wore a Roman uniform beneath my rough cloak, squinted toward the group of veiled females gathered around a pack mule. "One of them—Joanna—is married to Herod's minister of finance. I get tickled every time I think about Herod's money going to support Yeshua's disciples. Because it is, you know. The women pay most of the bills for that group."

I gave the woman a denarius for a waterskin, then bought a

bag of dried figs and settled into a corner to watch and wait. By the time the traveling party left Jerusalem, the group had grown to include eleven men, seven women, and three donkeys, one of them carrying blankets and food supplies, the other two loaded with water jugs. The men walked well ahead of the women, boldly striking out through Jerusalem's eastern gate.

I followed like a shadow.

I stopped when the group stopped, and more than once I saw men studying me, hands over their eyes to better see through the sun's hot glare. After a while I stopped trying to hide from them. After all, they had seen me in the upper room, so they had to know I was not an immediate threat. I studied them as carefully as they studied me, because at some point I hoped to spot Yeshua.

In the evening, as the sun lowered toward the horizon, the women camped near the men and hobbled the donkeys between the two camps' circles. Quickly and efficiently, the women passed baskets of dried fish and loaves of bread, which the men accepted with gratitude. Drinking gourds traveled around the circle, and more than once I found myself wishing I was part of the group. My waterskin had sprung a leak, so I had been relegated to sucking water from plant roots.

After eating and drinking, the travelers bedded down in sheltered spots among rocks or trees. The women kept to themselves, and a couple of men kept watch over both groups.

I slept beneath a rocky overhang and hoped they would not rise early and slip away from me in the darkness.

31

Rachel

So many names to learn in this new company. The women had made me feel welcome the instant Matthew introduced me. I was traveling with Mary of Magdala, who led the group due to her advanced age and wisdom, Miriam, Salome, Joanna, Susanna, and Mary, the mother of Yeshua. Joanna's husband was a wealthy man, yet she had been following Yeshua ever since he healed her of an illness. "I will return to Chuza when Yeshua leaves us," she told me, "but how can I remain at home when the bridegroom is among us?"

"And Israel is the bride?" I asked, trying to understand her analogy.

"Believers are the bride," she said with a smile. "Anyone who believes in Him."

"Yeshua often spoke of weddings," Mary of Magdala said, walking over to join us. She looked at Joanna. "Remember when He told the story of the wedding feast? The father had prepared a wedding feast for his son, but when he sent his slaves to summon the invited guests, they refused to come. So he sent more slaves, and they still refused to come. Then he said to his slaves, 'Go out to the street corners and invite to the banquet as many as you can find.' So the slaves went out and invited everyone, the bad along with the good, and the wedding hall was filled with guests."

"That's how it is," Joanna said, turning to me. "Everyone has been invited, but not everyone is willing to come."

Joanna had been one of the first to see Yeshua after his death, when she and Mary of Magdala were charged with telling the disciples of his resurrection. They had shared their story during yesterday's long walk, and I was so fascinated that my feet scarcely noticed the length of the journey. I had looked forward to hearing more stories of Yeshua as we traveled today, but now . . . I would have to think about Clavius.

I should have intuited the truth, but I didn't realize anyone was following us until the morning of the second day. I heard the other women whispering about "the Roman," never dreaming it could be anyone I knew until Mary of Magdala looked up from the fire and wondered aloud if the tribune was hungry.

My stomach swayed as the others craned their necks toward the south. I did the same and could see a leather-clad man standing beneath a distant overhang of rock, his face turned toward us. The shock of realization kept me silent for a long moment, and I turned away lest the other women read the guilt in my expression.

"He is persistent, I'll give him that," Matthew said, grinning.

"Adonai led him to us," Peter said. "Let him be."

Adonai led him? Somehow I doubted it.

What should I do? Should I ignore him? Should I tell the other women I knew him . . . and confess that he was my lover? These were holy women; they lived to serve Yeshua and the people who followed him. If they realized how unclean I was, how unworthy to be part of their group, they would ask me to go away. Bad enough that I was not married to the man who sometimes shared my bed, but even worse was the fact that he was Roman, pagan, and stained with Yeshua's own blood.

I worked quietly as we packed the donkeys, and when we set out, I walked beside the lead animal, pretending to be useful while I put space between myself and the other women. I would not force my presence on them. Once they learned about the sort of woman I was, they would be sorry they had ever shared their confidences with me.

Clavius, at least, was granting me one small mercy. So long as he kept a good distance between himself and the group, I might not have to say anything.

Of one thing I was certain: Adonai had not led him to us. Clavius had either followed me out of jealousy—an emotion that had no part in love—or he was following the disciples on some business for Rome.

Clavius had come for reasons of his own, and neither of them was good.

32

Clavius

THURSDAY, ANTE MERIDIEM

Squatting beneath the shelter of the rock, I had just spat out a barely digestible root when I heard the crunch of stones behind me. Taking care not to signal my intention, I gripped the hilt of my gladius, extended the blade, and spun around. My sword bit into flesh. When the man cried out and wheeled away, I crept out of my shelter. I straightened my back and stared at the bearded face of the disciple they called Peter.

"Water!" he yelled, glaring at the sword in my hand. "I brought you *water*!"

I grimaced when I saw blood on his leg.

"Did you not think to look before you struck?" he asked. He

retrieved a spilled gourd and pointedly dribbled the remaining liquid over his injured limb. Eyes narrowed, he hobbled about twenty paces away and, shaking his head, motioned for me to follow.

Once I had caught up to the big man, I insisted that he stop and let me tend the wound. The cut was not deep, and I managed to stanch the bleeding by placing a piece of my cloak over the wound and securing it with strips of leather. Peter looped his arm over my shoulder, and together we walked slowly back to his camp. "That will leave a scar, you know," Peter grumbled as we approached the circle of waking men.

The other disciples welcomed Peter back, exclaimed over his wound, and closed the circle around him, shutting me out. Later, as they sat and passed around a loaf of bread, Peter tore off a hunk and tossed it over his shoulder to me. I snatched up the bread and chewed thoughtfully as the big man stood and attempted to offer a prayer.

"Adonai, our Father in heaven, sanctified be your name," Peter began. "Your kingdom come, your will be done on earth as it is in heaven. Give us this day our daily bread . . ."

He hesitated. Another disciple then leaned over to him and whispered in his ear.

Peter nodded. "Yes! Forgive us our debts as we also have forgiven our debtors. And lead us not into temptation, but deliver us from the evil one."

At those words, ten heads turned toward me.

"Amen," Peter called, his voice ringing in the stillness.

The other disciples echoed his amen, turning to Peter with shining eyes, their concern about me apparently forgotten. They spoke about the day's journey, they wondered who they would meet on the road, and talked about how many people Adonai might lead their way so they could share the good news about Yeshua's resurrection.

I sat behind them and listened, quietly marveling at their joy and optimism. These men were neither wealthy nor highly educated. I did not think they owned much more than the clothing on their backs. They were not men of rank, even among their own people. A gossip at the market had whispered that one of Yeshua's men had even been a *tax collector*, a creature despised by Jews and barely tolerated by Romans. Yet the man had been so completely accepted that I could not tell which of them had once practiced that odious occupation.

Most of Yeshua's men, I had heard, were fishermen or common farmers before the Nazarene called them to follow him. But they had seen something in him, so they left everything and followed, wandering through difficult conditions like this because that was where Yeshua led them.

I could only hope he was continuing to lead them now.

Later that morning, after we set out, I fell into step beside Peter, still the only disciple willing to risk engaging me in a conversation. He had picked up a walking stick to compensate for his injured leg, and he seemed more than willing to let me bombard him with questions.

"Are you certain he wasn't a magician?" I asked. "I have seen some acts in Rome—"

"I'm most certain He was not," Peter answered.

"Did he have a twin?"

Peter chuckled. "You will have to meet His brother, James. They look nothing alike, I assure you."

"And you have seen no further sign of him?"

"Not yet."

"But . . . is he truly the son of your Adonai?"

"So He says."

"And you believe it?"

Peter smiled.

"*Do you believe it?*"

"I believed it even before the crucifixion," Peter said, "although until now I did not fully understand what it meant."

"Is the brother a god as well?"

Peter sighed. "I told you—there is but one God, and only Yeshua is of Him. Yet He is also fully a man, as we are, yet without sin."

"A man who rises from death. And eats and laughs . . . and disappears? How can that be?"

"I don't know." Peter gripped his staff. "But He has a body, the same vessel Adonai gives to all men. It is how He reached out to us." The big man shrugged to lower the pack from his back, then pulled out an empty gourd. "See this? Suppose it held a bug—a bug I loved dearly. Now suppose I needed this gourd to hold boiling water, so my little bug needs to leave. I could scream at the bug all day long, but still it's not going to move. How am I going to tell the bug he needs to move to safety?"

Confused, I looked over at the big man and asked, "Why would you love a bug?"

"That is not the point. Suppose I *created* the bug, so I loved it. Now—how could I save it from destruction?"

I shrugged. "You could turn the gourd upside down and spill the bug onto the ground."

"Not necessarily. He might cling to the side of the gourd."

"All right, you could fill the gourd with cool water. When the bug floats to the top, pour your bug out along with the water."

"You must have been an exasperating child." Peter stopped walking and pointed to the inside of the gourd. "I cannot speak bug language. The bug has always ignored me. So if I want to communicate with him, if I want to tell him I want to save him, I will have to become a bug myself. I will have to meet him where he is. *Now* do you see?"

I rubbed my hand over my stubbled chin. "And some say Roman religion is illogical."

Peter's face flushed as he blew out a breath. "I am not talking about religion. I am talking about communication! Adonai wanted to reach us, so He sent His Son, fully God and fully man, to live with us! To show us how to live! *That* is what I'm trying to get through your thick Roman head!"

I narrowed my gaze and stared. No man—Roman, Greek, or Jew—had ever spoken to me with such disrespect. If a legionnaire had said those words to me, I'd have had him flogged. If a Jew on the street had said such things, I'd have had him arrested and crucified. No one disrespected a tribune of Rome, because such an act was equivalent to disrespecting Rome itself.

But I was not traveling with these people as a tribunus cohortis. I was here as a student.

I drew a deep breath and resumed walking.

Peter glanced at me, shifted the walking stick to his other hand. "What I am trying to say," he said, his voice falling to a calmer note, "is that perhaps God had to become a man so that we could know He understands our trials." He smiled. "But trust me—I do not have every answer. We are as astounded as you."

"Where did you meet him?"

A smile split Peter's beard. "My brother, Andrew, was following John the Baptizer. One day Yeshua walked by. The Baptizer said, 'Look! There is the Lamb of God,' so Andrew and another disciple followed Yeshua. They asked Him where He was staying, and He replied, 'Come and see.' Andrew stayed with Him the rest of the day. Later, he came to my house and told me he had found the Messiah. I thought he had lost his senses, but he made me go meet Yeshua for myself. And when I looked into His eyes, I knew."

"What . . . what did you see?" I asked, genuinely wanting an answer.

"Love," Peter said. "And wisdom. When I approached Him, Yeshua looked at me and said, 'You are Simon, son of John, but you will be called Peter.'"

"Rock," I said, supplying the translation.

Peter shrugged. "Andrew insists the name means *stubborn*. But I have been called Peter ever since that day."

"So you left everything? Your home, family—"

"And wife," Peter said, giving me a sharp look. "She was not happy that I wanted to follow Yeshua, but she had her mother to keep her company. And we did not travel far. Yeshua preached every Shabbat in Capernaum, and afterward we would go to my house to eat. One Shabbat my mother-in-law was too sick to get out of bed, but Yeshua went into her room, rebuked her fever, and it left her instantly. She was able to get up and serve the Shabbat meal."

We walked in silence for about twenty more paces when I lifted my head and asked, "Can he fly?"

Peter snorted and quickened his step, wishing, no doubt, that he could leave me behind.

At midday we stopped at an outpost just west of Ephraim. The women went to the well and began filling the waterpots while we men settled in the meager shade cast by one of the buildings.

I knew Peter's patience had been sorely stretched by my theories and speculations, but I still had questions. Dozens of them.

"Why doesn't he simply show himself to all? Can he be slain once more? I know Pilate. If he believes that the Nazarene has risen from the dead, he will try to kill him again."

Peter wiped his brow and sighed. "I don't know. I don't know. I don't know . . . I wish I did, but I do not." He slapped a layer of fine sand from his cloak and dropped into a spot of cool shade.

I sat beside him, not caring that the right side of my body was still exposed to the sun. "The answers await us in Galilee?"

Peter shrugged. "We are followers. We are learners. We follow to learn the answers." Peter bent his head to check the scabbed wound on his leg, then cast me a sidelong glance. "I think He is preparing us."

"For what?"

"I don't—"

"You don't know," I finished for him.

"For a Roman, you learn quickly."

"Friends!" The sound of John's voice interrupted our conversation. A pair of travelers had stopped at the outpost and were attempting to load their donkey with an overlarge pile of wood. John walked toward them, a welcoming smile on his face.

"Have you heard the news?" John went on. "In Jerusalem, Yeshua of Nazareth has risen from death. From *death*! All sins are forgiven those who call upon His name. Eternal life can be yours. This man *is* the Messiah—rejoice!"

The men with the donkey looked at each other, then the eldest spat at John's feet. "Off with you! We have had our fill of false messiahs."

John kept smiling. "No, friends, hear me well. Did not the psalmist write of this? 'My body rests in safety; for you will not abandon me to Sheol, you will not let your faithful one see the Abyss.' The world has changed because He has risen. Do not turn your backs on God's gift. Don't turn away without hearing the glorious good news—"

Without warning, the younger man hunkered down and charged John, knocking the lanky disciple to the ground.

"I warned you," the first man said, flashing a humorless grin.

John lifted his head, still smiling. "You didn't mean it."

"I think I did." The first man kicked a spray of sand into John's eyes, then proceeded to pummel the disciple's ribs and face as the other traveler laughed.

Watching from the shade, I instinctively grabbed my gladius and stood, head down, ready to move into the fray. But before I could take a step, Peter gripped the edge of my robe. "Hold."

The second traveler sent a final spray of sand over John's face, turned and walked toward his donkey. "We've had enough of you messiah freaks."

The other disciples rushed forward, half of them to help John, the other half to stop the pair of travelers. Only Peter remained behind, probably to restrain me.

"No, friend—please," Thomas said, his hands lifted in petition. "He meant no harm. Please. We will speak another day, surely."

The first man snorted. "Look at you, thin and ragged—this is the life you want for us?"

He spat at Thomas, then turned and expended his anger on the poor donkey, whipping its flanks to drive it forward.

I shifted my attention to John, who was being tended by the others. James, who knelt at John's head, held a bloody tooth before his brother's wide eyes. "See the impression you made on his fist? He will not soon forget you."

John lifted his head, his mouth curling in a bloody grin that set them all to laughing.

I marveled at their spirit. I had seen courage before—soldiers in battle often rode a wave of fearlessness even though their bodies had been brutally battered—but these men were not professional soldiers.

Then again . . . perhaps they were becoming warriors of a different sort.

Peter released my robe. "We're learning," he said simply.

33

Clavius

I first noticed the rising dust as we prepared to leave the out-post outside Ephraim. Someone was tracking us—a large force, judging by the size of the dust cloud.

I said nothing to Peter or any of the others, but instead positioned myself between the men and the donkeys. While I didn't know who was following, I had a good idea as to who it might be. Lucius would have found my note before sunset on Wednesday. He would have wasted no time taking it to Pilate, and after several minutes of storming, cursing, and raving, the prefect would have sent the Italian corps to Hebron and ordered

Lucius to follow me with a detachment of cavalry. Who better to track down a wayward tribune than equestrians?

Pilate had two pressing reasons to find me. First, he still needed to settle the matter of the missing Nazarene in order to assure Tiberius Caesar that Judea would not soon be rocked by a religiously motivated revolt. Though the populace might be appeased by a bloated body on display, those people who had seen the resurrected Yeshua would know that Pilate and the religious leaders had lied. To soothe Caesar with confidence, Pilate would want to know for certain whether or not Yeshua still lived—and then he would try to kill the Nazarene again.

Second, while I did not consider myself a deserter, Pilate undoubtedly did. I had ignored his order to prepare for Hebron and left the city without permission. Lucius might even testify that I had found the man they were seeking and refused to turn him in. By now Pilate had tasked young Lucius with apprehending me, questioning me, and bringing me back to Jerusalem to stand trial . . . or face execution.

Lucius was probably already imagining his success and swift promotion.

We set out, and I remained in my central position until we came to a wide open area flanked by the rocky outcroppings of Mount Ebal. Realizing that Peter and the men were about to traverse the open space, I ran ahead and told them it would be safer to travel over the mountain.

Peter scowled, his brows knitting together. "Having cut me, are you now trying to *break* my injured leg? The rocks are treacherous, and the passage will slow us down."

I pointed to the dust cloud on the horizon. "Look behind us . . . past the women."

Peter and John lifted their hands to shade their eyes, then stiffened. "How long have they been following?" Peter asked.

John's jaw wobbled. "How many are they?"

"They've been tracking us for a while, and there are more than enough to wipe us out," I answered. "So please—travel over the mountain. Move beneath overhangs, choose the rocky paths, look for narrow trails. We may travel more slowly, but at least we will be alive."

Peter and John looked at each other.

"We could proceed across the open space in faith," Peter said.

John nodded. "But Adonai did send the Roman to us. Perhaps we should be prudent and listen to him."

"Agreed," Peter said.

I stood aside as the men diverted their course, leading the donkeys and the women through the mountain paths. I remained behind, my eyes intent on the horizon, until they had all safely entered the mountains. Then I followed.

———————•◦•◦•———————

The equites came on horseback, thundering over the sand until they reached the spot where I had sent Yeshua's people through the mountain pass. From my perch atop a rock formation, I watched Lucius slide off his sturdy draft horse and study the ground, then point toward the rocks.

I knew he would not be alone. Marcellus Drusus, a centurion from the Antonia, dismounted as well, his hands rising to his hips as he scanned the landscape. The riders had to be under his command, for Pilate would never dispatch cavalry under the authority of a mere beneficiarii.

Lucius lifted his gaze, as I'd known he would, and I stepped into his line of sight.

I was close enough to see his eyes widen beneath his helmet.

"Beneficiarii. Marcellus," I yelled, my voice echoing between the cliffs. "Leave and return to barracks at once. You have no business here."

Marcellus saluted me, his respect intact, but Lucius appeared to be engrossed with his surroundings. The rock I stood on was steep but not smooth, pocked with dozens of crevices and fissures, a ragged fretwork of limestone. He could always attempt to climb up, of course, yet the path was broken by ridges, cracks, and hollows, every step of the surface covered with scree.

I studied Lucius as sweat trickled down my spine. The air was heavy and still, the silence broken only by the squeak of saddles and the occasional whinny of a horse.

Lucius turned to confer with Marcellus. He then dropped his reins and motioned for half a dozen men to follow him. He was probably quoting Ovid and telling himself that fortune and love favored the brave.

My plan was simple. Since Lucius was unable to lead mounted riders through these treacherous rocks, I would draw him into the twisting labyrinth, doubling back, if necessary, to keep him from reaching the Galileans. While I distracted my beneficiarii, Peter could lead his party over the mountain and find a safe place to camp for the night.

Lucius wasn't interested in the Galileans. He wanted me because Pilate wanted me. And because ambition flowed through his veins, just as it once flowed through mine.

I hurried over the rock-strewn path as quickly as I dared, climbing boulders when necessary and slithering along narrow ledges. I waited until I heard Lucius approaching, then kicked a couple of pebbles to let him know which way I had gone.

Already the sunset had spread itself, luminous and brilliant, over the narrow strip of sky overhead. I tried not to think about the passage of time, for the longer I distracted Lucius, the safer Peter and his group would be.

I had descended a steep slope and was jogging along a curving path when I heard movement behind me. I darted into a fissure that opened to another passage, but then halted when I saw Peter. He had taken the rear position to protect the women. He looked at me, alarm in his eyes. I gestured for him to hurry, to keep moving forward.

Once Peter was out of sight, I readied myself to face Lucius.

While I waited I braced my hands on my knees and inhaled great gulps of air. The jagged mountains around me rose like armed sentries, confining us within a natural arena. When I heard the crunch of approaching footsteps, I drew my gladius and straightened.

Lucius appeared at the end of the narrow canyon, his face bright with exertion. "Tribune," he called, panting. "Will you come peacefully?"

"Beneficiarii," I answered, "I will not come at all."

"The prefect summons you." Lucius pulled his sword, tapped the flat of the blade against his palm. "He ordered me to bring you back—dead or alive."

My mouth curled in a one-sided smile. "If you bring me back dead, none of us will find the answers we seek."

"I doubt Pilate cares about the Nazarene anymore," Lucius said. "He is more concerned about the tribune who disappeared and left Antonia Fortress without a commander."

"I hadn't noticed that the Antonia was lacking in leadership," I called, a wry note in my voice. "Here you are, doing my job."

"I am only obeying the prefect's command. He is most concerned about your apparent desertion."

"That's only because Tiberius is coming—in what, five weeks?" Though I had no shield, I shifted my weight and assumed a battle stance. "I am not going with you, Lucius. So what say you?"

I flinched as an unexpected sound caught my ear. Holding my sword in a defensive position, I glanced over my shoulder and saw Peter and the other disciples. They had not hurried away; they had only moved the women forward to a safer location. They stood behind me, all of them, even John, whose face was still marked with blood and bruises from his encounter at the outpost.

I hesitated, blinking with bafflement. *Why* were they behind me? Then Peter held up one hand like a wall and butted the fingertips of his other hand into it.

No way out . . . except through Lucius.

"No quarter, Tribune." Lucius assumed a battle stance as well. "No mercy. That is what you taught me."

I tightened my grip on my sword and felt my hand warm to it. Lucius was but a boy—a bright-eyed, overeager, ambitious Roman son, trying to please his father and his empire. He was the young man I had been, before my living led me to far-flung reaches of the empire, and death. Lucius had lapped up everything I taught him, and even now he was mirroring me, determined to live up to my example and one day take my position.

He could have it now.

"If I taught you never to give quarter," I said, opening my hand and dropping my sword, "it was a bad lesson. I now surrender your teacher."

Lucius tipped his head back and searched the faces behind me. "The Nazarene?"

"Vanished." I stepped toward Lucius while motioning for Peter and the others to follow.

Lucius blocked our path with his gladius. I strode forward until the tip of his blade touched my chest.

"I don't wish to kill you," he said, mingled fear and bravado emanating from him like a scent.

"Then don't." I gestured to the men and women behind me. "There are no enemies here."

Lucius glanced behind him, where we could hear soldiers making their way through the rocks. All he had to do was shout and we would all be trapped like cattle in a chute.

I caught Lucius's gaze and held it. "Before you call out, know this—you hold the world in your hands, Beneficiarii. The future resides in these people."

Lucius looked down the line of fugitives, then blinked his hesitation aside. He drew back his blade to strike, but I had been anticipating his move. I caught his elbow, lifted it at an impossible angle, and forced him to drop the gladius. Before he could react I scooped up his sword and placed the point at the base of his ear.

"No one," I whispered, leaning in close enough to smell his breath, "no one dies today. No one."

His eyes showed white all around, like a panicked horse. But as I held him immobile, his eyes teared with relief. I could have killed him, and he knew it.

When all the Galileans had passed through the narrow opening to the chasm, I released Lucius and returned his weapon. "Walk back to the others in your unit," I told him. "Say nothing. I will wait here until you and Marcellus have led all the men off the mountain."

Lucius did not move, so I clasped his shoulder, squeezed it

gently and urged him forward. After he had disappeared into the canyon, Peter came up and wrapped me in a hug. "For a minute there I thought you were going to copy my move and take off his ear," he said. "I am glad you thought the better of it."

John walked toward me with obvious relief on his face. "You *were* sent to us." He smiled his gap-toothed smile. "Never doubt it."

34

Clavius

On the final night of our journey, all of us men sat around a campfire. The women, who had veiled themselves against blowing wind and sun in the daylight hours, folded their veils and served cheese, dried beef, and flatbread. In their way, they seemed as fearless and happy as the men.

"Offer the other cheek?" I asked Peter. "That is definitely not the Roman way."

Peter chuckled. "We try to . . . well, I try. But I failed when they came for Him. As you have heard, I struck a man's ear clean off, but Yeshua put it back on. I have a temper, you see."

I couldn't stop a smile. "Perhaps there's a bit of soldier in you."

"I'm afraid I cannot agree. That same night I denied I even knew Him—three times. I was hanging about the high priest's dwelling, trying to stay abreast of things, but my courage failed me. I knew what happened to zealots."

I nodded, remembering the battle against Barabbas and his group of fanatics. I shifted to meet the big man's gaze. "You know I was at Golgotha."

Peter sighed and tipped his head toward Mary of Magdala, who was talking with the others as she served our slender supper. "She told us. Ironic, isn't it? Yeshua has an unbelievable effect on men . . . even Romans."

Laughing, I shook my head. "Let me see if I have this right: your god sent his son for us to kill, to save you from a Hades he created to punish you for things he told you not to do, knowing you would still do them? That's not irony. It's illogical."

"If it amuses you so, why are you still with us?"

I turned my face to the fire. "To understand what I saw . . . and to see it again."

Peter stretched his wounded leg toward the flames. "Three years spent at His side and even I have questions. Yeshua simply . . . compels you. We thought He came to deliver us—from you, from Rome. Now we realize it's not about that. It's about something else."

"What then?"

"He came to set men free. Not from their circumstances, but from their fallen state."

A log on the fire shifted, sending a spray of red sparks into the night air.

"Did he speak of the tomb?" I asked. "Of where he was those two days after?"

Peter shrugged. "Where was He before He was born as a

baby? With His Father, surely. He said that He and His Father are one." The big man stretched out his other leg and pulled his cloak around a shoulder, preparing to rest for the night. "Sleep, Tribune. Tomorrow we reach Galilee."

But my thoughts were too restless for sleep. I tossed another bough onto the fire and sent a flurry of sparks upward, and their path drew my eyes toward the place where the women were settling down to sleep. Mary of Magdala was clearly their leader, though everyone—the men included—treated Yeshua's mother with respectful gentleness. I did not know the other women and was not particularly interested in meeting them.

I lay down and rolled onto my side, but a familiar laugh propelled me upright again. I looked toward the opposite circle, where a shapely woman was wrapping her veil around her shoulders. She turned, setting her profile against the firelight, and my heart stuttered.

Rachel.

As quietly as possible I walked to the edge of the women's circle and called Rachel's name. I only had to speak once. She turned immediately, and something like a smile flickered over her face, like gold in the firelight.

She whispered something to Mary of Magdala before stepping out to meet me. "I wondered when—or if—you would come to see me," she said. "You have been quite *intent* in your conversations. When I first saw you, I thought you had followed me. Soon I realized that you didn't even know I was here."

"Why *are* you here?" I asked, still reeling from my discovery. "How do you know these people?"

She looked back to the women and waved at Mary, who was

watching us with a concerned expression. "I met a woman who knew Matthew, the one who used to collect taxes for Rome." She discreetly pointed to the disciple who slept near Philip and Andrew. "You saw him leaving my house the other night."

Shock caused my words to wedge in my throat. "That was—"

"Matthew came to tell me about Yeshua. I did not know what to think, so I bade him good-night and let him go. But before he left Jerusalem, he sent a message by Nathanael and said I was welcome to join the group if I wanted to learn more. I did, so here I am."

We stared at each other in a silence so profound, all that could be heard were the snores of sleeping men and the faint whispers of the women. Finally, I said, "I am sorry I misjudged you, Rachel."

The firm line of her lips relaxed. "You have already been forgiven. Because I was noticeably upset when I spotted you, Mary of Magdala—"

"Counseled you to ignore me?"

"Counseled me to forgive you. She has counseled me about a great many things."

"I can imagine." I folded my arms to stop myself from pulling her into an embrace. "Are you now one of them? A follower?"

"Are you asking me if I believe Yeshua is alive? I do. All these people have seen Him."

"So have I, but that doesn't mean I want to practice what he teaches. I'm asking if you are going to give up your life in Jerusalem. If you, like these people, want to dedicate yourself to telling the world about him."

She turned and stared at the fire for a long moment. "I think . . . I want to dedicate my life to love, which is what Yeshua taught. Will you do the same?"

I grappled with the idea for an instant, then quickly dismissed it. "I'm a Roman soldier. My life is not my own."

"I see." An inexplicable look of withdrawal passed over her expression as she turned toward the women's circle. "Good night, Tribune."

35

Rachel

Mary, Yeshua's mother, had been kind enough to share one of the blankets with me, so I lay down beside her and tried not to disturb her sleep. Mary of Magdala had also settled down, so the only sounds were the soft whisper of the wind and the crackle of our fire. I rolled onto my side, pillowed my head on my hands, and tried to remain motionless as a sob rose from my chest and threatened to wreak havoc in my heart.

Oh, Clavius! Why do you cling so stubbornly to all things Roman?

I had learned so much since joining this group of women. Though I had never seen Yeshua or heard Him speak, Joanna, Susanna, Salome, and the two Marys had supported and traveled with Him for nearly three years. They had seen Him call children to His side; they had heard Him call out the hypo-critical Pharisees who trumpeted their good works and went about with sad faces while they fasted. They had listened while Yeshua warned the disciples about dangerous days ahead, and they had hidden their chagrin when the disciples argued over which of them would be assigned seats of honor in the kingdom of God.

"So many times they completely missed the point," Mary of Magdala told me as we walked through the rocks earlier today. "But if they would not listen to Yeshua, which of them would listen to a woman?"

The quality that had most impressed the women—and me—was Yeshua's example of love. He loved the outcasts, the sinners, harlots, and tax collectors. He stopped to touch lepers, gave clothing to half-naked madmen, and straightened the limbs of crippled children. He even loved the members of the religious council that ultimately condemned Him, welcoming Nicodemus and Joseph of Arimathea when they sought Him out.

"And He loved us, the simple people," Mary said, her voice dropping to a whisper. "Even before His arrest, He warned us that the world would hate us because the world hated Him first. 'But you are my friends,' He told us, 'if you do what I command you. You did not choose me, I chose you; and I have commissioned you to go and bear fruit that will last. Just as my Father has loved me, I too have loved you; so stay in my love. No one has greater love than a person who lays down his life for his friends.'"

Those words had stayed with me, replaying in my head doz-ens of times as the hours passed. *"No one has greater love . . ."* I heard it when I saw Joanna and Mary serving the disciples who had so often misunderstood their Master. I heard it when

I saw Peter stop to comfort John who, despite his bravado, was still aching from the blows he had suffered at the outpost. I saw it when Clavius dropped his sword in front of the young Roman who trapped us in the narrow canyon. Clavius, whose heart remained tender beneath that molded breastplate, would have given his life to make certain the disciples and their people went free.

And something told me he would have done the same thing for me.

I loved him. I could deny it no longer. Though I did not see any righteous way we could be together, neither could I find the strength to deny the way my heart turned over every time his image rose in my mind.

Beneath his armor, beneath his studied indifference to the people of Judea and his blind obedience to Rome, powerful passions surged and flowed. I had seen evidence of it in our time together, and I had seen proof of his strong convictions even on this trip when he had intentionally kept himself at a distance until Peter drew him in.

Even though he had been tentatively welcomed, Clavius still kept himself apart from the others. He sat outside the men's circle, though they left a space wide enough for three men his size. And he walked apart from the others, though he tended to trail after Peter in order to ask him questions.

What would it take for Clavius to breach the barriers he had erected to keep himself aloof from the world? From Yeshua? And from me?

I didn't know, and worse yet, I could not imagine an answer.

I bit my lip and lifted my gaze to the place where a cloud had reached out to wrestle with the moon for domination of the night. Because I trusted these people, believing in Yeshua had been easy for me. They told me about Him and my heart leapt within me, memories of the Scriptures melding with their words in an overwhelming conviction that I had finally discovered the truth about Adonai and His love for His people.

But Clavius did not find it easy to trust, and he had no well of memories from which to draw understanding. Even so, he had *something*, because he was still here. Still listening. Still searching for Yeshua.

Even though his true god was Rome.

"Adonai," I prayed, barely moving my lips lest I wake Mary, "I don't know what to do with this love you have given me for Clavius. Wrap him in your love and make his way clear. Out here in the barren land, remove Rome from his thoughts and show him your glory. And if it be your will, show me how to love him . . . in a way that honors you."

36

Clavius

I was one of the first to spot the Sea of Galilee, which Herod Antipas had renamed the Sea of Tiberias in a brazen attempt to win favor from Rome. I had climbed to the summit of a rocky hill while the others scouted for edible plants, and there it was, glittering like a blue diamond amidst the vast landscape. I let out a loud cry, and soon the others joined me on the hilltop.

"Fish!" Peter shouted, hurrying down the other side of the slope. "We will find a boat and have fish for supper!"

All of us scampered recklessly down the hill and, just minutes later, spread out along the shore, splashing into the water and washing three days' worth of grit and dust from our limbs and faces. We were, Peter told me, about a day's journey from Bethsaida, home to him and his brother, Andrew, as well as to Philip and Nathanael.

"Why do you think Yeshua told you to come here?" I asked him.

Peter grinned. "It was here that He called us to follow Him." Peter stood on the shore, shaded his eyes and turned slowly around, searching the hills, the plains, the lake. "He said we'd see Him here. But sometimes He is hard to recognize."

"How so?"

"One day—big day—we had fed over five thousand men as well as their families in a large open area. Yeshua was tired and wanted to pray alone, so the rest of us climbed into a boat to travel to the other side of the lake. The night came on, and we were several miles from shore when the wind kicked up."

"It was bad," Andrew chimed in. "Even worse than Peter says."

Peter ignored his brother's comment. "In the middle of the night, as we were all trying to stay afloat and keep from capsizing, we looked out and saw a man walking on the water."

"On the water," Andrew echoed. "With his robe fluttering all around him like a ghost."

"It wasn't a ghost," Peter said emphatically. "It was Yeshua. He called to us to stop being afraid, so I shouted back, 'If it's really you, tell me to come to you on the water.'"

I gaped at him. "You didn't."

"I did, Tribune," the big man said. "For about twenty paces. I was out there, walking over the waters as easy as you please. But then I started to think about what I was doing. The minute I did that, I began to sink. I cried out to Yeshua. He caught me by the hand and turned me back toward the boat."

"Finish the story," Andrew said, giving his brother a stern look. "You know, what He said to you."

Peter sighed. "He said, 'Such little trust! Why did you doubt?'" He thrust his hands on his hips and peered out over the water. "Why indeed? We could do anything with Him, if He willed it."

Andrew pointed to a clump of shade trees. "Enough with the stories. We can camp over there, but for now, everyone wants to eat."

"Then let's fish," Peter said. He started striding toward an overturned boat on the shore, yet no one else moved. Peter spun around, consternation on his face. "Is no one coming with me?"

The hungry disciples had become immobile, and Peter knew why. "Have you forgotten?" he asked, spreading his arms wide. "He'll find us."

One by one, smiles brightened their faces, and the other disciples joined Peter in marching across the beach. I glanced back at the women, who seemed content to make a camp beneath the trees. I ran forward to take a seat while there was still room in the boat.

The boat was a simple fishing vessel designed to hold a fifteen-man crew. We slid quietly into the lake, which had become a sea of molten glass as the sun approached the western horizon. A pile of fishing nets had been stored at the bow, and before long the seasoned fishermen—Peter, Andrew, James, and John—expertly lowered the nets into the deep.

Twice they raised the nets, and twice the nets came up empty.

"We're making too much noise," Nathanael said. "We're scaring the fish away."

We all quieted then and found ways to make ourselves comfortable while we waited. With our heads resting on our arms or on piles of spare netting, we listened to the light slapping of water against the hull as we rocked on gentle waves.

"So still," Bartholomew said quietly. "And where is Yeshua?"

Peter, who had been searching the distant shoreline, moved to the main mast, raised his arms toward heaven. "We're heeeeeerrrree!" he cried. The sound rang out over the waters, but no one answered back. Yeshua did not appear.

Peter sighed. "Let down the nets."

The nets were lowered once more, and again we waited, our stomachs growling. I extended my hand and let it trail in the water, sending a miniature wave riding up my wrist. The boat trembled beneath us, her boards brushed by something large.

Peter gave the order to haul up the nets. They did, but the nets were empty.

"Cast again?" Thaddeus asked.

Peter paused, scanning the lake in all directions. "Yes," he said, "and then we'll sleep until the morning sun wakes us."

The men shook their heads, some of them laughing, and let out the nets once again.

Before the sun disappeared over the horizon, we all slept on a tide of exhaustion.

37

Clavius

Saturday, ante meridiem

I sat up to the creaking of lumber and flapping of sailcloth. I frowned, trying to remember why I was on board a boat. Then I saw Peter standing near the mast and remembered where I was. We had drifted during the night. Instead of remaining near the center of the immense lake, we had moved closer to the shore, not far from where the women had established our camp.

The hour was still early, for the western mountains had only begun to glow pink as the sun appeared in the east.

When I heard Peter stumble over the nets, I looked up to see what had distracted him. A man in a cloak was walking along the shoreline, keeping pace with our drifting boat. "Friends, you wouldn't happen to have any fish, would you?" he called, his voice muted by the morning fog off the lake.

Peter lifted his arms and shook his head in a gesture of defeat.

"Throw the net off the right side of the boat," the stranger called, "and you will find fish."

"How would he know that?" I asked.

Moving quickly, with an air of repressed excitement, Peter roused the other disciples and told them to cast the net. No one questioned him, and within seconds the net hung off the starboard side of the boat.

Almost immediately I felt the boards beneath my feet vibrate. Timbers creaked loudly, men shouted and grasped at each other to remain upright, and the nets groaned in protest.

All the while, Peter stared at the man on the beach.

"Quick!" John said. "Pull it up before it breaks! Heave!"

Andrew gasped. "But we just—"

"Heave now!"

From my position on the opposite side of the boat, I held on to Matthew and Thaddaeus while the others on my side clung to whomever they could.

"It's caught on something!" Philip yelled.

Peter laughed. "Fish."

Working together we brought in a load so heavy that I feared the boat might capsize. Dozens of large silvery fish flipped and flapped on every surface of the boat. The men laughed and embraced each other, grinning as Peter told us to row back to shore at once. "If you can find an oar," he said, chuckling.

"How did you know?" John asked him.

Peter didn't answer, but leapt out of the boat and began to swim.

I found an oar and helped row, even as I kept an eye on Peter.

Once in the shallows, the big man found his feet and started running toward solid ground and the man on the beach. Peter threw his dripping arms around the stranger. The stranger hugged him back.

When we had reached the shore with the boat, the other disciples gave no more thought to their catch. They spilled out of the wooden vessel and rushed toward the man, embracing him and laughing with sheer joy.

I should have recognized Yeshua's handiwork.

I climbed out of the boat more slowly than the others and approached Yeshua with greater restraint. Still, I couldn't stop smiling, especially when Yeshua stepped forward to greet me. "Clavius," he said, with eyes that spoke far more eloquently than words. "I am glad you have come."

"Now," he said, opening his arms to all, "you are hungry. Bring some of the fish you've just caught." Three of the disciples returned to the boat and hauled the heavy net of fish onto shore. After the net was laid open, Bartholomew counted 153 fish, most of them big. "But not a string has broken," he marveled.

Yeshua, who had already prepared bread and a charcoal fire, called to us, "Come. Have breakfast." He took some of the fish and set them on a grate over the fire, then listened to the disciples' accounts of our journey while the fish roasted. He smiled at the story of John's attempt to talk to the men loading their donkey and gave John a sympathetic smile when he pointed to the gap between his front teeth. Yeshua's brow furrowed with concern when he heard about the Roman cavalry that had pursued us, and when Peter described how I had dropped my sword and offered myself to Lucius, I wanted the ground beneath me to open and swallow me whole.

"Clavius," Yeshua said, pronouncing my name with a clarity of feeling and purpose I had not heard before. Forcing myself to look into his eyes, I was surprised to see the shimmer of tears there. "You are not far from the kingdom of God."

I had no idea what he meant, but as the air had filled with the delicious aroma of roasting fish, I was grateful when Yeshua said we should eat.

As we stood to approach the grate to get bread and fish, I realized this day was Shabbat for the Jews. In Jerusalem, none of them would be cooking or fishing or doing any kind of normal work. When I bent to grab a fish off the grate, Yeshua looked at me. "The Son of Man is Lord," he said, "even over Shabbat."

I studied every detail of Yeshua's appearance while we ate: the wounded hands and feet, the easy smile, the quiet confidence of his presence. I couldn't help remembering the glassy, empty gaze of his eyes staring down from the execution stake.

Yeshua finished eating and sat silently, his eyes roving over each man in the group. At last he lifted his voice, saying, "I have told you these things before, but perhaps this is a good time to remind you of what will happen in the days ahead." His gaze fell on John, who sat beside him. "Remember that I told you 'A slave is not greater than his master.' If they persecuted me, they will persecute you too. If they kept my word, they will keep yours too. But they will do all this to you on my account, because they don't know the One who sent me."

He shifted to Peter. "Don't suppose that I have come to bring peace to the land. It is not peace I have come to bring, but a sword. For I have come to set a man against his father, a daughter against her mother, a daughter-in-law against her mother-in-law, so that a man's enemies will be the members of his own household.

"But you, watch yourselves." His eyes swept over the circle, taking in each man: Andrew, Simon Peter, James, John, Matthew, Nathanael, Bartholomew, Philip, Thomas, James, son of Alphaeus, Thaddeus, and Simon the zealot. "They will hand you over to the local Sanhedrins. You will be beaten up in synagogues, and on my account you will stand before governors and kings as witnesses to them. Indeed, the Good News must be proclaimed first to all the Gentiles before the end comes.

"Now, when they arrest you and bring you to trial, don't worry beforehand about what to say. Rather, say whatever is given you when the time comes; for it will not be just you speaking, but the Holy Spirit. Brother will betray brother to death, and a father his child; children will turn against their parents and have them put to death; and everyone will hate you because of me. But whoever holds out till the end will be delivered.

"Whoever receives you is receiving me, and whoever receives me is receiving the One who sent me. Anyone who receives a prophet because he is a prophet will receive the reward a prophet gets, and anyone who receives a *tzaddik*—a righteous person—because he is a tzaddik will receive the reward a tzaddik gets. Indeed, if someone gives just a cup of cold water to one of the little ones because he is my disciple, I tell you, he will certainly not lose his reward."

I heard the chatter of women and looked up to see Mary of Magdala and the others walking up the beach to join us. Mary, mother of Yeshua, sat between Yeshua and John, greeting everyone in the circle with something of her son's calm in her eyes. Miriam, Joanna, Susanna, and Salome made sure each of us had enough to eat, afterward sitting together and eating too.

I could not keep my eyes off Rachel, who was seeing Yeshua for the first time. In her wide-eyed wonder I saw how I must have looked when I found him in that upper room. A glow shone in her face, as though she contained a lamp that had just been lit.

Philip pulled a piece of roasted fish from the fire and offered it to Yeshua. "Another, Lord?"

Yeshua held up his hand, his pierced wrist clearly visible. Despite his easygoing manner and obvious physical presence, most of us could not move past our amazement. He was *alive* and *with us*!

Even Peter, who sat next to me, kept shaking his head.

"Did you know he would rise?" I whispered.

Peter blew out a breath. "He said He would, but truth be told, we doubted it. Or maybe it is more accurate to say we didn't understand. We thought He was speaking of the afterlife."

"Then what made you follow him?"

Peter did not answer, and a moment later I understood why.

A man had appeared in the field beyond the beach. Even from a great distance I could tell the stranger wore rags. He made his way toward us in a hunched posture as if suffering from some sort of infirmity. He had evidently smelled the roasting fish, because we could hear his voice on the wind, "Just something. A little bread. Please, I'm hungry . . ."

Rachel walked forward to serve him, but then abruptly backed away. Her hands flew to her face. "Leper!" she called, instinctively pulling back even farther. "He's unclean!"

Yet Mary of Magdala remained where she was. She looked to Yeshua, who did not disappoint.

Without a word, Yeshua pulled a good-sized fish from the hot grate and picked up a loaf of bread. As he walked toward the leper, I realized how truly courageous he was. Few physicians dared to be in close proximity to a leper, for the disease was extremely contagious.

"He's going to do it," Thaddeus said.

"Do what?" I asked.

Thomas nodded toward Yeshua. "Watch."

"Watch *what*?"

"He is going to heal that man."

Yeshua crouched at the leper's side, and the man recoiled. "Stay away," he cried, his voice as broken as his body. "I am an outcast."

I stared in astonishment as Yeshua handed the fish and bread to the horribly disfigured leper, then took the man in his arms, held him close, and spoke into the leper's disintegrating ear. So deep was our shocked silence that we heard the man weeping, and many of us gasped when Yeshua wiped the man's tears with his own hand.

"No one . . . no one touches me," the leper cried.

Afraid my eyes were deceiving me, I glanced around the circle. Mary of Magdala was soundlessly weeping too, as were Peter . . . and Rachel.

Yeshua kissed the suppurating skin at the leper's brow and rocked the pitiable wretch in his arms. I felt tears spring to my own eyes as I imagined Yeshua's arms around me—not to heal me, but to forgive me for what I had done to him . . . and hundreds of others.

The leper and Yeshua stood, and the leper walked away. He stood erect now, and as we could all plainly see when he turned to wave farewell, he was healed.

If I had not already been seated, my legs would have given way. "How?" I managed to ask.

"A miracle," said James.

Peter smiled. "We saw them often. He made blind men see with spittle and clay. Fed five thousand with a few loaves and fishes from a little boy's lunch."

"Paralytics, lepers, a woman with a blood hemorrhage—all of them cured," John added. "And demons driven away."

"Seven were driven from me," Mary of Magdala said, coming up behind me.

"He raised a Roman centurion's daughter from her death-bed," Philip said from across the circle.

Miriam nodded. "He raised Lazarus of Bethany from the dead after four days in the tomb."

I stared at them in silence, words failing me.

Peter turned to me. "You asked why we followed Him? That is why."

38

Rachel

I would never have had the courage to speak to Yeshua had He not spoken to me first. The other women had been happily serving Him, along with the disciples, while I maintained a safe distance between myself and the man who was no ordinary man.

I was somewhat prepared by the things I had heard and by the writings of the prophets, but I never dreamed that He, the promised Lamb of God, would speak to me.

After I helped serve the bread, I walked to a quiet spot and sat on the shore to watch the sea. I had not visited the Sea of Galilee since childhood and I'd forgotten how beautiful it was. When I heard grass swishing behind me, I thought Clavius was approaching, so I called out a teasing remark. "I was beginning to wonder if you would ignore me completely."

Then Yeshua sat beside me, and I wanted to run down to the lake and drown myself.

"I would never ignore you," Yeshua said, sitting cross-legged in the sand. "And you need not be embarrassed. I know all about you, Rachel."

My cheeks burned despite the cool morning air. "You . . . you should not even be speaking to me."

"Because you are not married to the Roman who shares your bed?" He studied me with understanding in His eyes. "I didn't come into the world to judge it, but to save it. Those who trust in me are not judged; those who do not trust have been judged already because they have not trusted in God's only and unique Son."

"How?" All of my loneliness, guilt, and confusion mingled together in a surge of intense yearning. "How do I trust in you?"

A smile flashed briefly in the darkness of His beard. "Do you believe in God?"

"Of course!"

"Believe also in me."

"*I do*. But how do I follow you? I am not holy—"

He caught my nervous, fluttering hand and held it between His own callused palms. "If you love me, you will keep my commandments, and the greatest of them is this: love Adonai your God with all your heart and with all your soul and with all your strength. This is the greatest and most important *mitzvah*. And the second is similar to it: you are to love your neighbor as yourself."

"Love?" I gazed up at Him. "Is it that simple?"

"Love is not easy for everyone." Yeshua's eyes crinkled at

the corners as He released my hand. "But it has always been easy for you."

Sitting there, wrapped in a silken cocoon of contentment, I began to relax. Yeshua knew me better than I knew myself and still He loved me. And if He could love me, He could love Clavius—even as He loved the entire world.

Yeshua gave me a sidelong smile, and the image snapped me back to a memory of that awful day when I saw Him stumble on the road to Golgotha. I hated to bring up such a horrific experience, but I had to know.

"Yeshua . . ." I hesitated.

"Go ahead. Ask what is on your heart."

"When I saw you in the road, you said something to the women behind me. I have thought about it many times since, but I still don't understand. Why did you tell them to cry for themselves and their children? Why are childless women the lucky ones?"

Yeshua's expression changed, compassion softening His eyes. "For if they do these things when the wood is green, what is going to happen when it's dry?"

"That's what you said? I am sorry, but I don't understand."

He looked me in the eyes. "Consider what they did to me, and then consider what they will do to Jerusalem when judgment comes. The day is coming, daughter, when not one stone of the Temple will be left upon another. In that day, the daughters of Jerusalem will envy the women with no children, for they will have no one to mourn. Oh, Jerusalem!" He closed his eyes and grimaced. "City that kills the prophets and stones those who are sent to her. I will return to Jerusalem again, but not until the city says 'Blessed is he who comes in the name of Adonai.'"

"When?" I asked, my voice fainter than air.

Yeshua opened his eyes and smiled. "When that day and hour will come, no one knows—not the angels in heaven, not the Son, only the Father. But you will be safe, Rachel, so do not fear."

Just then Matthew called for Yeshua. Yeshua stood, pressed His hand to my head, and went to join the other men.

He left me with a heart too full for words.

39

Clavius

SATURDAY

After speaking to Matthew, Yeshua wandered away, following a trail that led through the tall grass toward a rocky knoll. Before venturing out of sight, however, he glanced back and called Peter's name.

The big man set out, and I stood too. "May I come?" I called.

Peter turned and shrugged. "Why not?"

By the time I caught up with him, the sun had traveled halfway across the eastern sky. Yeshua was still several paces ahead of us, but I took a moment to catch my breath and scan the southern horizon.

"What do you search for?" Peter asked.

"Trouble. It will come." I gestured behind us, toward the camp, the other disciples, the women. "This development threatens Pilate, Caiaphas . . . even Rome."

"There's trouble this way as well." Peter pointed toward the rocky path that led to Yeshua. "People want to believe, but the life will not be an easy one."

Yeshua extended his arm. "Peter . . . let's walk together."

Peter squinted at the narrow passage through the rocks. Up ahead, where Yeshua stood, the path bordered a steep ravine.

"Why?" Peter asked.

Yeshua smiled. "To be closer."

I remained where I was as Peter edged toward his teacher.

"Do you love me, Simon Peter?" Yeshua asked as Peter slipped beneath his outstretched arm.

"You know I do."

"Then feed my lambs."

They walked on, out of my hearing, and I stopped when I saw Rachel approaching. "He's leaving soon," she said when she reached me.

"Is he?"

"Mary says so. And Yeshua told me He won't return to Jerusalem until the people there are ready to welcome Him."

I snorted, knowing that wasn't likely to occur anytime soon. "When he leaves, then what? What will his followers do?"

Rachel kept her eyes fixed on Yeshua's distant figure. "Count the days until they join Him, I suppose."

She remained silent for a moment, then gently took my hand. "I am different because of His love. Changed." A spark of some indefinable emotion lit her eyes. "When He embraced that leper, for the first time I understood what love is."

"Truly?" I took a wincing breath. "I thought we—"

"Love is not what brought us together, Clavius." She patted my hand, her chin quivering. "I thought I loved you, but what I offered was only a pale imitation, probably born out of neediness. I'm sorry for that."

We both watched Peter and Yeshua on the narrow path ahead. Yeshua leaned forward and shared something with Peter, words that seemed to leave the disciple astounded.

"What do you think Yeshua just told him?" I asked. "Do you think he promised promotion? Riches?"

Wiping a tear from her cheek, Rachel laughed. "Sometimes, my dear tribune, you can be as thick as mud."

Yeshua came toward us, Peter following behind. I sidestepped on the path to make room for Yeshua to descend, but he had vanished by the time I lifted my head.

I would never get used to his abrupt departures.

Peter halted beside me, a distinct line between his bushy brows.

Curiosity overrode my manners. "What did he tell you?"

Peter kicked a stone from the path, sending it over the cliff to bounce among the rocks below. "He told me how I am to die," he said, his eyes wide. "And how I'm to live."

"I'll leave you two," Rachel said, moving away from us. "I need to go help the other women."

Peter and I both fell silent, struck by her windswept beauty as we watched her walk away.

40

Rachel

I smiled as I stepped carefully down the rocky path, grateful that Clavius and Peter seemed to have developed a genuine friendship. Clavius did not have a lifetime of writings and prophecies to bolster his faith in Yeshua, but his quick mind was open and ready to receive the truth. He had already acknowledged that Yeshua lived, and surely he would soon grasp the complete portrait of redemption. HaShem had given us so many pictures of what we had recently witnessed with our own eyes: the Paschal lamb, the Temple rituals, even the Seder meal. If one had eyes to see, each element illustrated some aspect of Yeshua's death and resurrection.

The steady sounds of wind and waves accompanied me on

the walk downhill. The path curved around the mountain, flattening as it ran parallel to our makeshift camp. I relaxed as the boulders gave way to shrubs and grasses. In a few minutes I would be able to ask Mary about her travels with Yeshua, and she would tell me more about His miracles and teachings—

I stopped when a bush in the adjacent field shuddered violently. Was it a dog? A fox? Lions had occasionally been seen in these hills. . . .

I lowered my head and began creeping forward, ready to dart away at any moment, when I saw what had caused the disturbance. A Roman soldier was walking up through the underbrush, keeping low to the ground while focusing his attention on some point high on the hill.

I frowned and shaded my eyes. From where the soldier was moving, and from where I stood, Clavius and Peter were plainly visible. The soldier halted and looked down to pull his foot free of an entangling shrub, and I gasped when I recognized the youthful face of Lucius, Clavius's assistant.

Why would the young man approach Clavius like this? If he wanted to reach him, all he had to do was follow the path.

Unless he didn't want to be seen . . .

I crouched on the path as my thoughts whirled in confusion. I had not heard every word Clavius exchanged with Lucius when they met back at Mount Ebal, but I had observed enough to realize that Lucius had been dissuaded from taking Clavius back to Jerusalem. Had Lucius changed his mind and returned with reinforcements?

I scrambled over the path until I reached a boulder, then climbed to the top and surveyed the land around the base of the hill. I saw no other soldiers, only one horse browsing the grass at the edge of a meadow.

I squinted at the Roman again. I caught a glint of light reflecting from the scabbard at his waist, and the sight of his sword was enough to spur my feet. "Clavius! Peter!" Not caring if the youth heard me, I lifted my tunic and raced up the hill, my feet sliding on the scree and kicking up dust. "Clavius!"

My foot slipped and I fell, crashing face first into the hard-packed soil. For a moment, all color ran out of the hillside, and the soothing sound of the waves faded. Then I scrambled up and staggered until I found my balance again. I tasted blood in my mouth—had I cut my lip?—and a random memory came rushing back. Clavius in my bed, my finger running across his wounded lip, his comment about zealots . . .

"HaShem, help me!"

I screamed Clavius's name again, but the wind seemed to catch my words and fling them back at me. Finally, I rounded the corner that opened to the place where Clavius stood with Peter. I leaned against a boulder and struggled to catch my breath. Lucius had not yet reached the summit, so Clavius still had time to unsheathe his weapon and prepare to defend himself against the youth's sword.

With my hand to my chest, I looked down the hill, searching for the Roman. There he was, standing in the long grass, a spear in one hand—

A *spear*?

I whirled, seeking Clavius. Standing where he was, his face to the sea, he would not see the Roman coming, and in that instant I could imagine only one way to save his life.

I ran forward, my tunic flapping at my knees, my hair flying, my voice lifting. I knew I was doing the right thing. HaShem would surely hear my prayer, and who could know whether this act might be the effort necessary to bring a new life into the world.

From the corner of my eye, I saw the young Roman's face twist as he leaned back and threw the spear, its metal head wobbling as it flew upward into the wind. I turned and saw Clavius's eyes widen at my frantic approach. But I had to ignore him and stretch myself for the spear's arc, reaching for it as if it were the lover I had spent so many nights waiting for . . .

The spear found its home, nestling between my breasts, stealing my breath even as it knocked me off my feet. I fell back upon Clavius, whose arms caught and held me. And as I looked into his eyes, I wanted to say, *Why didn't you tell me he would be carrying a spear?* But this was not a time for levity, but for love and gratitude and certainty of purpose.

I heard Clavius's cry, followed by music filling my ears as the sky dissolved into brightness and Yeshua appeared, smiling, His hand extended, even as His smile told me not to worry, for I was finally safe and truly home.

41

Clavius

While the sun balanced itself just above the western horizon, I stood in a circle with Yeshua's followers, all of us gathered around Rachel's enshrouded body. The women had done their best for her, wiping away traces of blood and sewing a shroud out of sailcloth. After they placed her in it, one by one the women kissed Rachel's pale cheeks and stepped back. They called to me, but I remained by the campfire and pretended not to hear them. I had never shirked from battle, and I had willingly disobeyed a prefect of Rome, but I could not find the courage to kiss the face of the woman who had willingly, knowingly exchanged her life for mine.

"She spied him," Peter said, coming to stand beside me at the fire. "I looked across the way and saw her react to something she had spotted. Then I looked to see what had alarmed her. It was your young helper, standing on the hillside below. Rachel then ran toward the danger."

Lucius had disappeared, of course. By the time I recovered from my shock and roused myself to search for him, all that remained was his pilum, buried up to its metal collar in Rachel's chest. While the women tended to Rachel, I followed Lucius's tracks down the mountain to the place where he had left his horse while he carried out his attack.

After our confrontation at Mount Ebal, he must have had a falling-out with Marcellus Drusus the centurion. Lucius clearly wanted to go on searching for me, but since he had no authority over Marcellus's men, he followed us alone.

Hate beat a bitter cadence in my heart as I envisioned Lucius returning to Jerusalem . . . or Caesarea, if Pilate had already left for home. Lucius would report that he had tracked the traitorous Clavius Aquila Valerius Niger all the way to Galilee, where an anonymous Judean woman had inadvertently foiled his attack. Pilate would shed no tears for Rachel, nor for me when he ordered my arrest. Ever conscious of Tiberius Caesar's impending visit, Pilate might even offer a reward for my swift capture to avoid any disturbance during the emperor's visit.

As if Caesar were all that mattered.

When the time came for Rachel's burial, I stood beside Peter, who blinked tears away as he eyed the bloodred sun.

James lifted his hand. "The Master told us, 'Do not let your heart be troubled. Trust in God; trust also in me. In my Father's house there are many dwelling places. If it were not so, would I have told you that I am going to prepare a place for you? If I go and prepare a place for you, *I will come again* and take you to myself, so that where I am you may also be.' We know the way to Him because He told us, 'I am the way, the truth, and the life. No one comes to the Father except through me.'"

"Our sister Rachel walked with Yeshua today," Matthew added, "and we are confident she is now with Him. May Adonai grant us mercy, comfort, and understanding in the days ahead."

Peter stepped forward. "Because He was lifted from death, so shall she be. Praise be to God, who has caused us through the resurrection of Yeshua the Messiah from the dead to be born again to a living hope, to an inheritance that cannot decay, spoil, or fade, kept safe for you in heaven."

John cleared his throat. "We know that God has given us eternal life, and this life is in His Son. Those who have the Son have the life; those who do not have the Son of God do not have life."

"Rachel's life is not finished," Matthew said. "Didn't Yeshua tell us His Father is the God of Abraham, Isaac, and Jacob? God is not the God of the dead, but of the living. So Rachel lives with the Lord, and we will see her again."

"When?" I asked, my voice sounding strangled in the dense quiet.

Peter turned his gaze on me. "We will rise to be with Yeshua when He comes again."

The men worked quickly to fill in the grave. Once filled, they set rocks over the sand to prevent predators from disturbing the site. The women gathered wildflowers, tied them together, and set them in the center of the mounded earth.

"How should we mark the grave?" Thaddeus asked.

John found two pieces of driftwood and crossed them in an X. Peter pulled off his fabric belt and adjusted the pieces of wood, fastening them in the shape of an execution stake and crossbar. A cross.

My cheeks burned in shame. I know Peter did not mean to direct attention to my occupation, but in that moment I was helpless to withstand the avalanche of guilt that buried me.

That night we were not so merry. The grief of the day clung to us, despite Yeshua's promise and the disciples' reminders of their master's words.

Silence hovered over the women's circle; I suspected that most of them had already gone to sleep. The men sitting with Peter, however, had much on their minds.

"'There is no greater love than to lay down your life for your friends,'" Peter said. "That is what He taught us . . . and what Rachel demonstrated."

I did not speak, though I felt the pressure of their eyes on my back. I sat next to Rachel's grave, maintaining a private vigil for the woman who never should have considered trading her precious life for mine.

"The Master called us," Peter went on, his voice a low rumble that was both powerful and gentle, "to do good, even if it means suffering, just as He suffered for us. He is our example, and we must follow in His steps. Remember, His command is to love each other as He loved us. The world will know we are believers because we love. Love is our weapon. It is our defense and our sword."

He stood, his face glowing in the fire-tinted darkness. "Yeshua committed no sin, nor was any deceit found on His lips. When He was insulted, He didn't retaliate with insults. When He suffered, He didn't threaten, but handed His enemies over to Adonai, who judges justly. He bore our sins in His body on the stake so that we might die to sin and live for righteousness. By

His wounds we were healed. For we used to be like sheep gone astray, but now we have turned to the Shepherd, who watches over us."

Peter's words washed over me, shivering my skin like the touch of a ghost. Rachel once sang similar words to me, a lovely light filling her eyes as she shared the melody from her childhood.

The big fisherman moved around the circle, stopping by each man long enough to press an affectionate touch on each head. When he had finished, he left the circle and did the same for me.

A little later, the disciples slept, even Peter. I heard soft snoring and the occasional word spoken in sleep, but no matter how much I wanted to close my eyes and forget the events of the day, I could not.

The waves of the Galilee gently brushed the shore nearby as I stared into a starlit sky and wondered where Yahweh lived. I had heard that stars were holes in the heavens, their light only glimpses of the gods' glory. But the gods of Rome were temperamental, unpredictable creatures. I had spent my life offering them wine they never drank, food they never ate, and coins they never spent. As far as I could tell, they had ignored me altogether.

But Yeshua . . . I had been among those who murdered him, and yet he had smiled at me. He promised me eternal life and a new way of living on earth. A life for which I could never be worthy.

A movement on the hill caught my attention. I sat up and peered at a shadow near the ledge where Rachel had been slain. A man sat there, a man who could only be Yeshua. I stood and walked toward the path. When I was close enough to see that it *was* the Nazarene, I saw him pat the empty spot next to him in a friendly gesture. *Come and sit.*

I climbed so quickly I was out of breath by the time I arrived. Yeshua greeted me with a nod, and for a long moment we sat together in silence and watched the scene below: his followers sleeping, the lake at our right hand, the towns of Galilee on the horizon, the stars above us.

Finally, I found the courage to speak. "I don't even know what to ask," I began.

Yeshua smiled. "Speak your heart, Clavius."

"It is too full. I cannot reconcile all this . . . with Rachel . . . and the world I know."

"What will it take to convince you of the truth? With your own eyes you have seen, with your ears you have heard, yet still you doubt. Imagine the doubt of those who will never see what you've seen." He gestured to the sleeping disciples. "They will face a world that does not know me."

"That world knows other gods."

"The gods of man's own making." Yeshua shifted to face me. "What frightens you?"

I snorted softly. "Being wrong. And wagering eternity on it."

"No need to fear that. When you see Truth, believe it."

I nodded, but I was still unconvinced. Too many doubts crowded my head, and one of them loomed larger than the others.

He looked at me as if he had read my mind. "Speak freely."

"Why did you vanish today? Why couldn't you have stayed here to save her?"

Yeshua lifted his eyes toward the starry firmament. "'For my thoughts are not your thoughts, and your ways are not my ways,' says Adonai."

"What, then, are his thoughts?" I asked, my voice weak and bitter.

"To fulfill His purposes."

"Why couldn't Adonai purpose to save Rachel? She was good, perhaps the only good person I know. And I loved her." I heard the words roll off my tongue and almost laughed. Finally, too late, I was ready to admit how I felt about her. Was she laughing too?

"You could have come back sooner," I told Yeshua, "or we could go down to her grave now and you could wake her from death. You were in the grave three days, while she's only been dead a few hours—"

"Clavius." Yeshua touched my shoulder, cutting off the torrent of words. "You said you loved her."

"I did. I do. And—" my voice broke—"I want her back."

"If Rachel had made you a beautiful robe, and if you had spurned it after she presented it to you, how would she feel?"

I blinked, startled by the odd question. "She would be hurt. Brokenhearted."

Yeshua nodded. "Rachel's chief desire was to bring a new life into the world. Would you deny her dearest wish?"

I stared at him, baffled, as a tumble of confused thoughts and feelings assaulted me. Had Rachel been with child and not told me?

Yeshua's eyes warmed as he watched me struggle to decipher his meaning. "It is you, Clavius. You."

When it struck, comprehension crashed into my consciousness like a battering ram smashing through a thick stone wall. Rachel wanted new life—eternal life—for *me*.

Yeshua had suffered and died for the world, but Rachel had given her life for me. Yet it was too much—her goodness for my bloody past?

I felt the huge weight of that past, the shame and fear and hatred pressing in on me. I decided I would offer all of it to Yeshua. "In the name of Rome," I confessed, "I have killed hundreds of men, even women and children."

"I know."

"I have worshiped creatures and idols—more than I can count."

"I know."

"When you died on the stake, I was present."

Yeshua looked down to the wound on his wrist. "My Father willed it."

"I helped them kill you. I was *in charge*. And right now, in this moment, *my* chief desire is to slay Lucius Tyco Ennius."

Yeshua's dark, earnest eyes sought mine. "What do you seek, Clavius? A day without death? Forgiveness? Or vengeance?"

Shock flickered through me like summer lightning. How could he know all the conflicting truths about me and still smile so sincerely? If he was divine, then he knew all the evil I had done and all the death I had caused. How could he offer me the same love and forgiveness and healing he had shared with Rachel, whose greatest sin had been her loving me?

"I have sworn allegiance to Rome," I said, hanging my head. "For me there is nothing but life on this earth, followed by a bloody death."

"There is far more for those who believe," Yeshua answered. "For Rachel, and for you, if you will accept one thing."

"What is that?"

"Love, Clavius. I loved you enough to present my blood as your sin offering. Enough to give my life as your peace offering. Forgiveness is yours, if you will only accept it."

"It cannot be that simple," I argued. "Even the Jews know that a man has to live a holy life, do certain things, offer sacrifices—"

"Take my yoke upon you and learn from me," Yeshua said. "Because I am gentle and humble in heart, and you will find rest for your soul. For my yoke is easy, and my burden is light."

He straightened his back, hugging his knees as he lifted his gaze toward the heavens again. "The work of salvation . . . is finished. Even for you."

42

Clavius

I awoke on the hilltop boulder. I could see the disciples moving around below, and the women packing the donkeys. But I could not see Yeshua.

"Yeshua?" I called over my shoulder in case He had climbed higher. "Yeshua?"

No answer.

I scrambled down the path, found Peter, and caught his sleeve. "Yeshua—has He gone?"

Peter nodded. "From here, yes. But He told us to go back to Jerusalem."

To Jerusalem? To Pilate and the cohort and my old life? I

could not imagine myself reentering the Antonia Fortress or sitting behind my desk. I was no longer that man.

Last night, after talking to Yeshua, I had buried my head in my folded arms and heard Rachel's voice on a wave of memory. *"Because he doesn't return love. I don't know if he can."*

She had offered me love, yet I kept her at arm's length. Yeshua had offered life-changing love, and I stubbornly refused to accept it. Why?

I told myself it was because I didn't want to hurt anyone. I didn't want others to suffer the consequences of association with a Roman tribune. But that was a lie. In reality I didn't want to be hurt *myself*. Life as a tribune had taught me to keep people at a distance, because if I let them get close, *as close as a twin*, death could snatch them away, and I would be bereft.

But not anymore. Yeshua had conquered death, so I was free to believe . . . and love others without constraint, the way Yeshua loved. I had set out under a command to find the missing Nazarene, and after many trials I finally found Him, and He would be with me always.

I nodded at Peter. "What happens in Jerusalem?"

"Come with us," he said, smiling, "and see for yourself."

We spent the next three days traveling back to Jerusalem, living off dried fish and edible plants, dodging the occasional Roman patrol, and sharing our story with anyone who would listen.

At this point I believed in Yeshua with all my being, but simple belief did not answer all my questions, nor did it tell me what I ought to do upon our return to Jerusalem.

So I dogged Peter's footsteps again. "Tell me about Yeshua's birth and childhood," I asked. And later, "How can you say 'Yahweh is one God' when we know He has a Son?"

Peter looked at me as if he'd like to wrap his big hands around my neck and squeeze. "The mind cannot fathom certain mysteries," he said, "but the Shema says 'Listen, O Israel! The Lord is our God, the Lord alone.' In other words, our God is one."

"So?"

"The word is *echad*. It means He is one in nature, not one being."

One morning I asked Peter for details about what Yeshua had told him on the hilltop.

Pressing his lips together, Peter threw me a wary glance. "After asking me if I loved Him, He said, 'When you were younger, you used to dress yourself and walk wherever you wanted; but when you grow old, you will stretch out your hands, and someone else will dress you and carry you where you do not want to go.'"

I considered his answer for several moments before looking over at him. "Imprisonment, perhaps? Slavery?"

Peter shrugged. "I don't know. But I *do* know my death will bring glory to God. And if that's where He leads me, I will joyfully follow."

Glory—the prize every Roman earnestly desired for himself. Yet Yeshua's followers sought to direct glory toward their Adonai and His Son, Yeshua.

A memory ruffled through my mind like wind on water. "I spoke to a man at the garden called Gethsemane. He told me about your wild swipe with the sword. He also said that you followed Yeshua after the guards led Him away."

Peter's smile waned. "I'm not proud of what I did that night. None of us is."

"But you didn't run like the others. You had the courage to follow."

"Foolhardiness, maybe. I think . . . I was prideful. I wanted Yeshua to notice what I was doing for Him."

I frowned, finding it hard to imagine this gentle giant leading an attack. "What were you doing?"

"Spying. Or trying to." He closed his eyes as color flushed his face. "I followed at a distance as they took Yeshua to the high priest's palace. I lingered in the courtyard for a while before going inside and sitting down with the guards. When a serving girl accused me of being with Yeshua, I denied it. Then I went to the porch, where another girl said she recognized me. I denied it again. A third time, when someone said I had to be a Galilean because of my accent, I swore and claimed not to know the Lord."

Peter stopped walking, sighed heavily, and looked at me. "I wanted to die when Yeshua came out and saw me . . . and the rooster crowed, just as He'd predicted."

"You didn't run," I repeated.

"I might have done less harm if I had." Fresh misery darkened Peter's expression. "I had imagined myself a leader among the disciples, but I was a poor example of the man I should have been . . . the man Yeshua would want me to be."

In a barely comprehendible glimmer, I realized something. "Is that why He asked if you loved Him?"

"Three times." Peter gave me a rueful smile. "Because three times I had failed Him that night. But I will not fail Him again."

Yeshua did not appear in Jerusalem again, but we heard numerous reports of sightings outside the city. I was present when He appeared to more than five hundred people at a hillside meeting led by Peter, John, and James. Though some of those witnesses accused the disciples of trickery, they could not deny that Yeshua walked among them.

During that appearance, Yeshua told the believers not to leave Jerusalem, but to find the others and wait for what the Father had promised. "For John used to immerse people in water," He said, "but in a few days you will be immersed in the Holy Spirit."

"Lord," one of the men asked, "are you now going to restore self-rule to Israel?"

I tensed at the question, knowing that neither the religious leaders nor the Romans would tolerate such an uprising. The disciples' message was as unpopular with the Temple leadership as Yeshua's had been, and Caiaphas and other leaders of the Sanhedrin kept a wary eye on the Nazarene's followers. The threat of insurrection loomed as large as ever, and I suspected it was only a matter of time before some of my new friends found themselves imprisoned for sharing Yeshua's story with others.

Yeshua gave His questioner a tolerant smile. "You don't need to know the dates or the times; the Father has kept these under His own authority."

A few days later I was with the disciples in Bethany, at the home of Yeshua's friends Mary, Martha, and Lazarus, the man Yeshua had brought back to life after four days in the tomb. Yeshua appeared and invited His disciples to walk with Him.

I followed them and stood a little apart from the group when Yeshua turned to address His disciples. "In my name," He said, "proclaim repentance leading to forgiveness of sins to all nations, starting with Jerusalem. You are witnesses of these things. Now I am sending forth upon you what my Father promised, so stay here in the city until you have been equipped with power from above."

He lifted His hands and blessed them, His face shining with a light that seemed to emanate from within. "Go into all the world and preach the gospel to all nations. You will be my witnesses in Jerusalem, and in all Judea and Samaria, and to the ends of the earth. And know I am with you always, even to the end of the age."

While He spoke, His feet left the earth and He began to rise before our eyes. We craned our necks, desperate to keep Him in sight, but a scarf of cloud blew in and hid Him from our view.

"Do you see Him?" Peter asked. "Anyone?"

While we stared into heaven, two men in spotless white tunics appeared in the place Yeshua had vacated. "Men of Galilee," they said, smiling with kind forbearance, "why do you keep standing here looking up into heaven? This Yeshua who was taken up from you will come again in the same way you saw Him go."

The two men in white vanished. We glanced at one another, all of us amazed by what we had just seen.

"He said this would happen," Peter pointed out. "But He didn't mention how we would feel the pang of His departure."

"Shalom," Matthew said. "He has given us His peace."

"He is coming back in the same way." A note of awe echoed in John's voice. "Through the clouds."

As we walked the short distance back to the Jerusalem gate, an air of excitement pervaded our group. In high spirits the disciples kept interrupting each other as they recalled things Yeshua had said, utterances that had perplexed them at the time but now made perfect sense.

"He is our forerunner, our firstfruits," Matthew said, his

eyes wide with understanding, "the first to defeat death. He has ascended to heaven!"

"Where He has gone to prepare a place for us," Thomas added.

Peter nodded. "And where He is seated at the right hand of the Father. Remember what David wrote? 'Adonai said to my Lord, Sit at my right hand until I make your enemies a footstool for your feet.' David did not ascend into heaven, but Yeshua did! David prophesied of what we have seen today with our own eyes!"

Drawn by the disciples' fervor, a crowd gathered to listen. Never one to miss an opportunity to share the good news, John noticed the growing audience and hopped onto a limestone block to address those who had come near. "In the beginning," he began, "was the Word, and the Word was with God, and the Word *was* God. In Him was life, and the life was the light of mankind. This was the true light, which gives light to everyone entering the world. He was in the world—the world came to be through Him—yet the world did not know Him. He came to His own homeland, yet His own people did not receive Him. But to as many as *did* receive Him, to those who put their trust in His person and power, He gave the right to become children of HaShem, not because of bloodline, but because of God."

John lifted his eyes to the heavens, where clouds still sudsed the sky. "The Word became a human being and lived with us, and we beheld His *Shekinah*, the glory of the Father's only Son, full of grace and truth."

"What are you saying?" a man yelled. "Are you talking about Moses?"

John shook his head. "The Torah was given through Moses; grace and truth comes through Yeshua the Messiah. In the coming days we will be telling the story, friends, of life eternal and a new way of living by love. This news will change you"—he thumped his heart—"here."

Listening nearby, Peter smiled. "That's good. Very good."

"I may use it again," John said, grinning. "I ought to write it down."

James laughed. "Shouldn't you learn how to write first?"

"Maybe I will have it written," John answered. He clapped his brother on the shoulder as he jumped off the limestone block. "A man can speak to only so many people, but a written letter could reach hundreds."

"Thousands," James said.

I was about to volunteer to write John's story myself, but as we neared the city wall, I noticed Roman legionnaires stationed on both sides of the gate. I would have cautioned the disciples, yet I was the most likely one to be recognized. Pilate—and Lucius—had probably returned to Caesarea. The legionnaires, however, knew my face well.

I smiled at a sudden realization. Only a few weeks before, I despised the religious zealots who caused trouble for Rome. If Pilate were to see me now, he would count me as one of them.

Peter saw the guards, noticed my hesitation and my concern. "I'm not worried, because I will not die like this," Peter said, halting with me outside the city wall. "Yeshua told me so."

I nodded toward the others. "They don't have that assurance."

"None of us is afraid," he insisted. "Not anymore."

"Then go forward with what you have been entrusted." I placed my hands on Peter's shoulders. "Thank you, friend, for letting me badger you with questions. You were most patient and generous toward me."

Peter embraced me, holding me in place. "Will you join us, Tribune?"

I shook my head. "Jerusalem only bodes trouble for me."

"It is where we've been told to wait for the Comforter. The *Ruach HaKodesh* Yeshua promised."

Another phrase for my Hebrew vocabulary. "You had better wait and then go back home to Galilee. After all, your call is to fish."

"To fish for *men*." He laughed and released me. "To the ends of the earth, as He bade us. How could I do anything else? Will you fish too?"

I stepped back, rested my hands on my sword belt and shook my head, amused by his persistence.

"Farewell then," Peter called. "May Adonai bless and keep you." He took three steps toward the city gate, turned and raised his tunic high enough to expose the scar on his leg. "I will always have you with me."

I stood in the shadow of a lone fig tree until they had all gone into the city—the disciples, the women, and the curious bystanders.

Then I turned toward the wilderness.

Clavius

"And now . . . here I am." I looked up at the clouds through the inn's small window, then followed the slanting sunbeams to the tabletop, where shadows from the window frame's wooden inserts formed the shape of an execution stake on the dusty table.

I needed to make a decision. I had chosen to surrender my life to the one who redeemed it with His blood, but where did that leave me? I was a Gentile following a Jew, the Messiah from Nazareth. I was a Roman officer who had been absent without leave for nearly forty days.

"Tribune?"

I looked over at the innkeeper, who had refilled my cup countless times as I bore witness to what I had seen and experienced.

Now he sat with an elbow on the table and his chin resting in his hand, his eyes round and full.

"Tribune—amazing story, but do you truly believe everything you have said?"

I exhaled a slow breath. "I believe . . . and I will never be the same." My life belonged to Yeshua, and He could use it as He saw fit.

By the time I had finished relating my encounter with the Nazarene, my next step became clear: I would return to the Antonia Fortress and testify truthfully when questioned about where I had been. I would also testify as to Lucius's actions on the mountain in Galilee and leave his fate in Pilate's hands. I did not expect justice in his case, but Yeshua had not meted out justice to me either. He had shown mercy.

Pilate could easily decide to make an example of me. I had disobeyed his order and walked away from my post. Even though I'd done so to further explore a situation he had asked me to investigate, Pilate would not hesitate to order my execution.

Or he could have mercy and allow me to live, perhaps imprison me. I did not know. Either way, I would faithfully serve Yeshua and leave my future to Him. If it was Yeshua's will, someday I hoped to return to Rome . . . because I had a story to tell.

I stood, slipped my silver tribune's ring from my finger, and dropped it into the center of the shadowed cross on the table. "My payment."

As the innkeeper stammered in pleased surprise, I left him and turned my steps toward Jerusalem.

Author's Note

Readers always want to know how much of a story is fictional and how much is based on fact. While Clavius and Lucius are fictional characters, their roles are grounded in history. As I wrote, I tried my best to properly represent Scripture, history, and the *Risen* film/screenplay.

Though the premise—what would the Resurrection look like through the eyes of a Roman tribune?—is entirely fictional, I took a few small liberties for the sake of the story. For instance, when Thomas met the resurrected Christ, Thomas was actually in a locked room with the other disciples when Yeshua appeared and allowed Thomas to touch the wounds on His hands and feet (John 20:19). That event actually took place on a Sunday night, a full week after Christ's resurrection. And only seven of the disciples were present at the fishing episode on the Sea of Galilee: Peter, Thomas, Nathanael, James, John, and two others (John 21:1–3).

A screenplay is not nearly as long as a novel, so of course I found it necessary to add several additional developments in order to flesh out the story. Fortunately, both history and Scripture provided plenty of characters and situations for Clavius to investigate. The character of Rachel, who adds so much to the story, is a creation of Paul Aiello, the screenwriter, but her role had to be cut from the movie due to time constraints. I am happy that she lives within these pages and adds an additional point of view.

Simeon and Anna are real people whose story is told in Luke 2:25–38. I was searching for a development to emphasize the miraculous resurrection of Yeshua when I remembered the event described in Matthew 27:52–54: "Also the graves were opened, and the bodies of many holy people who had died were raised to life; and after Yeshua rose, they came out of the graves and went into the holy city, where many people saw them." I tried to think of holy believers who lived in Jerusalem and likely would be dead by the time Yeshua was thirty-three years old, and the names Simeon and Anna came to mind. What did these suddenly resurrected people do? Given what Simeon and Anna had done before, I believe they went right back to their work of proclaiming the word of the Lord.

Could Clavius have existed? Certainly, but I doubt he would have been in the upper room when the Holy Spirit descended. In the first few chapters of Acts, a document that records the history of the early church, Jews of many different nationalities (Parthians, Medes, Elamites, residents of Mesopotamia, Judah, Cappadocia, Pontus, Asia, Phrygia, Pamphylia, Egypt, parts of Libya near Cyrene, visitors from Rome, and Jews from Crete and Arabia) became believers in Yeshua, but no Gentiles—not until Cornelius, whose story is told in the tenth chapter of Acts.

Cornelius was a Roman army officer in the Italian Regiment, the unit stationed at Caesarea to guard Pilate. Cornelius was devout, a "God-fearer," and he prayed regularly to Adonai. One day an angel appeared to Cornelius and told him to send for Simon Peter, so he did.

Meanwhile, Peter was having a vision of crawling creatures, wild birds, and four-footed animals. A voice told him to kill and eat, but Peter recoiled from the thought of eating anything that was ritually unclean according to Jewish law. Then God said, "Stop treating as unclean what God has made clean."

Fellowship in the home of Gentiles—Romans, for instance—could defile Jews, so Peter learned this lesson at just the right time. Freed of religious restraints, he went to visit Cornelius and said, "I now understand that God does not play favorites, but that whoever fears him and does what is right is acceptable to him, no matter what people he belongs to" (Acts 10:34–35).

Peter shared the story of Yeshua with Cornelius and his household, they believed, and while Peter was speaking, the Holy Spirit fell on all who were hearing the message. They were baptized in the name of Yeshua, and Peter stayed on for a few days to teach them further. Can you imagine the questions they must have asked?

Cornelius and his household were apparently the first Gentiles to believe in Jesus Christ and receive the Holy Spirit.

Previously, another distinct group of people, the Samaritans, had welcomed Philip, who told them the story of Yeshua. Many of the Samaritans (who were descendants of the ten tribes of Israel that had been conquered by the Assyrians in 722 BC) believed in Yeshua and were baptized. But they did not receive the Holy Spirit until Peter and John went down and prayed for them to receive the Ruach HaKodesh, which indwelt them just as it had the Jewish believers.

Peter, you'll notice, was present when all three distinct people groups received the Holy Spirit and joined the universal body of Christ. Yeshua had said, "You are Peter [which means 'rock'], and on this rock I will build my Community, and the gates of hell will not overcome it" (Matthew 16:18). The book of Acts proves that Christ's words were fulfilled quite soon after His ascension into heaven.

What happened to the disciples? Of the eleven original disciples, ten were martyred for their faith. James (brother to John) was the first to die, killed by the sword after Herod Antipas ordered his death (Acts 12:2). Some were crucified (Peter was reportedly crucified upside down because he didn't consider himself worthy of dying like his Master), while others were boiled in oil, slain by the sword, or flayed alive. John was the last to die, dying a natural death while exiled to an island called Patmos.

These men, who based their faith and their confidence in eternal life on Yeshua's resurrection, died for a truth they had seen, heard, and handled. They and countless others willingly surrendered their mortal lives because they believed Yeshua's promise: "But if you give up your life for my sake and for the sake of the Good News, you will save it" (Mark 8:35).

For those of you who may be interested in knowing more about Yeshua's post-resurrection activities, my friend Harold Willmington has put together this list of Christ's appearances:

1. First appearance to Mary Magdalene as she remained at the site of the tomb: John 20:11–17.

2. Second appearance to the other women who were also returning to the tomb: Matthew 28:9–10.

3. Third appearance to Peter: Luke 24:34; 1 Cor. 15:5.

4. Fourth appearance to the disciples as they walked on the road to Emmaus: Mark 16:12–13; Luke 24:13–31.

5. Fifth appearance to the ten disciples: Mark 16:14; Luke 24:36–51; John 20:19–23.

6. Sixth appearance to the eleven disciples a week after His resurrection: John 20:26–29.

7. Seventh appearance to seven disciples by the Sea of Galilee: John 21:1–23.

8. Eighth appearance to the five hundred: 1 Cor. 15:6.

9. Ninth appearance to James, the Lord's brother: 1 Cor. 15:7.

10. Tenth appearance to the eleven disciples on the mountain in Galilee: Matthew 28:16–20.

11. Eleventh appearance at the time of the Ascension: Luke 24:44–53; Acts 1:3–9.

12. Twelfth appearance to Stephen just prior to his martyrdom: Acts 7:55–56.

13. Thirteenth appearance to Paul on the road to Damascus: Acts 9:3–6; cf. 22:6–11; 26:13–18.

14. Fourteenth appearance to Paul in Arabia: Galatians 1:12–17.

15. Fifteenth appearance to Paul in the Temple: Acts 9:26–27; 22:17–21.

16. Sixteenth appearance to Paul while he was in prison in Caesarea: Acts 23:11.

17. Seventeenth appearance to the apostle John: Revelation 1:12–20.*

* H.L. Willmington, *Willmington's Book of Bible Lists*, 168–69 (Wheaton, IL: Tyndale, 1987).

Where is Yeshua now? After His ascension into heaven, Yeshua sat down at the right hand of God (Hebrews 1:3), a position of honor. He is currently exercising His priesthood, interceding for believers (Romans 8:34), and serving as the defender of His community, the church, over which He is the head (Ephesians 1:20–21). One day soon He will return in the clouds, just as He left, to collect the believers and initiate the final stages of God's redemptive plan for creation (Revelation 21:1–4).

As John the disciple wrote during his island exile, "Come, Lord Yeshua!" May the grace of the Lord Yeshua be with you all!

—Angela Hunt

References

Aland, Kurt. *Synopsis of the Four Gospels*. Bellingham, WA: Logos Bible Software, 2009.

Balz, Horst Robert and Gerhard Schneider. *Exegetical Dictionary of the New Testament*. Grand Rapids, MI: Eerdmans, 1990.

Bridges, Linda McKinnish. "Antonia, Tower of," in *Holman Illustrated Bible Dictionary*, ed. Chad Brand, Charles Draper, Archie England, et al. Nashville, TN: Holman Bible Publishers, 2003.

Brisco, Thomas V. *Holman Bible Atlas*, Holman Reference. Nashville, TN: Broadman & Holman Publishers, 1998.

Borchert, Gerald L. *The New American Commentary*. Nashville, TN: Broadman & Holman Publishers, 2002.

Cargal, Timothy B. *So That's Why! Bible: New King James Version*. Nashville, TN: Thomas Nelson, 2001.

de Villiers, J. L., and G. M. M. Pelser. "The Roman Government and Judicature," in *The New Testament Milieu, Guide to the New Testament.* Orion Publishers, 1998.

Draper, Charles. "Letter Form and Function," in *Holman Illustrated Bible Dictionary,* ed. Chad Brand, Charles Draper, Archie England, et al. Nashville, TN: Holman Bible Publishers, 2003.

du Toit, A. B. "History of Palestinian Judaism in the Period 539 BC to AD 135," in vol. 2, *The New Testament Milieu, Guide to the New Testament.* Orion Publishers, 1998.

Edersheim, Alfred. *The Life and Times of Jesus the Messiah.* New York: Longmans, Green, and Company, 1896.

Edwards, Douglas R. "Gentiles, Court of the," in vol. 2 *The Anchor Yale Bible Dictionary,* ed. David Noel Freedman. New York: Doubleday, 1992.

Edwards, Elwyn Hartley. *The Encyclopedia of the Horse.* New York: Dorling Kindersley, 1994.

Feinberg, Jeffrey Enoch, and Kim Alan Moudy. *Walk Numbers!: In the Wilderness.* Clarksville, MD: Messianic Jewish Publishers, 2002.

Fiensy, David A. *The College Press NIV Commentary.* Joplin, MO: College Press Publishing Company, 1997.

Freeman, James M., and Harold J. Chadwick. *Manners & Customs of the Bible.* North Brunswick, NJ: Bridge-Logos Publishers, 1998.

Fruchtenbaum, Arnold G. *The Messianic Bible Study Collection.* Tustin, CA: Ariel Ministries, 1983.

Goodman, Martin. *The Roman World: 44 BC–AD 180.* New York: Routledge, 2012.

Gower, Ralph. "Cooking and Heating," in *Holman Illustrated Bible Dictionary*, ed. Chad Brand, Charles Draper, Archie England, et al. Nashville, TN: Holman Bible Publishers, 2003.

Grassmick, John D. "Mark," in *The Bible Knowledge Commentary: An Exposition of the Scriptures*, ed. J. F. Walvoord and R. B. Zuck. Wheaton, IL: Victor Books, 1985.

Hachlili, Rachel. "Burials: Ancient Jewish," in *The Anchor Yale Bible Dictionary*, ed. David Noel Freedman. New York: Doubleday, 1992.

Hagner, Donald A. Matthew 1–13, *Word Biblical Commentary*. Dallas, TX: Word, 1998.

Hindson, Edward E. and Woodrow Michael Kroll, eds. *KJV Bible Commentary*. Nashville, TN: Thomas Nelson, 1994.

http://www.britannica.com/topic/postal-system#ref367055, accessed August 18, 2015.

http://www.telegraph.co.uk/sport/olympics/equestrianism/81668647/Roman-emperors-horses-to-be-recognised-as-distinct-breed.html, accessed September 14, 2015.

http://www.tribunesandtriumphs.org/roman-army/roman-army.htm, accessed August 18, 2015.

https://universalparticulars.wordpress.com/2008/02/18/ancient-roman-prayer/, accessed August 18, 2015.

Hughes, Robert B. and J. Carl Laney. *Tyndale Concise Bible Commentary*. Wheaton, IL: Tyndale House Publishers, 2001.

Hurley, Virgil. *Speaker's Sourcebook of New Illustrations*. Dallas, TX: Word, 2000.

Jenkins, Simon. *Nelson's 3-D Bible Mapbook*. Nashville, TN: Thomas Nelson, 1995.

Keener, Craig S. *The IVP Bible Background Commentary: New Testament*. Downers Grove, IL: InterVarsity Press, 1993.

Kelpie, Lawrence. *The Making of the Roman Army: From Republic to Empire*. Norman, OK: University of Oklahoma Press, 1984.

Kennedy, David. "Roman Army," in vol. 5, *The Anchor Yale Bible Dictionary*, ed. David Noel Freedman. New York: Doubleday, 1992.

Knowles, Andrew. *The Bible Guide*. Minneapolis, MN: Augsburg, 2001.

MacArthur, John F. Jr. *The Murder of Jesus: A Study of How Jesus Died*. Nashville, TN: Word Publishing Group, 2000.

Manser, Martin H. *Dictionary of Bible Themes: The Accessible and Comprehensive Tool for Topical Studies*. London: Martin Manser, 2009.

Mathews, K. A. *The New American Commentary*. Nashville, TN: Broadman & Holman Publishers, 2005.

McGee, J. Vernon. *Thru the Bible Commentary: The Gospels (Luke)*, electronic ed. Nashville, TN: Thomas Nelson, 1991.

McQuaid, Elwood. *The Outpouring: Jesus in the Feasts of Israel*. Bellmawr, NJ: The Friends of Israel Gospel Ministry, Inc., 1990.

Myers, Allen C. *The Eerdmans Bible Dictionary*. Grand Rapids, MI: Eerdmans, 1987.

Packer, J. I., Merrill Chapin Tenney and William White, Jr. *Nelson's Illustrated Manners and Customs of the Bible*. Nashville, TN: Thomas Nelson, 1997.

Pelser, G. M. M. "Governing Authorities in Jewish National Life in Palestine in New Testament Times," in vol. 2 *The*

New Testament Milieu, ed. A. B. du Toit, *Guide to the New Testament*. Orion Publishers, 1998.

Radmacher, Earl D., Ronald Barclay Allen, and H. Wayne House. *The Nelson Study Bible: New King James Version*. Nashville, TN: Thomas Nelson, 1997.

Santosuosso, Antonio. *Storming the Heavens: Soldiers, Emperors, and Civilians in the Roman Empire*. Boulder, CO: Westview Press, 2004.

Shelley, Bruce L. *Church History in Plain Language*. Dallas, TX: Word, 1995.

Sloman, A., Brooke Foss Westcott, and Fenton John Anthony Hort. *The Gospel According to St. Matthew: Being the Greek Text, rev. and repr. with additional notes., Classic Commentaries on the Greek New Testament*. London: Macmillan, 1912.

Spence-Jones, H. D. M. "Leviticus," in *The Pulpit Commentary*. London; New York: Funk & Wagnalls Company, 1910.

Stewart, R. A. "Passover," in *New Bible Dictionary*, ed. D. R. W. Wood, I. H. Marshall, A. R. Millard, et al., 3rd ed. Leicester, England; Downers Grove, IL: InterVarsity Press, 1996.

Swindoll, Charles R., and Roy B. Zuck. *Understanding Christian Theology*. Nashville, TN: Thomas Nelson, 2003.

Thomas, Robert L. and The Lockman Foundation, *New American Standard Exhaustive Concordance of the Bible: Updated Edition*. Anaheim, CA: Foundation Publications, Inc., 1998.

Utley, Robert James. *The First Christian Primer: Matthew, Study Guide Commentary Series*. Marshall, TX: Bible Lessons International, 2000.

Utley, Robert James. *Paul Bound, the Gospel Unbound: Letters from Prison*. Marshall, TX: Bible Lessons International, 1997.

Venne, Paul, ed. *A History of Private Life: From Pagan Rome to Byzantium*. Cambridge: Belknap Harvard, 1987.

Watson, G. R. *The Roman Soldier: Aspects of Greek and Roman Life*. Ithaca, NY: Cornell University Press, 1987.

Wells, Colin M. "Roman Empire," in *The Anchor Yale Bible Dictionary*, ed. David Noel Freedman. New York: Doubleday, 1992.

Wiersbe, Warren W. *The Bible Exposition Commentary*. Wheaton, IL: Victor Books, 1996.

Wilkins, Michael J. "Barabbas," in *The Anchor Yale Bible Dictionary*, ed. David Noel Freedman. New York: Doubleday, 1992.

Yabin, Yigal. *Jerusalem Revealed: Archeology in the Holy City, 1968–1974*. New Haven, CT: Yale University Press, 1976.

Youngblood, Ronald F., F. F. Bruce, R. K. Harrison, and Thomas Nelson Publishers, ed. *Nelson's New Illustrated Bible Dictionary*. Nashville, TN: Thomas Nelson, 1995.

Angela Hunt has published more than one hundred books, with sales nearing five million copies worldwide. She's the *New York Times* bestselling author of *The Tale of Three Trees*, *The Note*, and *The Nativity Story*. Angela's novels have won or been nominated for several prestigious industry awards, such as the RITA Award, the Christy Award, the ECPA Christian Book Award, and the HOLT Medallion Award. Romantic Times Book Club presented her with a Lifetime Achievement Award in 2006. In 2008, she earned her doctorate in Biblical Studies and has recently completed her Th.D. Angela and her husband live in Florida, along with their mastiffs. For a complete list of the author's books, visit angelahuntbooks.com.